Hi.

I am only four and a half and can't write too good, so Thomas is doing it for me. Hoppy can't write at all yet, but he likes to color. He colored all over Mama and Daddy's plans for adding on to the house. Mama and Daddy were plenty mad, but then they said he was being ar-tis-tic. That must be a good thing, because he got a kiss. They say when Hoppy grows up he will be a picture-drawer or a chef. He likes to stir all his food together.

I'm going to be a well-driller like my Mama and Daddy and get my picture in the paper, like they did. Everybody said there was no water on the west side of the Waddell farm, but Mama said there was, and she found it, so she is famous now. I am just like my Mama, because Daddy says so and gives me a kiss. Mama says we are a wellspring of joy.

MOLLY

Ranch Rogues
1. Betrayed by Love
   Diana Palmer
2. Blue Sage
   Anne Stuart
3. Chase the Clouds
   Lindsay McKenna
4. Mustang Man
   Lee Magner
5. Painted Sunsets
   Rebecca Flanders
6. Carved in Stone
   Kathleen Eagle

Hitched in Haste
7. A Marriage of Convenience
   Doreen Owens Malek
8. Where Angels Fear
   Ginna Gray
9. Mountain Man
   Joyce Thies
10. The Hawk and the Honey
    Dixie Browning
11. Wild Horse Canyon
    Elizabeth August
12. Someone Waiting
    Joan Hohl

Ranchin' Dads
13. Ramblin' Man
    Barbara Kaye
14. His and Hers
    Pamela Bauer
15. The Best Things in Life
    Rita Clay Estrada
16. All That Matters
    Judith Duncan
17. One Man's Folly
    Cathy Gillen Thacker
18. Sagebrush and Sunshine
    Margot Dalton

Denim & Diamonds
19. Moonbeams Aplenty
    Mary Lynn Baxter
20. In a Class by Himself
    JoAnn Ross
21. The Fairy Tale Girl
    Ann Major
22. Snow Bird
    Lass Small
23. Soul of the West
    Suzanne Ellison
24. Heart of Ice
    Diana Palmer

Kids & Kin
25. Fools Rush In
    Ginna Gray
26. Wellspring
    Curtiss Ann Matlock
27. Hunter's Prey
    Annette Broadrick
28. Laughter in the Rain
    Shirley Larson
29. A Distant Promise
    Debbie Bedford
30. Family Affair
    Cathy Gillen Thacker

Reunited Hearts
31. Yesterday's Lies
    Lisa Jackson
32. Tracings on a Window
    Georgia Bockoven
33. Wild Lady
    Ann Major
34. Cody Daniels' Return
    Marilyn Pappano
35. All Things Considered
    Debbie Macomber
36. Return to Yesterday
    Annette Broadrick

Reckless Renegades
37. Ambushed
    Patricia Rosemoor
38. West of the Sun
    Lynn Erickson
39. A Wild Wind
    Evelyn A. Crowe
40. The Deadly Breed
    Caroline Burnes
41. Desperado
    Helen Conrad
42. Heart of the Eagle
    Lindsay McKenna

Once A Cowboy...
43. Rancho Diablo
    Anne Stuart
44. Big Sky Country
    Jackie Merritt
45. A Family to Cherish
    Cathy Gillen Thacker
46. Texas Wildcat
    Lindsay McKenna
47. Not Part of the Bargain
    Susan Fox
48. Destiny's Child
    Ann Major

Please address questions and book requests to: Silhouette Reader Service
U.S.: 3010 Walden Ave., P.O. Box 1325, Buffalo, NY 14269
Canadian: P.O. Box 609, Fort Erie, Ont. L2A 5X3

CURTISS ANN MATLOCK

WELLSPRING

Published by Silhouette Books

America's Publisher of Contemporary Romance

For Jim—
my lover, my husband,
and my best friend

SILHOUETTE BOOKS
300 East 42nd St.,
New York, N.Y. 10017

ISBN 0-373-88526-1

WELLSPRING

Copyright © 1988 by Curtiss Ann Matlock

Chapter One

Digging into the pocket of his denim jacket and into a small bag of candy there, Jack pulled out a yellow gummy bear. He slipped it into his mouth and wished it were a cigarette.

In anticipation of the drop in speed limit, he slowed his pickup as he entered the outskirts of Wensler, Oklahoma, a town of less than five thousand people. The pickup's engine roared and let out a staccato burst of small backfires as it worked to slow the fifth-wheel camper attached at the back.

Though the fuel gauge read half full, Jack decided to stop for gas. It would give him a chance to gather his wits. He was suffering the disconcerting sensation of the past and the present mingling in his mind as he looked around the familiar town.

He chose Cy Stanfell's garage over that of the coldly modern U-Pump station and grocery across the street. He wouldn't mind Cy's friendly face being the first he greeted. Carefully he eased the pickup and trailer from the road and skirted the giant potholes in the gravel before rolling up the concrete drive. Stopping beneath the canopy over the pumps, he lazily threw his legs from the cab and stepped out.

He took a deep breath and thought he caught the scent of rain. It was mid-March, the time of warming, sunny days and violent night storms spawned by summer's struggle to return and take over. Even now the bright sun made for a beautiful day, but the heavy, humid breeze from the south suggested the coming turbulence. By late evening, experience told him.

"Good morning."

He turned to see a thin man in greasy coveralls walking from the garage, wiping his hands on a rag. It was Cy.

"'Morning," Jack offered, taking off his sunglasses and allowing a wide smile to slip across his face.

Cy smiled; then his steps faltered. He studied Jack. "Well, I'll be . . . Jack Cashion! I heard you were coming—Mitchell Warner mentioned it the other day." With rapid steps, he came forward, stuck out his hand and encased Jack's in a firm shake. "I'd be hard-pressed to recognize you with that bristly face, man. Hell, you look like an outlaw—or one of those wild country-western singers."

Jack grinned and put a hand to his beard, feeling its thickness beneath his fingers. "Yeah . . . guess my face is pretty well covered." He'd left it that way on purpose, feeling the odd need to conceal his expressions.

"Sorry about Hoppy," Cy said.

Jack nodded.

"Mitchell said old Hoppy left you two acres that a well sets on. Oil leases aren't paying much these days."

"Tell me about it," Jack drawled with a lazy smile. He glanced around. "Looks slow."

"It is." Cy shook his head. "Savings and Loan closed six months ago, Steiner-White Oil sold out and closed down, and we've lost three stores in the past year. Hell, they're shutting down wells all over the state." He glanced at the pickup and camper. "Don't guess you've been out to the farm yet. Did you know there's an auction today?"

Surprise tingling in his bones, Jack shook his head.

"All the farm equipment, few other things of Hoppy's. Got to go to pay the bank debt." Cy shook his head. "Heck of a thing, but the land ain't to be sold, Mitchell said. Said the auction will pay."

It was the third time Cy had mentioned *Mitchell said*—and Jack didn't like it.

"Mitchell been handling everything?" he asked, watching Cy's expression turn a bit uncomfortable.

"Yeah…Willa's needed…well, Mitchell knows all about the legal stuff and such," Cy said, stumbling over his words.

Jack nodded. "That's good." And interesting, he thought. Damn Mitchell! Jack knew full well he had no right to feel that way, yet he did. He pulled out a twenty-dollar bill and handed it to Cy. "I'll pump it."

Cy nodded. They spoke of the weather, of Cy's family and of what the future looked like for the oil industry. Jack made comments and listened with only half a mind. His thoughts remained on what lay ahead—and on what Cy had told him about Mitchell.

"Let's get together for beers and poker," Cy called as Jack pulled away from the station.

Jack waved through the open pickup window. Then the road stretched out ahead of him. The powerful engine whined softly with the extra effort of towing the fifth-wheel trailer, then the pickup and trailer wheels sang along the blacktop.

Willa…Mitchell. In his mind's eye Jack pictured Willa's dark hair and how it used to feel between his fingers. His mind switched to Mitchell, and mentally he punched the image in the face. Then he tried to cool the anger. He had no right to it.

Well, he thought, determined, he was about to make it his right.

Fifteen minutes later, Jack came to the intersection of two county highways. He was only three miles from his desti-

nation. Stopped, he heard the clear call of the meadowlark, a sure sign of spring. Slowly, his eyes shaded by the
dark glasses and the wide brim of a black Stetson, he
scanned the surrounding pastureland, noting nature's rough
cuts in the earth, the brown grasses beginning to tinge with
green, two redbud trees in the first burst of violet.

He drank in the view, his heart swelling with feelings too
strong, too tangled to sort out. Like the meadowlark that
called sweet and clear, Jack had returned to Oklahoma, and
he, too, had the urge to call out the fact. To let loose with a
resounding holler, even to toss his hat in the air. A good,
southern yell signaling a charge. He grinned, settling for a
deep breath and a slow release.

Then his grin faded, inside and out. Thinking of his intentions, he slowly, deliberately shifted the pickup into gear
and headed across the intersection.

He saw the parked trucks and cars well before he arrived. They lined both sides of the road for a quarter of a
mile before and after the drive, as well as the drive itself.
Slowing the pickup, he glanced at the house. It was white,
neat and trim. The giant elm still shaded the west half. People crowded the backyard, children running, laughing.

He drove past the big auction sign with its fluttering red
flags and down to the far end of the line of cars, then pulled
the pickup and trailer onto the grassy shoulder. He turned
off the engine, reached into his jacket pocket and pulled out
a gummy bear. Slipping it into his mouth, he twirled it
around with his tongue, thinking.

Six foot two and stocky, he was a pretty big man. Not
much frightened him. It was his business to deal with the
unstable and always surprising earth, to drill deep into it and
claim its black riches, risking explosions and fires. The
danger involved rarely raised his blood pressure. But at the
moment, he noticed that his heart hammered, his palms
grew moist. It sort of puzzled him, took him several seconds to recognize it as nervousness.

He abruptly decided that drilling for oil was a hell of a lot
safer and more predictable than trying to put together the

pieces of his life. Still, nothing worthwhile in this life ever came easy. And more than work, it took persistence to get what you wanted—and he damn well knew he had persistence.

It flashed through his mind to drive on and return later. This wasn't exactly an opportune time to show up, what with all the people around and the goings-on. Then he pushed the thought aside. He was here, and here he intended to stay.

Pulling another candy from his pocket and popping it into his mouth, he alighted from the pickup and slammed the door behind him. He adjusted his hat low across his forehead and walked slowly past the parked vehicles, then down the drive. His boot heels sank a bit into earth softened by plenty of spring rain. Forsythia bushes bloomed bright yellow at the corner of the fence, and again he heard the call of the meadowlark.

Behind the shelter of the dark glasses, Jack scanned heads and figures, automatically looking for the familiar head of hair, auburn, the color of burnished mahogany. Would it still be long, flowing and curling wildly to the middle of her back? Instinctively he listened for her soft, distinctive voice, her low laugh.

He walked beneath the towering elm, close enough to check a long-remembered landmark—a lover's heart and initials he'd carved into the bark. His eyes found and lingered on the carving. Then, passing the small, portable concession booth, where two young boys guzzled soft drinks, he sauntered on across the large backyard, taking in the familiar surroundings.

Across the yard were the pump house, the grape arbor and the small orchard. Near the pump house, out of the way of the sale, sat a white pickup. Though he'd never seen it before, somehow he knew it was hers.

At the far rear of the yard was the long tin barn, and to its west side sat the equipment of Hoppy's trade: the massive water-well drilling rig, the water and gravel support truck, an old flatbed hauler and a pile of steel drilling pipe.

Jack stared at the rig, his gaze resting on the peeling paint of the company logo. Coyote Drilling. Hoppy's image came across his mind, and he pictured the old man's wiry arms straining to connect the pipes, his face, weathered by years of exposure to sun, animated and eager as the drill bit into the earth. Hoppy had been as excited about his quest for water as many a man got looking for oil.

Jack wondered if the drilling equipment was to be sold, and, for no good reason he could name, found the idea unpalatable.

The auctioneer's voice blared out over a microphone gadget. He stood on something near the big Massey-Ferguson cab tractor at the east side of the barn, where the more modern equipment was lined up. Men dressed in varying hues of blue denim and brown duck milled around, looking over the equipment, murmuring among themselves. A few were young men, but most were considerably older than Jack, middle-aged, longtime farmers and ranchers. The wise and established ones with money still to spend, looking for a bargain. Or to help out a neighbor.

Jack recognized a number of them: Mike Redbone, Charlie Seeley, W.D. Moses. And dressed more smartly in a western sport coat and slacks, a light brown Stetson on his head, was Mitchell Warner.

Jack's gaze lingered momentarily on Mitchell. The man was tall, good-looking, and more commanding than Jack remembered. He'd come far in the past two years, from junior partner in the family law firm to vice president of the family bank.

Jack and Mitchell had been good friends once, aeons ago, in their teens. They'd gone to the same swimming hole, shared Cokes, cars and first-time stories. That was before they'd each become interested in the same woman. Girl, she'd been at the time. So long ago. Jack had been the winner, and out of respect for the woman he loved, he'd managed what he termed a polite acquaintanceship with Mitchell, who'd stayed around as her friend.

Right now Jack didn't like Mitchell's familiarity with the farm. And he hated that Mitchell had been the one to contact him about Hoppy's death.

Deliberately moving his gaze, he looked at the women clustered to the side, talking in the sun. The only one he recognized was Charlie Seeley's wife. There wasn't a familiar mahogany head of hair among them.

The auctioneer called shrilly into his microphone, his rhythm picking up with the excitement of the bidding. Apparently it was getting hot and heavy over the Massey-Ferguson. Jack moved to where he could get a better look at the equipment displayed. His eyes skimmed down the attachments for the big tractor, then over a small front-loader, a smaller old tractor, mowing equipment and a hay baler.

Pivoting, he walked rapidly to the auctioneer's booth to secure a bidding number. He wrote his name on the card and watched the woman look at it. She glanced up quickly.

"Relative?" she said, noting his name on her list.

"Yes."

"That's good. Missus Cashion can use all the help she can get. Too many people out of work around here to bring in high dollars." She handed him his number, her expression curious.

Missus Cashion . . . the name echoed in his mind.

Turning from the woman's close study, Jack slipped the number into his shirt pocket and walked in long strides to the corner of the barn, an out-of-the-way place to view both the auction proceedings and the wide yard. He leaned against the stout frame and again dug for a candy, pulling out a red one this time and rolling it a moment between his fingers before slipping it into his mouth. With deliberate slowness, his gaze swept the faces and shapes, looking for Willa, the woman he'd left behind two years before. His wife.

Willa looked at Darlene Woolard and thought the woman had eyes much like her brother's had been: close together, one smaller than the other. Somehow they had added character to Hopkins Lowe. On Darlene, his only sister, they simply looked mean. And Darlene was mean, and greedy. At this thought, Willa prayed for Christian charity, a mighty elusive commodity in that moment.

"I was brought up in this house," Darlene said, glancing around. At fifty-five, she was over fifteen years younger than her late brother. She had bright, bottle-red hair, heavy breasts and buttocks and strangely skinny legs. "My father built this house." She emphasized the word *my*.

Willa just stared at Darlene's bright hair, feeling no need to argue the point. It seemed that Darlene had visited the farm more in the previous eight weeks than she had in the past eighteen years. Once Darlene had left the "backwoods," as she considered them, and had found heaven in a prosperous husband in Dallas, she'd been adverse to returning to the humble beginnings she found embarrassing.

Now, catching the scent of money, Darlene was trying to reclaim rights she'd forfeited years ago—and Willa wasn't about to let her do it. The land was hers, and Molly's. She intended to keep it, for she had, like Hoppy, the love for it. It was her firm foundation, her heritage, the only home she'd ever know.

As if sensing Willa's inattention, Darlene said, "Our lawyers say we can put a hold on everything. You won't be able to touch the money from this auction—or the oil leases, either—until the court decides who gets what."

Willa took a deep breath. "That's fine, Darlene." She'd been through all this with Darlene before, several times, and she felt it futile to discuss it any further. "I boxed up some of Grandpa's things, some pictures I found and thought you might like. I also found two of your high-school yearbooks. I'll just get them...."

She went to the hall closet and brought back a green dress box heavy with pictures and other mementos. Though she didn't think for one minute they would mean all that much to Darlene.

"If you think I'm settling for you going through my brother's things, you'd better think again." Darlene's eyes seemed to get smaller. "I'm his sister, his very next of kin. I'm going to go through this house myself." She looked around and sucked in a breath, making her ample breasts heave. "In fact, I might as well begin now. I know Hoppy had a valuable coin collection. Or have you already sold it behind Mitchell's back?"

Willa jutted the box toward her, smacking her in the stomach. "You'd better think again about going through my house, Darlene. If you were so all-fired interested in Hoppy's possessions, you should have come around a bit more while he was alive and talked to him about them."

Darlene's fleshy face was mottled with red. The veins of her plump hand shone as she grasped the box, and her flashy rings seemed to cut into her fingers.

"You ain't going to get away with all of this, Willa." Her voice rose as she moved to the door. "You ain't nothin' but Jimmy's bastard and won't ever be anything else. That counts in a court of law. I'll get my due!"

Darlene jerked open the door, then slammed it behind her. Willa was relieved to see her go, because her palm just itched to slap the woman, and she knew she'd regret such crude behavior. All her life she'd struggled to control her fiery temper.

A second later the porch screen door banged. Her insides shaking in anger, Willa moved to the window and watched Darlene call to her husband, Ray, as she stomped heavily toward the drive. Ray turned from where he was examining the antique John Deere tractor. Ray Woolard knew the worth of the machine, which had been the first one in the county back in 1920.

A soft smile touched Willa's lips. Hoppy would've been glad to know W.D. Moses had bought the John Deere—and at a good price. Old Moses had always wanted it, had tried repeatedly to talk Hoppy into selling it. But Hoppy had stubbornly refused, and for no better reason than enjoying irritating the man.

Remaining at the window, Willa looked out at the people milling about the yard. Slowly her anger faded, and a deep, sad loneliness took its place. She missed her grandfather; he'd been the stability in her life, the only one who'd always been there for her.

She looked off across the yard to the big, dull-red drilling rig, its paint rusting and peeling in a million places. It was a symbol of Hoppy, of her own life.

At the age of twelve, Willa had walked up the gravel drive of the farm for the first time to meet a grandfather she'd never even seen before. She'd been scared, but more angry than anything else, and had harbored a great yearning for a home, for someone to belong to. Her mother had given her the bus fare and directions, needing to be rid of the daughter who was a daily reminder of a love affair that had not ended in marriage. She couldn't remember her father, had seen him last at the age of two, and he'd died in a boating accident when she was five.

She hadn't expected Hopkins Lowe to welcome her, but he had, in his gruff way. He'd recognized her as belonging to his son, accepted her and done the best by her that he could. He'd given her his name, his home, his heritage.

For a bare instant her mental image of Hoppy blended into that of Jack. The stab of loneliness plunged deeper.

She became aware of clutching the rose-colored percale curtain in her hand. Releasing the cloth, she smoothed out the wrinkles with her fingers. Her gaze strayed to the envelope tucked behind the ceramic sugar container. It had remained there since the previous month when she'd dug it out to provide Mitchell with the address—Jack's address. Willa wasn't certain why she'd even saved it. A vague hope at the time, vague daring, she supposed, though she'd done nothing about it.

Mitchell had sent Jack a wire informing him of Hoppy's death and the inheritance left to him, and in response Jack had called Mitchell. Their conversation was brief, Mitchell had told her. He didn't say what he'd told Jack; Willa didn't ask. But he did say Jack planned to come as soon as possible, to settle things in person. Jack was coming. Though no one knew when. Just that he was coming.

Willa took a deep breath and let it out. She wondered when Jack would come. She wondered what she would say to him. "Well, hello, how have you been?" sounded a bit inadequate to say to the man she'd once lived with for ten years—until he'd walked out on her nearly two years ago.

As a faint sound caught her attentive ear, Willa turned and walked softly to the bedroom across the short hall from the kitchen. She reached the doorway just in time to see Molly, stomach down, lowering her tiny body from the bed where she'd been napping.

"Hello, sweetheart," Willa said, crossing the room. Kneeling, she hugged her daughter to her. The child's curls were damp where she'd lain on the bed. "Have a good sleep?"

Molly snuggled sleepily into Willa's arms and murmured around the thumb in her tiny mouth, "Potty."

Fifteen months old, still a baby, Molly thought she was ready for toilet training, but her body didn't cooperate on a regular basis. Which at this moment proved to be the case, for her pants were wet. Dutifully, Willa carried her daughter into the bathroom anyway, pulling off the moist clothes as she went. Twenty minutes later Molly, dry, cleanly dressed and wide-awake, sat on a stack of books on a chair at the kitchen table, sharing a snack of vanilla wafers and sips from her mother's cup of tea.

After their snack, Willa worked on Molly's high-top shoes and snugged her into a warm, zippered sweater, then reached for an old, oversize sweater for herself, one of Hoppy's. She thought little about her looks these days; there seemed no point to it.

She didn't want to go out among all the people, the auction being what it was—a sale to pay debts—but she couldn't afford to pass up the opportunity to have the auctioneer announce that she was once more in the drilling business.

Molly's tiny hand in hers gave Willa courage. If she were to provide a good home for her daughter, she'd have to begin building up the business again as soon as possible.

Nothing like today for getting on with it. Together they stepped from the kitchen to the screened porch and on out into the bright sunlight beyond.

Molly tugged away and toddled off to play with W.D. Moses' grandchildren at the tree swing. The eldest, June, waved at Willa, signaling that she'd take care of Molly. Willa proceeded across the yard to where the auctioneer was presiding over the sale of a backhoe attachment.

She wondered who'd bought the big Massey-Ferguson and what price it'd brought as she joined the edge of the crowd, listening and discreetly studying faces. The bored expressions, the folded arms and ball-cap brims pulled low over the forehead were as much a part of the auction as the rapid rhythm of the auctioneer's call.

The bidding for the backhoe rose quickly. Still, at the prices offered it would be a steal. W.D. Moses saw her and nodded in greeting. Willa nodded in return.

"Sold!" the auctioneer called, throwing his hands into the air in a dramatic gesture. The man who'd won the bidding, a man Willa didn't recognize, smiled and nodded his pleasure. A steal, Willa thought again, though she didn't let the thought show on her face as she made her way to the auctioneer and spoke quietly into his ear.

The crowd regrouped in a loose semicircle around the smaller, plain farm tractor, the one Hoppy had used when Willa first came to the farm. It was silly, but she had a soft spot for it in her heart. She'd spent many an hour on it, cutting hay, plowing up dirt. Self-conscious, she kept her face proud and straight, her eyes averted from any one particular person as the auctioneer stepped onto the stool provided by his assistant and spoke loudly into the microphone.

"Missus Cashion wants to let you all know the Coyote Drilling Company is once again in business." He nodded politely to her and looked out over his audience. "We all know Miss Willa worked alongside Hoppy—he taught her— so pass the word. We got a good well drilling man, er, woman here."

Willa, blushing at the compliment, felt eyes upon her. She kept her face impassive, her hands balled into tight fists and jammed into the sweater pockets. It was natural to be stared at, she told herself, under the circumstances.

Slowly, she made her way to the back of the group, fearing her presence could be awkward for the bidders. Then she stopped and turned, curiosity compelling her to wait and see just who would buy the tractor and for what price.

Mitchell appeared out of the crowd and came toward her. The hazy, bright sunshine glinted on his light brown hat. "We got a good price for the Massey-Ferguson, Willa." He stopped beside her and folded his arms across his chest. He was a tall man, and Willa had to look upward, shielding her eyes with her hand.

"How are the prices in general?" she asked.

"Low," Mitchell said after a moment.

Willa nodded, knowing the poor state of the economy. Still, she'd elected to go this route. She'd keep the land free and clear of debt. Mitchell cleared his throat, and Willa instinctively braced herself for his words of disapproval.

"Willa, well drilling is no work for you."

"Why not? I did it with Hoppy."

"That was different." He wrenched his hat from his head and slapped it against his thigh. "Hell, Willa, you're five foot five, one hundred and twenty pounds soaking wet. You don't need to be doing a man's job."

His expression of concern tugged at her heart. "I won't be doing the heavy stuff—I'll have Thomas working for me. When I need more men, I'll hire them."

Mitchell looked far from convinced. "Charlie Seeley's upped the price he's willing to give you for the land," he said, sidestepping the subject of drilling.

"That's fine," she replied, raking her hair behind her left ear. "He can offer me triple the going rate, and I'm still not going to sell."

She fought rising irritation. Mitchell couldn't be expected to understand how she felt about the land, about her heritage. He'd always known exactly where he came from; he took it for granted.

"Willa, it's a damn good offer. You'll still have the house and ten acres. What more do you need?"

"I don't need any of it," she told him, looking up again. "I just want it. And that's reason enough. I will lease to Charlie, if he still wants to."

Mitchell gave a reluctant nod. "He does. At least his son, Jared, does. I'll relay the information."

"I'll call Charlie and talk to him," Willa said firmly.

Frustration knitted Mitchell's brow. "Willa..." He waved his arm. "All this is a beautiful dream, but it could end up being a costly one. That electronics firm has decided to build up near Chickasha. Land prices are going to stay down around here for a long time ahead."

Willa shrugged, knowing that she didn't care about land prices. She cared about the land, having it to look at, knowing she walked land where people with her blood had walked before her. How could she explain that what she knew of herself was tied to the land and a way of life her great-grandfather had established? It was something a person felt, without putting it into words.

"Willa," Mitchell said, looking so frustrated that her heart softened, "sell the land and the house...and that stupid rig." He waved his hand toward the drilling rig. "The money you'd make would be a good investment in the future for you and Molly. It could work for you. You could move to town or down to Duncan."

She shook her head. "No, Mitchell. This land and that rig are my investment in the future."

She knew what Mitchell left unsaid: that he thought her foolish. And she conceded to herself that she probably was—but it was her own choice, and she liked it that way.

"You want to go to dinner tonight?" Mitchell asked then. "You and Molly. No sense in you cooking after a day like today."

Willa shook her head. "Not tonight," she said, not because it wouldn't be pleasant but because she'd allowed

Mitchell to do enough for her, with the auction and all the legalities of the will. She had to be careful to keep their relationship from growing into anything deeper. To soften her answer she laid a hand on his arm. "I think I just want to have a sandwich, a hot bath and get to bed early when this day is over. It's best for Molly, too."

Disappointment crossed his face, but he nodded. "Another night, then."

"Yes . . . thanks. And thank you, Mitchell, for all you're doing."

"You bet."

He stayed beside her, rocking back on his heels occasionally, and they both turned their full attention to the auctioneer. He'd gotten the bidding going on the tractor, but it was very low, beginning at five hundred dollars.

"If this tractor doesn't bring a high price," Willa said to Mitchell, "Hoppy will haunt whoever buys it."

Mitchell chuckled; she did, too.

"Now this tractor is old, gentlemen," the auctioneer stopped to say, building up his product, "but it purrs like a kitten. We all know Hopkins kept his machines in top working order. Don't embarrass yourselves with these low bids."

"Twelve hundred!" came a call.

Willa sighed and imagined Hoppy getting ready to stomp up and down on the clouds of heaven.

"Twenty-one!" came a counterbid.

There was bid and counterbid between two men, until finally the bidding appeared stopped at three thousand dollars. Willa knew if he were watching, Hoppy was fighting mad.

Suddenly another voice called out. "Thirty-five hundred!"

There were murmurings of surprise. Every head turned to find the voice that had spoken. Willa herself strained to see. The tempo of her heartbeat picked up. Something in the man's voice . . . there was something familiar . . . but she couldn't see who'd spoken.

The auctioneer could see him, though. Looking above the crowd, he grinned at the man. "Okay, sir!" He waited expectantly for a counterbid.

Willa eased over to try to get a look at the man who apparently was to be the tractor's next owner. She thought she located him—he seemed to be the one everyone had made space for, the one who drew everyone's attention. He was a big man, broad-shouldered, with a thick, dark beard and a black Stetson on his dark hair.

Recognition dawned at the exact moment the auctioneer cried, "Sold!"

Cold and heat flashed through Willa at the same time. Her head swirled; her legs felt weak. As if from far away, she heard the auctioneer call, "What's your number, sir?" The man held up his card. Willa stood rooted to the spot, staring, as the big man then turned her way.

He looked right at her. It was too distant to see the color of his eyes, but she knew very well their pale blue shade, the color of a clear morning sky in winter.

"And who is the proud new owner of this fine workhorse of a tractor?" the auctioneer called out in a friendly fashion.

"Jack Cashion," came the answer loud and clear, in a deep, achingly familiar voice. With movements that seemed to be in slow motion, he put a hand to his hat and lifted it in a gallant gesture. A small smile split his beard.

Willa didn't know if there was actually dead silence in the yard or if the beating of her heart in her ears drowned out all sound. She felt everyone's gaze on her.

Taking in a sharp breath, she turned and walked rapidly away.

As Jack watched Willa's long-legged stride, his stomach knotted. He saw her profile, the sharp curve of her high, pale cheekbone. Her rich, mahogany hair was cut now to just brush her shoulders, emphasizing her square jawline. A small gold hoop earring glimmered in the bright light as she raked her hair behind her left ear in a familiar habit that caused his heart to squeeze.

And she was walking—more like running—away from him.

He hesitated, wondering if it'd be better to give her a few minutes alone. He should have planned a better arrival—something a bit more romantic. Then he glanced at Mitchell, who was staring at him. That was enough to propel him into action, whether it be wise or not.

"Hell," he muttered aloud, stepping across the yard to follow Willa. He'd just quit a profitable job and come over three thousand miles, and not for any pitiful bit of inheritance—but to see Willa. *To get his wife back!*

Suddenly there came the jingle and creak of leather harness and wood, the plodding of horses' hooves as an old-fashioned wagon drawn by a pair of massive draft horses appeared around the corner of the house. Two young men sat on the wagon seat. Strapping and handsome young men, Jack realized. One waved; they both called friendly greetings to Willa. To his wife! he thought angrily.

He paused, then continued, walking more slowly, and watched Willa hurry forward to greet the two men—eagerly, he noticed. A sharp pang touched him. He felt left behind, out of her life. As, of course, he was.

He reached the corner of the small well house and stopped. Willa's voice came to him. "Yes." She sounded breathless. "I'd welcome it. I'll just get some things...."

She turned and looked at him across the short distance—a matter of yards—separating them. He waited for an invitation from her. None came.

She jerked her gaze away and looked toward the children at the swing on the apple tree. "Molly!" she called.

Into Jack's line of vision came a tiny girl, running with a clumsy, baby-child gait across the yard toward the wagon. Willa bent to swoop the child into her arms and hold her close.

Something like ice-cold steel sliced into Jack and down his back. His heart beat loudly in his ears as he watched Willa enter the house and return minutes later to have the young man help her and the child into the wagon. Then they were leaving, the horses clomping slowly away down the drive.

Away. From him.

Who was the child? Was she. . . .was she *Willa's child*?

Willa gazed straight ahead and tried to keep her breath even, her face without expression. She felt Jack's gaze drilling into her back. Realizing she was clutching her hands together, she forced them to relax and spread them across her denim-clad thighs.

"Mom wouldn't let us bring the truck," Thomas Spangler said, sitting beside her, turning the team to head back down the drive. Willa heard his words as if from far away and tried to bring her mind to the present. Thomas continued. "She's getting so she wants us to take this dang wagon everywhere."

"She'd have us taking this thing on dates, if she could," Temple called from behind where he sat with Molly. Temple and Thomas were the only two males Molly ever had much to do with. "But I put a stop to that the first time she suggested it." The two young men were twins, though it wasn't readily apparent.

Willa pushed her hair behind her ear and tried for a smile for Thomas.

Jack. *It had been Jack.*

The beard did a good job of hiding his features, but she'd known him, had recognized the proud tilt of his head, the charming, lopsided smile, the very boldness of his stance.

Puzzlement touched Thomas's eyes just before he looked back at the horses and clicked the reins for them to pick up speed and pull the wagon out onto the blacktop. "Mom figured you wouldn't have ate," he said. He smiled. "Has a big supper waitin'."

Willa did a better job with her smile this time, but still, she couldn't find her voice.

She was running away. She didn't even know why. Except she had to have some time to. . . to prepare herself.

Gather her wits so as not to make a complete fool of herself before him.

She listened to the sound of the horses' hooves against the pavement, to Temple teasing Molly, to Molly's laughter, Thomas's whistling. She looked around at the rolling land awakening from winter sleep. Another memory from long ago filled her thoughts: the sun upon Jack's dark, lustrous hair, his even, white teeth beneath his mustache when he smiled.

Nearly two years—twenty-two months—and he'd returned.

She'd have to face him now.

Have to face herself—and her guilt in having a daughter, his daughter, she'd never told him about.

Chapter Two

Twenty minutes later, the sight of Carrie Spangler waving to them from the porch pulled Willa from her jumbled thoughts.

Carrie Spangler was considered a character in the county. A tall, large-boned and attractive woman, she carried herself with uncommon pride. One hardly noticed her usual attire of baggy pants and oversize men's shirts as being a bit odd. With her adherence to old-fashioned customs, some believed her a member of the small Amish community who lived in the area, but in actuality she was a sociology professor from a northern university who'd "dropped out," as she put it, some fifteen years ago. A widow, she'd come south and bought a farm. With a good deal of her income coming from essays in national publications, she'd done everything she could to return to a simpler style of life, and she had raised Thomas and Temple in such a style.

Carrie was also the one person Willa counted as a true friend. Though a generation apart, they shared a love for the land and the fact of both being single mothers. And with

Carrie there was never any pressure to explain actions or feelings.

Allowing Carrie the rarity of an embrace, Willa felt the older woman's calm strength emanate to her. Carrie pulled back and studied Willa's eyes.

"Thanks for sending Temple and Thomas for me," Willa said.

"I'm glad you came," Carrie replied. She turned to take Molly from Temple. "Come on up and relax. We'll eat directly."

Throughout the leisurely meal, Jack lingered in Willa's mind. It was odd, she thought, how a person could carry on perfectly normal conversation while her mind remained swirling wildly. She'd wanted to blurt out the news about Jack, but she couldn't with Thomas and Temple present. And even later, when she was alone with Carrie, cleaning up, her innate reticence held her in check. Some things were too private to share, hurt too much, were too confused to fit into words.

"Has Darlene paid any more visits?" Carrie asked, squeezing liquid detergent into the sink. She resisted buying a dishwasher, saying it was just another machine to break down.

Willa nodded and sighed. "This morning. She's determined, I'll give her that. She says she's starting legal proceedings to contest the will." Willa gathered the dirty plates from the table and took them to the counter, in the process stepping over Molly, who was playing with empty pots and pans on the floor.

"She can't think she'll get much money from the estate," Carrie said, puzzled. "Why in heaven's name does she think there's an auction of all the equipment, if not to pay off the bank note?"

"She knows there's not much money. She wants the land."

"The land? Whatever for? Surely not to farm from her drawing room down there in Dallas. And the price of it is at rock bottom."

"I think she caught wind of a possible electronics plant going in."

"Really? I hadn't heard."

"I hadn't either until Charlie Seeley mentioned it when he approached me about buying part of our place." She winced at the slip. "*My* place. Then the next time Darlene and Ray came up, poking around, Darlene made this comment about dividing sixty acres into five- to ten-acre tracts. She wants to sell it as residential acreages—I just know it." Willa gathered empty glasses from the table. "Mitchell told me today, though, that the electronics firm is going up to Chickasha. Still, Darlene knows land prices won't stay down forever."

"You got that right," Carrie agreed. "And I imagine she sees a free and ready investment."

Willa nodded. "She can afford to let it sit there, waiting for a ripe time to sell, no matter how many years it takes." Molly began banging a pot lid unmercifully, and Willa bent to pick her up. "Hey, Squirrel, enough noise."

"I can hardly believe Darlene is from the same womb that bore Hopkins Lowe," Carrie said. "Pardon my bluntness."

Willa chuckled. "I've had the exact feeling. But let's face it, Hoppy had a stubborn streak, too. While I wouldn't describe it as mean, he could be downright ornery."

She paused and gently raked her fingers through Molly's short brown curls and brushed her lips across Molly's velvet cheek. She studied her daughter's blue eyes, her button nose, her full lips surrounding the thumb within her mouth. Sometimes she felt she couldn't get enough of looking at her.

"Darlene called me a bastard this morning," Willa said, almost before she realized it.

Carrie, both hands in the sudsy water, looked up. "Did it bother you?"

"Yes," Willa admitted after a moment. "And I'm certainly surprised at myself. I'd thought I was over all that years ago. But the *way* she said it, as if I didn't belong there at the farm—which, of course, was what she intended." A soft smile broke into the bleakness of her spirit. "But you know, Hoppy took that stigma from me when he took me to live with him. I can still remember him driving me into town and going right into the school to enroll me. He said he wanted to enroll his granddaughter. Said it loud and clear."

Carrie smiled. "In any event, you are one hundred percent Lowe, temper and all." A wicked gleam lit her eyes. "Maybe that's why you and Darlene clash so."

"You're stepping on dangerous ground," Willa said in mock warning.

Carrie turned serious. "You doing better now? Sleeping okay?"

Willa nodded. "Better now. I'll never quit missing Hoppy, but I've come to accept it." She gave a wry smile. "At least I'm not so mad at him anymore."

"Good sign . . . you're progressing through the grief," Carrie said. "And I'm glad to see you carrying on with your plans for the business, too. You need it."

"Yes." Willa nodded. "I had it announced at the auction today—Coyote Drilling is officially in business again. Now we just have to get some jobs."

"Thomas is still intent on working with you," Carrie said. "He told Ben Wheatley he'd help him at the ranch for a while, but he means to come drill with you full-time when you'll have him. He didn't want to say anything to you today, knowing you were already weighted down with concerns, but I could see he was itching to ask about it."

Willa smiled. "I'll speak to him about it before I go. I should have before, because heaven knows I'll need him. I'm just afraid that for a while I can't promise steady work. It will take time to get our name spread around."

"Thomas knows that."

"Carrie, I want you to know I'm grateful for yours and the boys' friendship."

Carrie motioned with a wet hand. "Go on now . . . take that child out on the front porch and nurse her. She's about to pull the buttons off your shirt."

Willa enveloped Molly's tiny hand within her own, arresting it from plucking at the material of her blouse. Molly let out fussy whimpers, furrowing her brows, mumbling, "Nap...naapp."

Willa chuckled and kissed her as she walked out to the front porch to sit in one of the three rope-bottomed wooden rockers. The sun was warm in the afternoon sky, and there was no longer a need for sweaters. Opening her blouse, she unfastened her bra and nestled Molly to her breast. Molly's eyes smiled up at her, and Willa bent to kiss the child's soft forehead. A sudden contentment settled over her as her milk let down. Leaning her head back, she pushed the chair to gentle rocking, allowing the peace of a rare, balmy day to envelop her.

She'd wanted Molly, had prayed for years, and at last the miracle had happened. At a time when something was taken from her, something had also been given. She never let a day go by that she didn't give thanks and take care to observe her daughter's every tiny step in her journey of growth. Oh, she knew that she clung to the baby stage, but children grew up fast enough. There was no need to push. So, despite the righteous shock of some, she continued to nurse, didn't firmly press for toilet training, and picked Molly up and held her at the slightest whim. She wanted for her daughter the childhood she'd never had herself.

What would Jack say when he learned of Molly—providing, of course, he stayed around long enough to learn?

She knew very well she should have told him, if not before Molly's birth, at least afterward. From the very first she'd received periodic notes informing her of his address changes. Occasionally there'd been telephone numbers. And for the first twelve months, there'd been checks, which she'd always returned without an acknowledgement of any kind. She wouldn't take, didn't need, his money.

Her pride in shreds, she'd wanted nothing from Jack. She was perfectly capable of standing on her own two feet. Finally the checks had stopped coming, but the notes continued, containing only his address. These she'd kept, pressing them to the back of her lingerie drawer.

A hundred times she'd grabbed pen and paper to write, once even dared to dial the latest number he'd sent, to tell him about Molly. He should know he'd fathered a child; both he and Molly had that right. Yet she'd hung up before he could answer, and she'd never written.

How could she tell him she'd been carrying his child when he'd left, when he'd said he simply didn't want to be married anymore? The pity and guilt on his face had driven the pain even deeper into her heart. She wondered how long he'd felt that way and had stayed with her out of a sense of obligation—not love.

What had happened between them was to her like an uneven gash, too ragged to ever come together and heal.

Her husband hadn't wanted her anymore. He hadn't wanted the love she offered; his love for her had died. There was not much that could hurt a woman more, Willa reflected now with a detached sense of calm she'd learned to employ when going over it in her mind.

Jack's leaving had severely wounded her sense of self-worth. For a long time all she could see were her faults: her hot temper, her tendency to pout. It had been her fault he'd gone away. There was something wrong with her that no one could love her. Hadn't it always been so? Her father had gone away, died before she even knew him. Her own mother hadn't wanted her. No one had ever wanted her, but Hoppy. And now he, too, was gone.

Brushing a trickling tear from her cheek, she sniffed. Silly self-pity, she told herself, and she wouldn't have it!

All those memories were in the past. What had been done by both herself and Jack was as new-mown hay that couldn't be put back to its stems again—it was done, no way to undo it. She must deal with the present.

Jack was here. There was explaining to be done. Both dread and a strange, inexplicable anticipation swirled within her heart.

The door creaked, and Carrie stepped out onto the porch. She smiled down at Willa. "I'd turn back the clock if I could," she said. "Few things more fulfilling than holding a sleeping child."

"The key word there is *few*," Willa quipped as Carrie went to sit in the swing. With gentle movements she shifted Molly and readjusted her clothes. Molly snored softly as Willa again pulled her close.

"Ah, yes," Carrie breathed. "There is eating—chocolate cake being very fulfilling—and there are men." She gave a throaty chuckle.

"Yes, there are men."

Then they each fell into their own thoughts.

"Weatherman says there's a cold front coming," Carrie commented after a minute. "Storms tonight."

Willa nodded, only half hearing. She thought of Jack's most recent address way up in northwestern Canada. She wondered if he liked the area, the weather there.

"You brooding over Darlene's threats?" Carrie asked then. It was unusual for Carrie to ask any question that pried into a person's thoughts. Knowing the concern that prompted the question now caused Willa to smile.

She shook her head, wanting so much to speak of the worries in her heart but finding it hard.

"It's Jack," she said finally, forcing her voice from her throat. Tears blurred her vision. "He's come back." There, she'd said it aloud.

"Oh," Carrie said after a moment. "You knew he was coming sometime soon."

"Yes. I knew." Willa rocked the chair.

"So, what'd he say?"

"Nothing." Willa looked sheepish. "I didn't talk to him. He showed up this morning at the auction. He just showed up! No warning. And in front of all those people! I couldn't face him, Carrie. Not without some kind of…preparation. Then Thomas and Temple pulled into the yard, and I ran away over here."

Carrie's lips twitched, her eyes understanding. "How do you feel now?"

A full half minute hung in the air while Willa tried to answer the question in her mind.

"Like a stiff southern wind has knocked me down and won't let me get up again." She gave a dry chuckle. "I can't imagine why in the world I feel so... so unbalanced."

She paused, still trying, unsuccessfully, to understand herself. "I'm not mad at him anymore—a person can't be mad at someone for not loving them. And Jack didn't set out to deliberately hurt me—I can't lay blame on him anymore. Besides, it's sort of hard to sustain anger for so long a time at someone you don't even see." She shook her head. "I guess I'm scared. There's a lot I have to face now—telling him about Molly, seeing to a divorce." The pain, almost as fresh as it had been two years earlier, washed over her. "I'm wondering how it will feel when I see him face-to-face, talk to him. It's going to be so hard, Carrie."

"Uh-huh." Carrie moved the creaking swing. "If the hurting remains, Willa, could it be that some feelings still do, too?"

Willa hesitated. "I don't know. That part of my heart is numb, or dead. Sometimes I think I'll never be able to love any man again." Her heart hardened, and she met Carrie's gaze. "Jack Cashion isn't a man easily forgotten, but I don't intend to waste my life mooning over him."

Carrie looked noncommittal. "What about you and Mitchell?"

"I've been considering it, Carrie, some. Mitchell's made no secret of his affection." She smiled. "You know he was the first boy I ever kissed?"

Carrie smiled. "Oh, yeah?"

Willa nodded. "Behind the church, of all places, right next to Lath Tanner's tombstone. Mitchell's the only man besides Jack I ever kissed. I never had many dates—no more than two with Mitch before I met Jack. I just was never at ease with people." The lonely girl she'd been filled her thoughts. "Mitch was nice, but Jack, well, he had a way about him. Mitchell married Beth not long after Jack and I married. I thought they made a good couple. Mitchell never talks about her, hasn't ever said what went wrong between them."

"Have you ever talked to him about Jack?"

"No." She couldn't talk to anyone about Jack. Carrie was the only one to know Willa hadn't told Jack of the existence of a daughter. She looked at Carrie.

"Mitchell's a good, steady man. Maybe I'm not all hot and panting after him, but I do care for him. And he'd be there for me." She frowned. "But I'm not certain I could make him happy. I couldn't be the little wife greeting him in the evenings with a martini in hand and wearing a ruffled apron. I'd put my land before him, and as for drilling—well, he doesn't understand that at all. It's not in his picture for a woman, much less his wife." She chuckled. "Now, can you see me moving up to the Warner mansion and parking the rig out back?"

Carrie chuckled, too, then said, "You can build a love on many different things, Willa. Question is, do you want to?"

"That's something I have to figure out. I'm not thrilled with going through life without a man, but the more I go along, the more I believe it does have its advantages. I don't have to accommodate anyone but Molly."

"There are more disadvantages," Carrie said emphatically.

"You chose to do it, Carrie."

"I did. It suited me for a while. But sometimes I think of the two men who came into my life after Richard, and I regret not choosing one of them. The nights can be lonely, Willa, and the days long." A shy and unfamiliar twinkle lit Carrie's eyes. "Ben Wheatley has asked me to go over to Ruidoso for the weekend after next. He's entering a horse."

"Ruidoso?" Willa was amazed. She'd known Carrie and Ben had been close friends, but she hadn't known about romance. "Well...are you going to go, and what is all this?"

Carrie nodded, looking much like the cat who's caught the canary. "Yes, I am. Ben is interested. I can hardly believe it after all these years, at my age. And he's something—fifty-two years old and a body as hard as a rock. He knows a thing or two about pleasing a woman.''

"Carrie," Willa said gently, "you're a handsome woman and quite a catch yourself."

The older woman blushed and touched her hair. "Well, what I'm getting at is that man and woman go together. It's the way of this world, the way the Almighty made it." Her eyes turned dark. "Don't make the mistake I made, Willa, by turning inward in your hurt. Don't close your heart to love that can be there for you if you'll let it."

Willa nodded thoughtfully. Jack's image and the way his kisses used to make her feel filled her mind. Maybe no man could ever come after him.

"Well," she said with finality, "one thing's certain now— I can't put off telling Jack about Molly any longer."

Carrie chuckled. "I don't think there'll be a lot of 'telling' involved. One look is worth a thousand words."

Amusement touched Willa, too. "Yes, the evidence speaks for itself," she agreed, chuckling. As her gaze met Carrie's, they both erupted into full laughter. Long ago, when still a small, lonely child, she'd learned the strength to be found in seeing the funny side of every situation.

But, she thought in the next instant, she doubted very much that Jack would consider the news he had a daughter no one had told him about very funny.

The sun was far to the west, rays shining upward behind gathering purple clouds, when Thomas drove Willa and Molly home, this time by car. Temple, by far the more outgoing of the two, stayed home to ready himself for a date.

Willa held Molly on her lap and strained her gaze ahead as they approached the house, looking for a vehicle or any sign of Jack's presence. Even while doing so, she chastised herself for her silly behavior. Did she expect him to sit on the porch step and wait? Perhaps, after the way she'd run away, he wouldn't even return. Her heart beat apprehensively at the thought.

The vehicles that had lined the road and drive were gone. The place that only that morning had teemed with people was silent, felt exceedingly empty. Willa noted that W.D. Moses had already taken the antique John Deere away, and the large Massey-Ferguson had also disappeared. The remaining equipment would be claimed by the new owners at various times over the following week.

The tractor Jack had bought still sat where it had that morning. Why had he bought it? she wondered. Did he perhaps have a place on which he could use it? The idea hurt. He could have a place, and another woman.

"Mom says that bad weather's coming," Thomas said as he pulled to a stop. He nodded toward the woodpile. "Want me to help you get in some wood?"

Willa smiled. "Thanks, Thomas. That'd be nice." Carrie had raised a pair of uncommonly polite boys, she thought.

Thomas looked sheepish. "Well...Mom told me to ask—and she's sure to ask me if I did when I get home."

Willa laughed aloud. Molly called out, "Potty! Potty, Mama!" Whisking her daughter to her hip, Willa ran to the house, calling to Thomas over her shoulder, "The wheelbarrow's right there by the pile."

This time Molly was very proud of keeping dry pants, and Willa praised her excessively. Then, with Molly trying to "help," Willa and Thomas filled the bin beside the fireplace nearly to overflowing with wood.

Willa stood on the back step and waved goodbye, offering, "I'll call you as soon as we get a drilling job." Thomas flashed her a smile and a wave.

Willa looked west, toward the growing cover of thick clouds, and wondered if Jack would return that evening, or the next day...or the next.

She imagined telling him about Molly. Nothing seemed to fit. She imagined talking about divorce. How hard it all was.

And for the first time, she fully admitted she still cared for Jack Cashion. She couldn't honestly call it love, for she didn't know for sure. But something remained within the hidden places of her heart.

"Fool," she murmured.

The setting sun sent rays peeking through a break in the purple clouds and reflected gold in the rearview mirror as Jack drove east out of town. He'd enjoyed a hamburger and beer and visited with several old acquaintances at the Township Café. Now he again headed toward the Lowe farm. He rephrased the thought: Willa Cashion's farm.

Images swirled in his mind. He saw her rich hair gleaming in the sun, saw her again as she'd looked standing beside Mitchell. His ire rose.

The child—*who was the child*? Regret stabbed deeply into him. He'd never been able to give Willa a child, and she'd so longed for one. When Mitchell's image filled his mind again, dread settled upon his shoulders. Was the child Mitchell's? Was it like that between Willa and Mitchell now? A hole, big and deep, seemed to open up within him. If Willa and Mitchell were together, then why no divorce? Lord, he had too many questions. Questions he intended to have answered tonight.

Jack was nearly past the cemetery before he realized it and decided to stop. He pulled the pickup and trailer to a fairly reckless halt at the side of the road, alighted, and walked through the entry gate.

Light was fading fast now, early dark brought on by the growing clouds. The air had taken on an eerie stillness that spoke of gathering winds miles away. Jack knew he'd have to hurry if he were to find Hoppy's grave.

Not having any inkling of where to look, he strode rapidly along the small paths, searching for newer looking graves. There were few, and the cemetery was small. He shoved his hands into his jacket pockets, then, with one, pulled out a candy and slipped it into his mouth.

Luck was with him; in just a few minutes he found the marker near the far west corner of the cemetery, where the land dipped toward a gully. *Hopkins B. Lowe* the temporary flat marker read. Looking at the close proximity to the gully, Jack had to chuckle. He'd bet Hoppy had chosen that place for himself, thinking that if a good flood came up, the gully could possibly wash and unearth his casket, maybe even carry it away into the next county. Hoppy would have found such a happening hilarious.

Jack looked at the marker and the fresh earth with bits of grass and weeds just beginning to grow. It wasn't Hoppy, yet he found himself inwardly talking to the man, remembering.

He thanked Hoppy first, for all the old man had given him, friendship and fatherly guidance, acceptance, which didn't come easily from Hopkins Lowe. And for Willa; she wouldn't have married him if Hoppy hadn't given his approval.

The first time Jack had seen Willa was when he and his father had come to drill a well on the Lowe farm—the same acreage that Hoppy had given Jack in the will. Jack's father was working in partnership with Kinsey Oil, a small, loose association of wildcatters.

In memory, Jack traveled back to his teens. He and his father weren't overly close, but they got on well together. His mother had left them both before Jack's fourth birthday. To this day he knew little of her; his father wouldn't say anything more about her than that one day she'd run off with the circus. Jack's outspoken Aunt Mary said his mother *was* a circus. It had been Aunt Mary who'd finally told Jack his mother's full name and had provided a picture of her. He'd thought to look her up, but soon after word had come of her death. It seemed better for her to be dead than to go to her and find she wanted nothing to do with him.

Willa had come out with Hoppy to watch the drilling that very first day. Jack had noticed she was pretty, with skin the color of heavy cream and wide, luminous hazel eyes. But it was her hair that struck him most. He'd never seen anyone with such beautiful hair, long past her shoulders, the color of Aunt Mary's polished mahogany drop-leaf dinner table.

In short order, he'd discovered the amazing fact that Willa knew an awful lot about drilling, having been taught by Hoppy all about the process of sinking water wells. She even worked with Hoppy, seemed to share the passion for the land and for the quest of drilling into it. That very first day he'd asked her out to a movie. He guessed they fell in love within the following two weeks. She'd been fifteen, he a bare nineteen. They had in common a hurtful childhood, a fascination with drilling, and a mutual, burning physical attraction.

It had come as something of a shock to discover that Willa was the same girl Mitchell was interested in—deeply interested. But though Mitchell was a longtime friend, Jack wouldn't give up on Willa. The friendship ended, in blows.

For the next two years, Jack spent the summer traveling around, working on drilling crews all over the state and down into Texas with his father, gaining experience as well as earning college money. But he'd made sure to get up to see Willa often. Each fall, he went to college. Letters to and from Willa flew through the mail. Jack got away only once at Christmas to see her, because any time he wasn't in school, he was working to pay for going.

Then came the third summer. Willa was seventeen, graduated from high school. That fact seemed to make time feel as if it were rushing along. Again Jack worked around the state with his father and traveled back and forth between wherever he worked and Willa.

How he wanted her. He begged her a hundred times in the seat of his pickup. But she refused repeatedly... until one night, one late-summer, starry night when the air was heavy, humid and sweet.

In two weeks he'd be going back to college. The inevitable separation hung heavy on both their hearts. Jack kissed her and stroked the velvet skin at her waist, afraid to go farther for fear of being unable to stop. Feeling a fool, but with the driving need pressing him onward, he whispered in her ear, "Please, Willa..."

Her answer sent his blood pounding through his veins. She didn't speak, merely sucked in a sharp breath and pressed against him.

So they'd made love there in the truck. And Jack had always wished their first time had been in a soft bed with smooth sheets. And that he'd gone slower. But, oh, how she'd taken him to heaven that night with the sweet abandonment of her inexperience, trusting in him to show her the way. He'd been a boy; she'd made him step a long way into manhood. At least for a few minutes he'd thought of someone besides himself.

He'd loved her, couldn't bear to leave, wanted to make things right. Against all practicality, he'd asked her to marry him. And had been astonished when she'd hesitated and said they had to ask Hoppy. He'd sweated that one, especially when Hoppy had fixed that cold, stern eye upon them. Jack felt in his bones the old man knew what had transpired in the front seat of that pickup. He hardly heard Hoppy say fine and offer them his blessing.

He and Willa loved each other. Except for wanting a child that didn't come, that doctors suspected Jack couldn't father, they were happy. Truth be known, Jack liked it being just himself and Willa; all her attention remained focused on him. And they could do what they wanted, when they wanted.

He couldn't say just when things went wrong. Only that they did.

At the young age of thirty-one, Jack was called throughout the southwest, as well as to such places as Peru, Mexico, Alaska, Canada, for his expertise as an independent oil consultant. The demand for oil grew, and the industry boomed. Heady stuff. Money flowed, women gathered, and Jack's head turned.

He felt his marriage foundering, knew it was mostly his fault, felt guilty and didn't like it. He didn't want to lose Willa, couldn't bring himself to sever the marriage tie, but neither could he resist the lure of excitement, power and flattery. It seemed he'd sort of been swept away, in the process losing sight of the jewel he left behind.

"Lord, Hoppy," Jack murmured. "I made a hell of a mistake, and I'm sorry. I'd do anything to wipe it all away."

The heavy weight of regret settled upon his chest. He'd known he'd made an enormous mistake almost from the first. He'd wanted to come home for well over a year, he mentally told Hoppy, fully admitting his cowardice. The plain fact was that he'd been afraid to face Willa, couldn't stand to see the accusation he feared would be in her eyes. Every time he thought about coming, he'd remind himself that she was safe and secure with Hoppy, was better off without him. He'd messed up her life; it was best not to interfere. But then he'd heard Hoppy had died, leaving Willa alone. Unless she'd found someone else. She was alone, and she might need him.

And heaven knew, he needed her. He wanted her.

"I can't change what I did, Hoppy," he murmured. "But I'm going to try to make it up to her." He thought about the child and coughed into his fist. "I'll be good to the child, Hop. I promise. If you have any influence from up there, I'd sure appreciate it." He turned to go, then stopped. "I love her, Hoppy."

It remained now for him to prove it, to win back the woman he'd loved since he was nineteen years old. The woman he'd carried in his heart throughout all the struggles of the past two years to find himself again. That the chances for success weren't in his favor, he refused to consider. A man determined his own chances, he figured. A man chose his own place in life. And he was stubborn enough to still believe he could reach the stars if he just tried hard enough.

Suddenly, realizing it had grown too dim to make out the words on Hoppy's marker, Jack turned and strode from the grave site. Colder air blowing from the north now tugged at his hair and nipped at the collar of his jacket.

The air sucked at him as he opened the door to his pickup and slipped behind the wheel. He pulled out onto the road, impatient at the slow response of the truck as it struggled to pull the trailer. He pressed the accelerator. The headlights illuminated leaves blowing across the road, rapidly swirling in the gusty wind. There came the sound of distant thunder.

While still far down the road, he spied the light from the pole lamp at the opening of the drive. As he got closer, he saw the second pole lamp at the rear of the drive. Its glow illuminated a car—a brown sedan.

Jack had no knowledge of who owned the vehicle, but he could take a calculated guess at what sort of person would drive that car. Some inner sixth sense told him he'd find Mitchell Warner in the house with Willa. He glanced over at the flowers lying beside him in the seat and prayed Mitchell didn't live there with her.

Chapter Three

Mitchell watched Willa's eyes widen in surprise as he told her about Jack's purchases that afternoon.

"He bought the flatbed truck, too?" she asked, turning her puzzled gaze to the papers Mitchell had insisted she take a look at.

"He bought that and all the equipment for baling hay," he told her flatly.

He watched her carefully, trying to judge how much of her reaction was surprise, how much indicated a deeper feeling for Jack Cashion. She looked better than he'd seen her in months, and a dull ache touched his heart. He knew she hadn't dressed up for him; she hadn't known he was coming.

No, it wasn't for him that she'd dressed in slim-fitting designer jeans and a soft peach sweater that brought out the creaminess of her cheeks. It wasn't for him that she'd taken time to put on makeup. She expected Jack.

With determination, Mitchell tried to let the hurt go. It wasn't important now, he reminded himself. What mattered was what happened after Jack left.

Jack Cashion was a fool, Mitchell thought vehemently, for letting Willa slip through his fingers, for ignoring a daughter he'd sired. But that was all right with Mitchell, because Cashion's stupidity was his good fortune. He wished Cashion hadn't decided to come back at all, but maybe it was for the best. Now Willa would be able to get it all settled, free herself from the man legally and mentally. And Mitchell intended to be there for her when she did.

"I don't understand," Willa said, pushing her thick hair behind her left ear and raising hazel eyes full of questions from the papers. Mitchell's heart tugged. She looked so young and vulnerable. "What can he want with all that stuff? Did you talk to him?"

Mitchell shook his head. "No. He paid by check and left. Nina said she told him all the equipment had to be claimed by this coming Friday, and he told her that'd be fine."

Willa looked back at the papers. "He certainly got it all fairly cheap."

"None of the bids were high. But you'll pay the debt and have a bit of money left over. Even after Darlene gets her thousand. It's what you wanted—the land free of debt."

"Yes...it's what I wanted." She studied the sheets of paper, as if to find answers there. Mitchell longed to lay a hand upon her shiny hair, to test its warmth. But fearing to drive her from him, he restrained the impulse. Willa had been hurt badly by Jack. Mitchell needed patience to get beyond that hurt and into her heart.

There came the sound of a vehicle in the drive. Willa's gaze flew to his; then she moved to look out the window above the sink. He watched her shoulders tighten as she leaned forward. Suddenly the wind seemed higher, buffeting the house. Or was it just so quiet in the kitchen that every sound seemed louder? Mitchell could even hear Molly's faint singing from her bedroom beyond the hall.

Willa turned from the sink and grabbed a towel to wipe her hands. They weren't wet; she just needed the activity. She imagined the large figure she'd seen alighting from a tan pickup walking across the yard to the back porch. She couldn't hear his footsteps—the wind made too much noise—but imagination conjured up the sound for her.

She heartily wished Mitchell hadn't come out. In her effort to be polite and kind that morning, apparently she hadn't made it plain that she wanted to be alone tonight. Nor had she been able to tell him point-blank when he showed up, bearing pizza and soft drinks, to make certain she ate. Irritation sprang up suddenly toward both men who'd appeared at their own convenience to complicate her life.

Heart pounding in her ears, she met Mitchell's gaze.

"It's Jack," she said, then thought it was an unnecessary statement. No doubt Mitchell had a good idea of whose hand had just opened the screen door to the porch and made it creak, whose footsteps scraped the porch flooring.

Quite suddenly, as she forced her legs to walk to the back door, Willa heard very clearly Molly's sweet singsong voice floating from her bedroom.

Flipping on the porch light, Willa opened the door before Jack could knock.

Like a massive chunk of granite, he seemed to fill the doorway. Always a hefty man, he was heavier now, especially around the middle. His shoulders stretched the denim fabric of his jacket to its limit. His eyes were dark beneath the shadow of his hat, his face mostly hidden by the thick beard. So different...and yet so much the same. It was Jack, the boy she'd fallen in love with, the man who'd been her husband for twelve years. And now, after so many months, he stood on her doorstep, awkwardly holding a large bouquet of roses, daisies and baby's breath. For her? she thought with wonder.

In that moment the longing to run into his strong arms swamped her. But she stood where she was, feeling the wind tug at her hair and suck at her sweater.

"Hello, Willa." His voice was deep and soft. He removed his hat, and she saw clearly his pale blue eyes.

"Hello, Jack." How odd to be looking at him after such a long time. To speak in a perfectly normal fashion when she could hardly breathe. She moved back. "Come in."

Jack caught her fragrance as he stepped past her into the kitchen. Behind him lightning cracked across the sky, and out of the corner of his eye he saw Willa jump slightly.

His gaze fell on Mitchell unwinding his lean body from a chair at the table. His first thoughts were ones of grudging respect. Mitchell had filled out over the years. His suit coat hung well on his tall frame, and there was a strong, commanding air about him. Jack met the man's gaze and nodded politely. Mitchell didn't offer his hand, and Jack didn't, either—he hadn't missed the challenge in his former friend's deep blue eyes.

He twirled his hat a half circle and, realizing he stood like a fool with the flowers still in hand, held them out to Willa.

Her gaze on the flowers, she slowly reached for them with slim fingers. She cast him a shy glance. "Thank you." Her words came softly.

She was more beautiful than he remembered. It didn't embarrass him to just look at her for a minute, to study her golden-brown eyes when she again gazed up at him and to search for feeling there. For the moment everything else faded from his consciousness.

He didn't think he imagined it—there was something there. In her eyes. On her face. Something definitely still sparked between them. Jack continued to gaze at her, taking immense pleasure in something so long denied him.

"You bought quite a lot at the sale today," Mitchell said, his voice cutting into the private moment. Willa jerked her head to look at him, then returned her gaze to Jack, her eyebrows knitting with a question.

Jack turned more slowly to Mitchell and searched his mind for an acceptable way to tell the man to get the hell out of his business.

Just as he opened his mouth to speak there came a bright, searing flash and the sound of a horrendous explosion above their heads. It sounded as if all hell had broken loose right over the house, destroying every bit of light in the process.

Jack acted instinctively, throwing himself toward Willa, pushing her against the near wall, shielding her with his body. Her scream of surprise echoed in his ears.

"Willa?" Jack stared into the darkness but couldn't see her face. Yet he could feel her trembling body against his own, and he recognized after a second that she was struggling to push him away. "Willa? Are you all right?"

"Yes, but I have to get Molly!" Urgency vibrated in her voice.

Stepping back and releasing her, he stood a moment, trying to get his bearings, listened to make certain the house wasn't crashing down around them. Myriad sounds came to him: a child crying for Mama, a chair crashing to the floor and Mitchell's muttered oath, wind rattling the windows, lightning crackling in the air.

A flash of lightning illuminated the counter, and Jack tossed his hat onto it. Using the counter as a guide, he searched for the cabinet where he knew flashlights used to be kept. Mitchell called for Willa; Willa answered.

"Smoke... I smell smoke, Jack," Mitchell said in a low voice.

"I smell it, too," Jack said, keeping his voice calm. "Hold on—I'm getting a flashlight." He also heard what he recognized as the sizzle of broken electrical wires up above them. And the roaring sound of rising wind. His hand felt carefully inside the cabinet and closed around the slim cylinder of a flashlight.

"Willa?" he called, training the flashlight on the far end of the kitchen in the direction of the hall. The beam of light played across her figure and that of a bundle beneath a quilt in her arms. "Come on. We'll get you two out to the storm shelter." He moved forward quickly, showing the others the way with the flashlight. He opened the back door and held it steady against the wind. Heavy drops of rain began to splat against the porch roof.

"Jack...the house..." Willa said, coming forward to duck beneath his arm. "If it's on fire..."

"We'll worry about that after we get you out of here," he told her, pressing a hand to her back and directing her out onto the back porch. "Wait." He shrugged out of his jacket. Moisture smacked his face and shoulders where the wind blew rain against the screens.

Mitchell moved around Willa to the screen door, saying, "Hurry up!"

Positioning himself against Willa's back and a little to the side, Jack held his coat over her head. Sheltered by the denim and Jack's huge body, Willa held Molly tight and stepped out from the porch. The wind jerked the screen door and slammed it back. The rain lashed at her, the ground squished under her feet and the wind seemed to take her breath away.

They ran the few feet to the storm cellar, where already Mitchell struggled to open the door. Relying heavily on Jack's supporting hand, Willa hurried down the steep steps. Using his flashlight, Jack located the battery lantern on a shelf alongside jars of canned beans. It worked, if dimly. Mitchell pulled the cellar door closed.

Willa slipped the now damp quilt from Molly's head. Molly stared up at her with wide, curious eyes. Willa smiled reassuringly and stroked Molly's curls. "We're having an adventure," she said softly.

Molly blinked, fearfulness turning to curiosity.

"She okay?" Jack asked, holding the lantern high to shine on Molly.

"Yes," Willa answered, breathless. "She's never been afraid of storms." *Just like you and me,* she thought, leaving the words unsaid.

Jack stood very close. He stared at Molly, and Willa wondered what he thought of his daughter. His expression told her nothing—except that he was thinking something, very deeply. Slowly he turned his gaze to Willa. She put her hand to his chest, almost without realizing, and looked up at him, seeing his face shadowy in the dim glow of the lantern. Rivulets of water dripped from the thick hair on his forehead and beaded on his beard. He grinned.

"Want to open the door and have a look?" he asked, a touch of mischievousness in his voice.

Willa nodded. "Yes . . . wouldn't we, Molly?"

Before the words were out of her mouth, Jack moved to comply. The rain poured in the opening, soaking the steps and their faces as they stared upward. The wind swirled, seeming to entice Willa's spirit with it. Lightning flashed, illuminating the angry clouds and the house for a split second. Willa strained to see, wanting very much to go check the house.

"It's okay, Willa," Jack said from beside her. "Whatever fire there was will be drowned by the rain."

He was right, she thought, her mind eased.

It was too dark to see much of anything, but it was all there to be felt—the wild, free, soaring sensation of untamable nature. Molly solemnly held her face up to the rain. Mitchell stood at Willa's back, close enough for his suit coat to brush her shoulder blade. Jack stood at her side, one foot upon the step, his hip brushing her arm. They waited and watched. For the moment personal concerns were forgotten.

Then Willa heard a change in the wind, a new sound joining that of the gusty buffeting, the tree limbs clacking together, and the bushes brushing the house. A new roar. A glance at Jack told her he heard it, too. Willa stepped back out of the way while Mitchell joined Jack in fighting the wind for the door. For an instant she wanted to smack both their behinds because they paused and peered out, no doubt wanting to see what couldn't be seen in the dark—until it was too late. Then the door was closed.

Puffing from the exertion, Jack stepped from the narrow stairway to one side, Mitchell to the other. The roaring grew louder—maybe a tornado, maybe on the ground, maybe in the air. Maybe not even one at all. Jack would have liked to stay above and watch. There was something magnetic to him about storms. But he didn't want to leave Willa, and it was safer for her and the baby in the cellar.

He looked at her now in the shadowy light from the small lantern. She stood between him and Mitchell, gazing down at the child, murmuring softly. The low light lit the baby's hair with a feeble glow, making it the same golden brown as Mitchell Warner's.

Jack looked at the tall man. Mitchell was staring at Willa; then his gaze moved to Jack. His eyes were darkly shadowed, his face hard. Again Jack sensed a challenge from the man. The pain sliced deep as he turned his gaze back to Willa. And the baby.

The fact remains, he told himself, that she is still my wife.

He wouldn't give up. He wouldn't turn away until Willa told him to go—and maybe not even then. And focusing his eyes upon Mitchell, Jack silently told the man so.

The roar from above diminished. Jack listened, then hopped up the steps and threw back the door. The rain had turned to a cold drizzle, and the lightning faded into the distant northeast, the storm leaving only a tail of wind to whip the ground.

"Looks clear," he said. "Let's see what the damage is."

"Jack?" Willa called up in an anxious voice. "The house...is it okay?"

He trained the flashlight in the direction of the house, found the wall and followed its line.

"It's there, Willa, in one piece so far."

Then he reached down and took her arm, helping her and the baby from the cellar. He didn't release his hold on her arm but walked beside her back to the house, leaving Mitchell to follow behind.

They saw several scattered tree limbs near the back door, but if a tornado had touched down, it hadn't been in the yard near the house. Neither the barn nor the drilling rig and other heavy equipment could be seen in the dark.

The house indeed remained in one piece, but the horrendous crash that had taken out the electricity had been the result of a giant limb from the old elm tree falling into the attic bedroom—Hoppy's bedroom—creating a gaping hole in the roof.

Jack got a powerful flashlight from his truck and went to survey the area, reporting back that lightning had apparently blown the top off the electric pole and cut into the tree at the same time, sending the entire mess right into the house. Mitchell's car had escaped damage by inches. Emergency switches down the electrical lines had tripped, cutting the power to the broken lines within minutes, and the rain had drowned the fire that had begun in the tree, just as Jack had surmised.

Willa stood looking at the bare branches just beginning to bud that poked right into her house and scratched at Hoppy's bedstead. In the glow of a kerosene lantern they resembled the tentacles of a monster. The wind seeped in and swirled coldly around the room. Walking to the dresser, she shook debris from Hoppy's old-fashioned brush and comb set, the one he'd used for most of his life, and clutched them in her hand.

Oh, how Hoppy would have loved to see a storm such as this, she thought.

Molly picked up a stick and began tapping it on the floor scattered with limbs, splintered wood and nails. Gently taking away the stick, Willa lifted Molly, protesting, from harm's way.

"We'd better try to cut away some of this tree and block the hole." Mitchell turned from where he was examining the damage. "It's sure to storm again tonight."

Willa looked at Jack, who was studying the ceiling cracks that spread out from the hole. "Will you go check on the rig and equipment?" Her need to know forced her to ask it of him, though she couldn't say why she turned to him instead of Mitchell. She'd have gone herself, but it wouldn't be good to drag Molly out into the weather, and Molly wouldn't stay behind without her mama.

Jack nodded, and his eyes, curiously warm, rested on her. "Mitchell's right about the roof. We can get what we need to cover it from the barn—if it's still there.'' He reached to take her upper arm. ''We'll go check everything. You call the electric company and get changed into dry clothes. You're soaking wet.''

''You are, too.'' Willa looked from Jack to Mitchell. She wondered if Mitchell's suit would ever be the same.

''So we are,'' Jack said. ''A bit more won't hurt.''

Standing on the back porch, watching the men disappear into the blackness of the night, she fought the impulse to cry. A reaction to all that had happened, she knew. She would have given so much to go and look around herself and thought that at times motherhood was a definite inconvenience. Then, kissing Molly's curls, she reached for two cookies to pacify her. It was eight-fifteen and seemed as if it should be past midnight.

Moving rapidly, Willa turned to necessities. Quickly she called Carrie and was greatly relieved to hear her friend say that her family and farm were untouched. Willa quickly related what had happened and promised to get back to Carrie in the morning, then hung up and dialed the electric company to report the damage. They said a crew was already working in the area and would get to her place in the morning.

In the living room, she lit a blazing fire in the fireplace. The men would be cold when they returned, and since the furnace was electric, the fireplace was now the only source of heat.

Back in the kitchen, she paused when her gaze fell on the flowers wrapped in green tissue paper. A bit rumpled, they lay upon the table, though Willa wasn't certain just how they'd come to be there. She'd dropped them when the lights had gone out and Jack had hurled himself over to protect her.

Gingerly, she reached for the bouquet and for a brief instant pressed it to her breast, recalling how concerned he'd been about her when the storm hit the house. She looked at the delicate petals. Early in their marriage, he'd often brought her small, inexpensive bouquets that he'd gotten at the market or from the roadside vendors. It was a kind gesture now, one she appreciated.

Tears sprang to her eyes, and she blinked them back. Silly to remember things so long past and gone, she told herself as she moved purposefully to get a vase from the cabinet.

Don't attach more significance to these flowers than was meant, she cautioned herself. They're just a way for him to express sympathy over Hoppy and apologize for what has happened. That's all.

The water came slowly when she turned on the faucet to fill the vase, reminding Willa that electricity ran the pump in the well. There was a five-gallon holding tank in the well house. When the water it contained was gone, there would be no more until electricity was restored. At this realization, Willa developed a powerful thirst.

Putting the kettle of water on the gas burner, she ran upstairs to gather a shirt and pair of pants. Hoppy's clothes would do for Mitchell but wouldn't come close to fitting Jack, and she had nothing of his. What few things he'd left behind, she'd thrown away. Refusing to allow her mind to think of times past, she carried the shirt and trousers downstairs. No doubt, she thought, Jack had plenty of dry clothes in his camper.

Thoughts of Jack, Molly, Mitchell all swirled around in her mind, but she couldn't give them place yet. The storm, with its more pressing problems, had taken away normal reality, providing an odd escape route from things she didn't want to deal with.

The barn, rig and all the rest of the equipment were intact, the men told her when they returned, bringing with them old tarps, boards and a chain saw. But there had been a tornado. It had turned the tractor, which now belonged to Jack, on its side, taken out the chicken house, mangled the east fencing and left debris in its wake. Everything else as far as they could see appeared untouched.

They all gathered near the warming fire in the living room, Mitchell standing to one side of the hearth, Jack crouching in the middle. Molly came to stand in front of the fire, too, as if to discover what everyone found so fascinating there.

Willa stole glances at Jack. The fire illuminated his features, highlighting his gleaming beard, dark hair and pale eyes. When he looked at her, she averted her gaze to pour the coffee.

She handed Mitchell his cup, and then passed one to Jack, saying, "It's instant," almost as an apology, remembering how Jack abhorred instant coffee. Then she flicked her gaze to Mitchell, for some odd reason needing to include him in anything she said.

Reaching for the milk carton on the tray beside her, she handed it to Jack. She looked away from his eyebrow raised in surprise and let go of the carton so quickly that he had to grab for it to keep it from falling. She sipped her own coffee, and her gaze fell to Jack's hands, so big and rough, recent scrapes showing. They were the hands of a man who worked hard for a living. The same powerful hands that had once gently caressed her cheek.

Again she tore her gaze away. Picking up the ashtray she'd automatically brought, she extended it toward him.

He smiled and shook his head. "Gave it up," he said, reaching into his jacket pocket. He pulled out a small something and held it up between his forefinger and thumb. Willa recognized a red gummy bear. "Exchanged one addiction for another, I'm afraid."

Slowly, he slipped the candy into his mouth, and his pale eyes seemed to burn right into her, as if he wasn't thinking about cigarettes or gummy bears. He was thinking about something...hot...and sensual, and his gaze made a quivering begin deep in Willa. Molly touched her knee, and Willa welcomed the distraction of helping her daughter up onto her lap.

The room was quiet, tension seeming to grow and fill the air. Even Molly was quiet, her eyes wide and round as she studied the adults.

"I got you a shirt and pants, Mitchell." Willa indicated the folded clothes on the couch. "Hoppy's. I think they'll fit pretty well." She turned to Jack to find him still looking steadily at her. "I didn't have anything I thought would fit you."

He nodded. "I've got clothes in the camper." He downed the rest of his coffee and rose, saying, "We'd better get at it while we can without getting drenched."

Mitchell nodded in agreement and set his cup on the tray. "Thanks for the clothes, Willa," he said gently, "but these are already a mess. Might as well leave them on." As he spoke, he removed his suit coat and hung it over the newel post, then mounted the stairs.

"Be right there," Jack called after him. Taking one of the lanterns, he walked from the room.

Again Willa watched them go off together and wondered at what they were feeling. Necessity made strange bedfellows, she thought. Suddenly she wished very much she were equipped to handle the damaged roof herself. Mitchell had done enough since Hoppy's death. She didn't want to be further beholden to him—already she felt the choking tie of gratitude growing tighter, tugging her in a direction she wasn't at all certain she wanted to go. And she definitely didn't like the idea of Jack up there doing work on her home. She wanted nothing from him.

Anger at both men sparked, then flamed inside her. They were men, butting into her life, taking over as they saw fit! She rose and even walked halfway across the room, intending to call them down. The hole could just stay there until she could hire someone to take care of it. And surely, if she couldn't run a chain saw, she could use a handsaw and manage well enough herself. She wasn't helpless.

A chain saw sputtered, and then its roar echoed through the house.

Willa stopped and stared at the dark stairs. The hole in the roof should be covered. They were up there, would do a much better job than she ever could. She hated the fact but knew it would be foolish to stop them. Molly toddled over and raised her arms, wanting to be held. She didn't like the noise.

"Whatszat?" she asked, clutching Willa tightly around the neck.

"A chain saw. The men are cutting away the branch in Pa Pa's bedroom."

"Where's Pa Pa?"

"Gone to heaven, sweetheart. To be with the angels," she said, repeating the answer she'd given before and feeling it inadequate. Molly knitted her brows thoughtfully. "Come on, Squirrel, we need to get you into warm pajamas." She pressed Molly to her, taking comfort in the action.

"Wet." Molly shook her head and made a face as she ran a pudgy hand across Willa's shoulder.

"I sure am," Willa laughed. "I'll get warm clothes on, too."

Two things stuck in Jack's mind as he looked at Mitchell's lean face in the glow of the lantern: the image of the child's deep blue eyes as she'd stood before the flickering fire, eyes the same shade as Mitchell's—and that Willa had offered Hoppy's old clothes to Mitchell, which meant the man had no clothes of his own at the house. It told Jack the all-important fact that Mitchell didn't live there with Willa.

Hoisting the chain saw, he raised an eyebrow at Mitchell. "You or me?"

"You. I'm not much of a hand with one of those things." Mitchell spoke without embarrassment, as a man confident of doing other things well.

Jack nodded, his respect for the man rising one notch higher, though his dislike didn't change. He managed the chain saw while Mitchell stood back and held a lantern high. In less than fifteen minutes, Hoppy's bedroom was littered with wood chips and limbs, but the hole was clear enough to cover with the tarps. Jack shut off the saw, lowered it to the floor and shook the wood chips from his shirt and jacket.

Without speaking, Mitchell took the two tarps, stood on a chair and crawled out onto the roof, avoiding the big main limb, which still jutted above the hole. Without being asked, Jack handed out one of the lanterns, then passed the boards, hammer and nails through the opening. Lastly he, too, hefted his bulky frame up onto the roof. It was no easy trick to squeeze past the huge limb, but Jack intended to go every step of the way on this job with Mitchell. It seemed important somehow.

Pausing to slip a gummy bear into his mouth, Jack then helped Mitchell spread the tarps. Nothing beyond "Hand me another nail" and "Pull that edge tighter" was said, yet they worked together with amazing synchronization.

Amusement over their situation touched Jack, but not enough to chuckle aloud or to share it with Mitchell. Again he thought of Willa offering the clothes to Mitchell. This fact had taken a weight from him. He thought about how she'd remembered things, like his aversion to instant coffee, his fondness for milk in his coffee, and his smoking cigarettes. And he became more certain there was a lot to offer him hope.

The hole was covered. Jack picked up the lantern and led the way toward the back porch roof. From there he and Mitchell jumped easily to the ground.

In the kitchen, Jack set the lantern on the table and turned to face Mitchell. "Thanks for the help tonight." He stuck out his hand.

Mitchell looked down at Jack's hand, then back up to meet his gaze. "I didn't do it for you."

Nodding in understanding, Jack withdrew his hand, letting it rest on his hip. He assessed Mitchell, his opponent.

"What do you want here, Cashion?" Mitchell asked.

"That's between Willa and me."

Mitchell's jaw tightened. "You can see me in town about the inheritance. Anything else you need to discuss with Willa, get it over quick. You've hurt her enough."

"Mitchell . . . I suggest you leave now and let me be alone with my wife."

Chapter Four

Y ou still consider her that? Your wife?'' Mitchell asked, watching Jack carefully.

"Yes, I do.'' Jack's voice was low but hard as steel.

"Why don't you just get what you came for without playing your games, Jack? Willa doesn't need to be put through any more than necessary.''

"I'm not here to hurt her, Mitchell.''

"What are you here for?''

"I repeat, that's between Willa and myself. It's none of your business.''

A muscle twitched in Jack's cheek, and for an instant Mitchell had the distinct impression of staring at a massive stallion intent on protecting his territory. He sensed that just maybe Jack had returned for something other than a divorce. It surprised him—and made him mad as hell.

Giving in, for the moment, because there wasn't anything else to do, Mitchell inclined his head. "I'll just get my coat and say goodbye to Willa.''

Jack nodded. His voice stopped Mitchell at the hall entry. "Thanks for your help tonight, Mitch, and for all you've done for Willa."

It cost him dearly, but Jack felt the need to say it. It seemed to clarify just where he stood. And to call a debt paid.

Mitchell strode away without a response, and Jack turned to putting the chain saw and other tools out of the way on the porch. He wanted to be completely out of hearing distance for whatever might be said in the living room.

Mitchell's remarks had hit home. Maybe none of this was best for Willa. Lord, he hadn't come back to hurt her. He wanted to make her happy. Maybe he was being selfish and fooling himself by thinking he had something to offer. For the first time a crack appeared in his confidence.

Then the thought came to him: Willa hadn't gotten a divorce. And she lived here, with her child, alone. So apparently she wasn't in a powerful hurry to join her life with Mitchell's. Jack slipped a gummy bear into his mouth and once more felt hope kindle and burn brightly within him.

The wind had picked up again, and rain splattered against the roof. Willa had placed four pots in strategic areas beneath the ceiling in Hoppy's bedroom to catch drips. She'd also set her biggest pan outside the back porch to catch rainwater. There was no telling how long the house would be without electricity. She kept the portable radio on low, listening with one ear for storm warnings. So far, the heavier storms and tornado alerts had been staying to the north of them.

Molly slept, stomach down and curled in a ball, oblivious to the frequent crackle of thunder and lightning coming from a distance. Wound up by the night's excitement, she'd fought sleep until crawling onto the couch and sitting there a few seconds. Once she was still, sleep had overcome her so quickly, she'd seemed to pass out. Willa covered her with a blanket, then added two more logs to the fire. She and Molly would bed down in the living room near the fire's warmth. Her mind flickered to Jack, wondering where he intended to sleep. Irritated by the turn of her thoughts, she pushed them from her mind.

The feeling of suspended reality had left with Mitchell, and since then Willa had waited for Jack and what would have to be said between them. Every fiber of her being seemed to listen for him, to wait curiously, apprehensively. She hadn't seen him since he'd disappeared up the stairs to help cover the hole in the roof. Lights shone from his fifth-wheel camper. He'd obviously gone there to change clothes, but it seemed awfully long ago.

Mindful of the small supply of water, she heated just enough for a single cup of coffee. Leaning against the counter for a few seconds, she found her gaze straying to the vase of flowers. The roses looked a deeper red, the white daisy petals tinged golden by the lamplight.

Giving a small sigh, she turned her gaze away, took up one of the two lanterns and carried her coffee into the warmer living room.

Maybe Jack didn't intend to return tonight, she thought, looking around the room lit only by the flickering glow of the fireplace. The very idea kindled Willa's ire. He'd seen Molly. It was time they spoke about his daughter. The least he could do was care enough to come to holler in outrage at not being told.

Preoccupied with her thoughts, she took a deep sip of coffee and scalded her tongue. Setting the cup aside, she bent to pick up baby books, a colorful plastic windmill and the stuffed bear Molly had managed to drag from her darkened bedroom.

The sound of a light rapping against wood surprised her, and she jumped slightly, jerking her gaze upward to see Jack leaning against the hall archway. Though he stood in deep shadows, she could tell his eyes were upon her. He'd shaved his beard.

Slowly she straightened. "Molly must have X-ray vision. She managed to find these in her bedrooms in the dark," she said, indicating the things in her hands. "This guy here is George."

Jack sauntered forward, his gaze moving to Molly on the couch. Willa studied his face, going over the familiar planes of his freshly shaved cheeks. There were a few nicks from the razor. His mustache was neatly trimmed; his dark hair was damp. He still had that ruggedly handsome look.

"She's not afraid of the dark?" he asked, his eyes remaining fixed on Molly.

Willa shook her head. "No, she never has been."

Setting the books and windmill aside on a table, she moved to lay the stuffed bear, George, beside Molly. Straightening, she turned to see Jack standing behind Hoppy's chair and still staring hard at Molly. Willa braced herself.

Slowly Jack's gaze moved upward to meet hers.

"Is she Mitchell's baby?"

Stunned, Willa couldn't respond. The words echoed in her mind, and her breath seemed to leave her. Clamping her teeth together, she pivoted and headed from the room, choking back the scream that rose within her.

"Willa!" Jack called in a hoarse whisper.

She ignored it. She wasn't fleeing so much from him as from her own burning anger. It swirled and tangled within her, taking over in a frightening fashion.

His boots sounded upon the floor behind her, and his hand fell on her shoulder, forcing her to stop. In a fluid movement she spun around, bringing her hand up. The sound of her palm striking his cheek seemed to echo in the hallway.

She didn't know who was more shocked—Jack or herself.

His expression was hidden by the darkness. There came a crackle from the distant fire and the sound of their breathing. Willa's heart plummeted, and regret at her loss of temper flooded over her. Again she turned and fled toward the kitchen, and again Jack followed.

Her hands clutched the sink. Its porcelain was cold beneath her fingers. The rest of her felt flaming hot. Vaguely she realized she was angry at more than what Jack had said, but the question had been the last straw.

Jack knew he had no right to any questions. He stared at her quivering back lit by the flickering lantern. He stepped closer and put his hands on her shoulders. "Willa..."

She whirled to face him, shaking with anger. His hands slid down and gripped her upper arms. He pulled her, struggling, into his arms, hugging her to him. Willa...Willa... Lord, how he wanted to hold her. He tried to calm her, to keep her to him, but she would have none of it. He released her and watched her step backward, her eyes wide with fury.

"Oh, I suppose Molly could be Mitchell's," she quipped, raking her thick hair behind her left ear. "Or maybe she's Brad Marlow's. He's a bartender down at The Corral. Maybe she belongs to Deputy C.C. Boone... or the guy at the all-night grocery. I saw a lot of him. I'm really not sure."

"What do you mean by all that?" Jack asked, baffled at her fury. And dear God, it *was* wild talk, wasn't it?

"Well, I was so crushed when you walked out that I just ran to every man who'd have me."

"Stop it."

"Well, that is what you think, isn't it? I couldn't get along without you—without a man."

"You damn well didn't get pregnant without a man!"

"You got that right, cowboy!"

Her eyes blazed plainly even in the dim light, her contempt cutting into him. He strained to control his voice.

"I just asked if she was Mitchell's. I know it's none of my business what's been going on in your life the past two years, but I think I have a bit of a right to know that one thing."

"You have rights? Where did you get them?"

"You're still my wife."

"On paper."

"That counts."

"You've been away a long time. We women have the vote now."

He leaned forward, trapping her against the sink, his arms planted on the counter on either side of her. Her sweet scent floated to him. Her face was very close, her breasts moving rapidly as she breathed. His eyes fell to her lips. They were moist and quivering, and the strong desire to kiss them rose within him, as did a pressure in his loins.

"No," she said.

He blinked and looked back to her eyes. "No?" Her eyes told him she'd read his thoughts.

"No, the baby isn't Mitchell's."

Relief and anger stirred within him. Well, who in hell did the kid belong to? That she could have adopted her, that the child might not be Willa's at all, occurred to him. He stared at her, willing her to answer a question he refused to voice.

She raised an eyebrow. "Quit using force on me, Jack," she said in a steely voice.

Slowly, reluctantly, Jack removed his arms. He debated about pressing the matter of the child's parentage, but his pride held him in check. If Willa wanted him to beg to know, she'd have to wait a lifetime. She remained where she was, watching him.

"So Mitchell's been helping out around here," he said. Almost absently he reached into his pocket and pulled out a candy to slip into his mouth.

"Just in handling the auction. His bank holds the lien on the farm. He drew up the will for Hoppy, and Hoppy made him the executor."

"Why didn't you contact me about Hoppy?"

"Mitchell is the executor," she repeated. Anger and pain flickered across his face. "I just thought it'd be less awkward all around for Mitchell to talk to you," she said more gently. "And Hoppy was dead—there wasn't anything you could do."

"What happened? How did he die?" he asked after a moment.

Willa swallowed. "His heart just gave out. He had a severe attack last October that forced him to stop drilling. That took a lot of his spirit. Then one day, he simply went;

his heart just quit. I'm really grateful it was like that. One minute he was walking among his fruit trees, the next, he'd gone.'' She watched him nod in understanding and forced the lump down in her throat.

"I'm sorry," Jack said.

The comment didn't require a reply. She wanted to run into his arms, but she remained where she stood. She'd built a life of her own in the past twenty-two months. She might as well learn to keep it that way.

"Heard Mitchell has been taking care of other things for you, too," he said after a long minute, his eyes narrowing.

"Yes," Willa replied sharply. "Mitchell was here to help. I appreciated it. But his help was offered in friendship, without strings. I stand on my own two feet, Jack Cashion. I don't mean to shock you, but a woman can exist in this world—and quite nicely, thank you—without the constant assistance of a man." She pushed around him. "Molly's stirring."

Jack followed. "I don't hear anything."

"You're not a mother," Willa quipped.

Just as Willa reached the living room entry, Molly let out a wail. She was sitting up on the couch, the blanket tangled around her legs, staring in confusion around the room. "Mamaaa..."

"Shush...it's all right, sweetheart. Mama has you." She cuddled Molly to her and looked around at Jack. "It'll take me a few minutes to get her back to sleep. We can talk then, if you want to wait."

His gaze flickered quickly from Molly to Willa. "I'll be here," he said after a moment. Then, taking the hint from her expression, he left the room.

Molly pulled sleepily at Willa's sweater. "Nap...naap."

Moving to the wing-back rocker, Willa settled Molly at her breast. "Hush, little baby, don't say a word," she sang in a low voice, "and Mama's gonna a buy you a mockingbird..."

Jack looked around the dimly lit kitchen. He saw that Willa had put the flowers he'd brought her in a vase. Papers of some kind lay on the table alongside the lantern; a jar of instant coffee sat near the sink. The room was cool; wind and rain lashed the south windows. It was a night to watch for storms, he thought vaguely, having more pressing concerns on his mind than the house being blown away.

Going to the stove, he lifted the kettle and shook it to see if it held water. It did. Setting it back on the burner, he turned on the flame.

People changed. Jack knew he had in the past two years. And Willa was different. There was a tough guardedness about her now, a reserve she wasn't about to let anyone breach. And it was his fault—he was to blame!

Restless, he paced, his mind recalling their recent exchange. She didn't owe him anything, he reminded himself. He had no right to question her about the child—Molly. He had no right to question her about anything.

Still, a powerful curiosity gripped him as to who had fathered the child, and he puzzled over a discreet way to find out.

Willa's child, if indeed she was that. He didn't think Willa would lie about Mitchell not being the father. Had it been just someone passing through her life? Did Mitchell know? The thought that Mitchell could be close enough to Willa to know something so private didn't set too well.

Jack wondered darkly if he had another rival for Willa, someone he didn't have a chance in hell of beating out.

He made his instant coffee, then found himself wandering toward the living room. In the hall he heard Willa's soft voice singing a lullaby. He stood very still, listening. Emotion stirred within him as he remembered how she used to gaze wistfully into the maternity shop display window.

Something drew him on to the living room. Willa sat in her chair there, the firelight flickering on her face. Jack's gaze skimmed downward, seeing the golden light on her sweater and the child held to her breast. It dawned on him that Willa was nursing the little girl. The fact hit him with surprise, bringing with it a sweet, warm marveling. The child was indeed Willa's. And they looked so... right together.

He couldn't move, could only stare at the mother and child. He wanted to see. And this wanting grew quickly into a desire to become a part of the closeness between them.

Willa looked up. Her eyes widened. Reluctantly, feeling an intruder, Jack turned to go.

"Jack."

"Yes?" He didn't turn around. Something was breaking inside him.

There was a brief pause. "Come in."

Treading cautiously, he crossed the room. "Do you need something?"

"Come over here."

He complied, his insides churning with confused emotions. Feeling the need to be smaller, he squatted on his haunches in front of the rocker and rested his arms upon his thighs. He looked up into Willa's face. Her mouth tilted upward in a gentle smile.

"She's sure pretty," he whispered, his gaze moving back to the baby.

"Yes, she is."

Her voice seemed to choke, and Jack searched her face for tears. He found one slipping down her right cheek. Immediately, he started to move away.

"I didn't mean to interrupt—"

"Jack..." Her hand fell to his shoulder. She sniffed, and a funny kind of smile lit her lips. "Jack, Molly is your child."

He froze. A chill ran from the base of his neck down his spine, then traveled to his stomach. He looked at the baby. *Molly. His child?*

He searched Willa's face for evidence of a cruel joke, but he found only tender truth. No, Willa never lied. He felt then as if he'd been punched in the gut.

Gently, shifting in the chair to modestly hide herself from his gaze, Willa eased her sleeping daughter from her breast and pulled her sweater down. When she looked again at

Jack, she saw he remained exactly as he'd been, a stunned expression on his face.

"Would you like to hold her?" she whispered, extending Molly toward him.

It was a moment before he moved to raise his arms. "Won't she wake up?" His loud whisper echoed with panicky concern.

Willa shook her head and choked back a chuckle. "I don't think so." She put Molly fully into his hands, forcing him to hold her.

Molly sucked in a ragged breath and threw out an arm, causing Jack to jump.

"She's so small." His whisper echoed with wonder. "How old is she?"

"One year, three months."

For what seemed a very long time, they stood side by side, staring at the child who was a product of them both. Hope grew within Willa that no matter what went wrong between herself and Jack, Molly would have a father. Please, let it work between them, she found herself praying. She wanted her daughter to have what she'd never fully known, a father's love. And she found herself vowing to do whatever was necessary to insure her daughter received that chance.

Jack moved to hand Molly to Willa, but she stepped back, shaking her head.

"Lay her on the couch."

Looking every bit as awkward as any new father, Jack took hesitant steps and bent to place Molly on the couch. She handed him the blanket, and he carefully spread it over Molly.

"Mustn't forget George." Willa tucked the stuffed bear down beside Molly. Then, as a precaution, she propped a pillow against Molly to keep her from rolling to the floor.

Jack walked away to the kitchen. Willa came more slowly, pausing in the archway to take a deep breath and straighten her shoulders.

He stood at the sink, his back to her. His broad shoulders looked tense beneath the ever-present denim jacket. The wind and rain had abated for a few minutes. The room was so quiet and still, Willa thought she could have heard a flea sneeze.

"I didn't know I was pregnant when you left, Jack," she said, breaking the silence. She walked forward and put her hands on a chair back. Seeing the lantern flicker rapidly, she reached over and turned up the short wick.

When Jack didn't turn around, she added, "Even after I finally realized I'd missed perhaps more than one period, I didn't consider the possibility of pregnancy. After all those years . . . and I was under a great deal of strain."

There wasn't anything left to say, and she refused to speak again until he turned around. She waited. After what seemed an eternity, Jack slowly faced her. His expression hovered between fury and confusion.

"How? The doctors . . . the tests . . ." His tone carried a reproach against the world.

"The doctors said only that it would be difficult for us to conceive a child—not impossible, Jack."

His pale eyes bore into her. "Why didn't you tell me?"

Willa looked at him. "You didn't want the burdens of marriage. You surely wouldn't have wanted the additional burden of a child."

"Thanks for thinking for me. You could have asked."

"You weren't here to ask."

"Don't give me that. I sent you my addresses all along." He raised an eyebrow. "Were you ever going to tell me?"

Willa raked her hair behind her ear and fought the sudden, embarrassing lump in her throat. "I didn't not tell out of revenge, Jack." She searched for honesty, not blame and not pity. "I truly thought maybe it was best to wait for a time like this, when you were back, to tell you. What difference does it make, Jack? You've been gone to the far corners of the earth. What did you have to offer Molly? And, at the outset, two years ago, would you have wanted me to be pregnant?" Knowing she spoke the truth gave her fortitude.

He looked away, took a deep breath, then shook his head. "I don't know." He looked back. "I sent you money, Willa. For one solid year, I sent you checks. You returned them all."

"I didn't want or need your money, Jack. You left plenty in the accounts, and I got a job right after I moved back here with Hoppy."

She watched his eyebrows arch in surprise, and it pleased her.

"Because of my condition, I couldn't drill with Grandad, so I got a job with Steiner-White as a land man," she said, using the term applied to people who secure land leases for oil companies. The further amazement slipping into his eyes was gratifying. "I knew enough of the business, and I knew the people who owned the land. It was a perfect job. I made my own hours, which weren't long, and I could take Molly with me after she was born. The commissions were good. I worked for them until this past November, when Corley Steiner had to sell out to a Dallas-based company to keep from going bankrupt. Hoppy needed me home then, anyway."

"I wanted you to have the money," Jack said after long seconds in which he stared at her. "You should have taken it, for Molly."

"I'm perfectly capable of providing for all Molly or I need. It's not your responsibility."

His jaw hardened. "I didn't say you weren't capable. I'm her father. I share in the responsibility."

"I realize that, Jack. It's just that I carried her. I bore her. She seems so totally mine." *You weren't here,* she thought, not attempting to hide the cold accusation she felt.

A helpless expression crossed his face before he averted his gaze to the table. He was a bear of a man who'd just been handed a surprise big enough to take all his strength.

Compassion welled in Willa's heart. "I'm truly sorry about not telling you about Molly before, Jack," she said quietly. "I didn't do it to keep Molly from you. It just seemed that I had time yet. She's a baby. She doesn't know about fathers. She wouldn't have understood my telling her about you when you weren't here for her to see. And I didn't think it would make any difference in your plans."

Jack nodded. "I know." Absently he moved to the counter, thinking, *a kid. A girl. I've been a father for months and months.* It felt odd. He looked at his reflection in the black window. Molly was his child. Not Mitchell's, not some Joe's he didn't know. His. And Willa's.

Turning back to her, he felt his face breaking into a wide smile. "I'm a father."

"Yes, you are," she said with a low chuckle. Her eyes were warm.

The next instant, without thinking, he crossed the distance between them and gathered her into his arms. "Ah, Willa...Willa..." he murmured, rubbing his cheek against her soft hair. Joy sort of spilled from his heart and flowed all over him. It was an unfamiliar and heady feeling. Willa's shoulders beneath his touch felt femininely small, and good. She was warm and smelled like sweet flowers. And his body reacted.

The next instant, with mild shock and puzzlement, he felt her struggling from his embrace. Once free, she nervously tucked her hair behind her ear, then looked up at him. He saw her chest move rapidly up and down.

"I want you to be a father to Molly, Jack," she said. She wet her lips. "I want you to get to know her. A little girl needs her father. You can see her any time you want—we can leave the matter of custody wide open."

Willa felt exceedingly self-conscious; her words sounded wooden even to her own ears. She hated the moment, the fact she must face.

"Custody?" Jack gazed intently at her. "As in divorce?"

She just looked at him, wondering at such a question and telling herself to remain cool. Aloof. She could do it. It wouldn't do either of them any good for the pain to come out. Why was he looking at her so strangely? For some irritating and irrational reason her gaze strayed to his wide chest, and her mind recalled what it looked like beneath the fabric of his shirt, thick-muscled, sparsely covered with black hair.

"I didn't come here for a divorce, Willa," Jack said then, his words seeming to plunk into the quiet kitchen as water drops into a tin pan.

Chapter Five

Willa just stared at him for long seconds, wondering at his words. And how to talk without making a fool of herself.

"Well, what did you come for?" she asked at last, peeved that he'd forced her to do so. "You don't need to see me about the acres Hoppy left you. Mitchell will handle that."

Jack shifted against the counter. His eyes remained steadily fixed on hers. Willa's heart fluttered.

"I want us to try again, Willa." It wasn't easy, and Jack didn't think he had found the right words. God had blessed him with a right handsome face and strong body but not a gifted tongue.

Willa simply stood there staring at him. Her gaze flickered to the vase of flowers on the counter and then back to him.

"Oh, Jack." She crossed her arms and rubbed her elbows. He watched and waited. She looked up at the ceiling, then back to him, a helpless and confused expression on her face. "You don't have to think like that. You can see Molly, be a father to her. I know it won't be the same as being right here with her, but when she's older, she can go wherever you're working, wherever you can have her."

"I'm not talking about Molly. I'm talking about us."

Again she looked at him for long seconds. He couldn't tell what she was thinking, but he had a hunch she was going to doubt anything he said. He reminded himself it would take persistence on his part to get her to see he was right.

"Maybe we'd better go back into the living room," he suggested. "It's pretty cool in here, and I think that lantern's about to give out."

"I think we'd better stay right here. It's not feeling too cool to me. That lantern'll last the night." She reached over and turned the wick a bit. The lantern sent up a puff of black smoke, then glowed brightly.

Willa walked around the corner of the table, putting it between them, resting her hands on a chair back.

"I can't imagine what it must be like to suddenly find out you're a father, but I know it has to be . . . well, a bit unsettling. And I feel the effects of old memories, too. But, Jack, the fact remains that we've been separated for two years—"

"Twenty-two months," he cut in.

She nodded and nervously tucked her hair behind her ear. "Okay. Anyway, I know what you found out today makes you feel obligated, but there's no need, Jack."

"Why not? Molly's my daughter. You're my wife. And I hate it when you try to be rational."

"Well, pardon me." Willa bristled. "But I have to be rational. I have Molly to think of—and my own life. You can't just up and say you want to come home, want us to be married again. It doesn't work that way. Turning emotions on and off like water faucets. What did we just have—a twenty-two month vacation from each other and now you've come home?" She raised her hand in an angry motion, then dropped it.

"You never got a divorce," he said, pleased that he'd broken into her cold, common-sense reserve.

"I didn't feel it necessary. Legal papers didn't give me a marriage—a legal divorce wouldn't make any difference, either."

"You remembered I took milk in my coffee." He dared her to deny it.

"What does that have to do with anything?" she protested, but he saw the understanding flicker in her eyes. She gave a dismissive wave. "I lived with you for ten years. Every day for ten years you had milk in your coffee. I'll probably remember that for the rest of my life."

"You loved me for ten years."

"Yes," she said in a solemn voice. "And for the past twenty-two months I've had to live with that memory. It tends to change a person."

"I'm sorry, Willa, for hurting you." He paused and raked a hand through his hair. He knew his words sounded stiff and all wrong, but it was truly what he felt. He hoped she saw it in his expression. "I made the biggest mistake a man can make. I know I can't change what happened, but I don't think we need to throw away what we could have because of it. I love you."

She flinched at his last words. The skepticism he saw in her eyes caused his heart to squeeze near to cutting off his breath. He wondered if what he wanted was possible after all.

"We had a good thing," he said stubbornly.

"Yes," she said quietly, remembering. "We had a good thing."

Don't cry, she thought frantically. Don't make a fool of yourself in front of him.

She looked up at his face. He meant what he said, she saw, and for a moment her heart swelled with sweetness. Then immediately the clear voice of cold reality returned. He meant it now, at this moment. It was natural, she supposed, when they were both open and bleeding, remembering how it had been. And when he'd just found out they'd produced a child. But it was a fleeting feeling, one sure to fade when hit with the bright light of morning.

"It was good," she said, taking a ragged breath and trying to swallow the lump in her throat. She forced herself to look him in the eye. "But that was over two years ago, before...everything. There's no way to turn back the clock."

"Is it Mitchell? Are you and he..."

"No, it isn't Mitchell!" she replied, irritated. "Or anyone else. Why do all you men immediately think if it isn't one of you, it has to be another? I've made a good life, Jack. On my own. And I happen to like it that way."

"What about Molly? She has a right to have both parents."

"Yes, she does. And she can, if you make a place for her in your life."

"Don't you even want to give it a try?" His jawline tightened.

"We gave it a try. We had the best there is. It wasn't enough. I don't want to go down that road again, Jack Cashion—not for you, not for anyone."

"What do you want me to say? To get down on bended knee? I said I was sorry...I'm not going to grovel."

"Who asked you to say anything? What do you expect me to do? Fall over in a faint, thankful that you condescended to come back to me?" She shook with anger and gripped the wooden chair back. "I didn't shrivel up and die when you went away, Jack. I made a life of my own. I can't just turn around in midstream and change it, even if I wanted to. And I don't. This life suits me fine."

She saw the fury in his eyes before he turned his face away. He stood there a moment, staring at the counter. His hat sat there, propped against the toaster. He reached for it and settled it with extreme care over his hair, then turned and gave her a nod and a tight smile. Without a word he walked to the back door, opened it and stepped out onto the porch. The cold wind rushed in. Willa heard distant thunder.

"Jack..." She moved to catch the door before he closed it. "Please, if the weather gets bad, don't stay in that trailer. Come to the storm shelter."

Giving a nod to show that he'd heard, he pushed through the screen door. Quickly closing the back door, Willa didn't watch him walk away. To keep from running after him, a most foolish impulse, she walked purposefully to the table and turned out the lantern. She then went rapidly through the darkened house to the living room.

On the couch, Molly slept soundly. Willa got blankets and made a bed before the fire. She lay there staring at the flames and listening for an approaching storm, alert in case she needed to grab Molly and run for the shelter. If it'd just been herself, she'd never go to the shelter. She'd watch the storm from the windows. But she had Molly to think of.

Molly to think of . . .

Had she done the right thing in turning down Jack's proposal? Perhaps, for Molly, she should have jumped at the chance of a reconciliation.

How long, Willa wondered, had she waited and longed for Jack to say what he had tonight? She used to imagine him coming, wanting to make up. But when the months passed and it hadn't happened, she'd forced herself to accept that it could never be. She couldn't allow her life to hang on a hope. It was killing her. So, with Hoppy's help, she'd made a life on her own. She'd grown used to sleeping alone, to having two pillows to herself, to checking the oil in her car and even rotating the tires because Hoppy insisted she learn these things, too.

She'd had no other choice but to tell Jack no, had she? They couldn't possibly make it work, not after so long a time. And heaven help her, she'd forgiven, but not as completely as it would take for her to live with him again. She'd always be afraid he'd tire of her, or that she'd make a mistake and he'd be off again. Their lives would be miserable, and it wouldn't do Molly any good.

Her heart felt like an old-fashioned flatiron in her chest. She'd loved him so very much. Once.

Turning to her side, she fluffed the pillow and tried to get comfortable. Half the night was gone, and tomorrow she had a lot to deal with. Again she pictured Jack. That he'd asked to try again did a lot for her ego, she admitted. But he'd sure given up quickly enough, she thought tartly. It just went to show, she was right. Their marriage was water under the bridge, and she might as well quit mooning over it.

She remembered him saying *I love you*.

She didn't believe it, though she also didn't believe he'd lied. He simply thought he felt it in that moment.

She rolled onto her back and stared at the ceiling. How their marriage had fallen apart, she wasn't certain. Jack had grown further and further away from her, and she'd reacted by pulling within herself, seeking shelter from the hurt. Often she'd pouted, or raved at him when he'd at last come home. His changing had made her so angry.

The problem with their marriage hadn't been all his fault, she could see now, but what she did blame him for was leaving. No matter what problems they'd had, if he'd loved her, he would have stayed to work them out. But he hadn't. He'd left because the lure of his job and all that surrounded it—the meetings and parties with powerful people, the money and the inevitable feminine attention it brought—was more important to him than she'd been.

One day he'd come home to say he'd taken a job in Mexico. They'd fought. And Jack had said he didn't want to be married anymore. He was sorry, so damn sorry. He just didn't love her anymore.

The tears started then as she remembered, and the pain welled up inside her. She turned her face into the pillow to bury her sobs. And she vowed she would never be in that position again, where her life and happiness could be ripped apart by another person.

Willa awoke when Molly snuggled down on the floor beside her. She opened her eyes and found herself staring into the deep blue ones of her daughter. The room was so light, she knew morning was well along.

And then she smelled the coffee. Wonderful coffee, she thought, her body and mind still hazy with sleep. ''Good morning, Squirrel,'' she said, stretching. Molly giggled and turned her face into the pillow.

With arms in midair, Willa remembered Hoppy was dead. There was no one to make coffee. She took a sniff. It was coffee she smelled.

Wriggling from the tangle of blankets, Willa hoisted Molly onto her hip and hurried into the kitchen. The sun peeking over the horizon sent a golden ray through the back door window and across the room to strike the shoulder of Jack, who was sitting at the kitchen table. A coffee cup, milk carton and papers were on the table before him. He wore his usual denim jacket, light colored shirt, and jeans. He rather dwarfed the kitchen chair. His dark hair was freshly combed, though a bit unruly on top, as it always used to be.

"Good morning," he said, lazily looking up and giving a friendly smile, as if it were the most natural thing in the world for him to be sitting there. The chair creaked when he shifted his weight. "I made coffee in the trailer. Thought you'd like some, so I brought it over."

A glass pot sat on a burner on the stove, with a low flame underneath it. The oven door was open, the burners on within it, too.

"Pretty cold in here this morning," Jack said when he saw her look at the oven. "It's better now."

Willa still couldn't think of a thing to say. She blinked against the brighter light and looked around the room, seeing Jack's hat on the counter, the vase of flowers, the sun glancing off the refrigerator. Her gaze fell to the papers he had been studying. They were the papers Mitchell had brought the night before, the listing of equipment sold at the auction. Why was Jack looking at those? And why was he even here? she thought as she watched him stand, move to the stove and pour a cup of coffee. He held it out to her.

"Thank you," she said then, stepping forward to take the cup with her free hand. Her eyes flickered across his wide chest before she looked into the cup and took a sip of coffee.

Willa's eyes still held sleep. With warm amusement, Jack remembered how it always took her a long time to wake up—and that it used to be dangerous to try to talk to her before she'd had her coffee. The morning light glistened off her rumpled hair like a halo; her face held the peach glow of first awakening, her lips the texture of dew on a wild rose. Jack was suddenly amazed to realize he'd come up with such poetic thoughts. But they were apt, he thought with amusement. An ache settled within him. Lord, he wanted to hold and kiss her. And his daughter, too.

"Can I hold her?" he asked, indicating Molly.

Willa held Molly toward his extended hands. "This is Jack, sweetheart. You remember him from last night. Can you say hello?"

It hurt when Molly pulled away from him, back against Willa's chest, and buried her head beneath Willa's chin. Jack didn't insist, telling himself it was bound to be awkward for a while. He didn't know the first thing about kids. But he would learn.

"She's shy, especially with men," Willa said. "It'll just take some time."

Jack nodded and sat down. Willa took a chair across from him. Sitting on Willa's lap, Molly stuck a thumb in her mouth and snuggled close. Willa raked her fingers through her hair, hoping for a semblance of order, then sipped the coffee. It was very good; Jack had always made the best coffee.

"Why did you name her Molly?" he asked.

At the question, Willa looked up into his pale eyes and tried to gather her thoughts. "I got one of those baby name books, went through every possibility and just finally decided on Molly. I think it fits her."

"Yes," Jack agreed thoughtfully, "it does." His gaze moved back and forth between her and Molly. "When's her birthday?"

"December second." Willa smiled softly at his questions, pleased at his avid interest in his daughter, regretful that he didn't already know the answers. "She weighed six pounds, two ounces and was twenty inches from head to toe.''

Again Jack's gaze rested on Molly.

"She loves vanilla wafers and applesauce," Willa said, wanting to help him feel closer to his daughter. "She isn't afraid of the dark or storms but does seem to have an abnormal fear of fire. And already she's particular about her clothes."

Knowing they were talking about her, Molly peeked at Jack and grinned widely when he winked at her. Staring at Molly, Jack seemed to slip into deep thought. Willa sipped her coffee.

"Why are you looking at those papers?" she asked after a moment. "My papers."

He ignored her clarification of ownership, appeared not in the least ashamed of prying.

"You didn't do too good with the sale," he said.

"Times are hard. No one around here is doing any good.'' She felt the odd need to defend her decision to sell the farm equipment. "Mitchell thinks we did okay." Immediately she wished she hadn't mentioned Mitchell's name, because Jack's jawline tightened with irritation.

"Why did you sell all this stuff?" he said, waving a hand at the papers. "Why not farm like Hoppy did? You could have done it, could have hired someone to help." He pulled a candy from his pocket and slipped it into his mouth.

"I didn't want the work, or the responsibility. Hoppy had always handled it all. There's too much I don't know. Besides, we'd had two years in a row—rain took out the cotton and peanut crops in the best years they'd had. Because of that, and to save the big Massey-Ferguson and some other things, Hoppy mortgaged the land several years ago.

"It wasn't a hefty mortgage, but it would have taken the bit of life insurance Hoppy left and a good deal of what I'd saved. And the bank was nervous with Hoppy gone. They really wanted the money. I just didn't want to chance losing the land. I want it clear."

Jack nodded in understanding. He'd always had the same sort of feeling for land that she had, she recalled.

She sipped the coffee again. "You still make the best coffee I ever tasted."

In answer he gave a small grin, then said, "So the land is safe now?"

Willa nodded. "The bank debt is paid. All I have to do is keep up with the taxes. And I have working capital."

"You going to start over farming it?"

"Maybe, later." Willa looked into her cup. "When I get ahead again."

"So you're going to drill?"

Willa nodded and drank deeply from her cup, feeling Jack's gaze upon her. At last she looked at him.

His mustache twitched, a grin tugging at his lips. "Oil's down, but people always need water."

"That's what I figure. Hoppy had times drilling when he made good money. It was just in this last year, with his health going down and his having to cut back on jobs, that his profits were poor."

"The rig looks to be in pretty good shape," Jack said.

"It's not bad for twenty years old. I just had some work done on it—Cy in town overhauled the engine. He assures me it'll go another twenty."

"You'll need some help," he said.

"Thomas Spangler will work for me. He worked with us before Hoppy took sick. Hoppy taught him like he'd taught me." She found herself smiling in answer to Jack's smile. He had no doubts about her ability, she saw, and she felt a pricking of pride in her chest.

Jack looked again at the papers.

"Why did you buy all that equipment yesterday?" Willa asked. "Have you bought a place somewhere?"

Though she took care to sound casually interested, she flinched inwardly at the idea. Lifting her gaze, she met his over the rim of her coffee cup. He seemed to deliberate about something and make up his mind.

Rising slightly from the chair, he pulled his wallet from the back pocket of his jeans. Willa set her cup on the table and watched him take out a piece of paper. Unfolding it, he tossed it beside her cup. Slowly Willa picked it up. It was the receipt for the equipment—the tractor, mower, baler, flatbed truck—that he'd bought at the auction.

She looked at him, an unspoken question on her face.

"Now you can still cut the pasture Hoppy planted for hay. That's something. No need to pay someone else to cut it or let it go to waste." He rose, moved toward the counter and picked up his hat. "And what's a farm without a tractor?" he quipped.

"But . . . these are yours now."

"I paid cash," he said, "with the money you wouldn't take for the past twenty-two months. If you don't want to consider the money yours, you can't argue about it belonging to Molly. This is her farm, too. And I guess I can buy what I want for my own daughter."

His pale blue eyes held a self-satisfied gleam that dared her to object.

She looked back at the receipt he'd handed her and realized he'd bought the equipment before he even knew of Molly's existence.

"Thank you, Jack."

He settled his hat on his head, gave a nod and walked to the back door. "I brought you a bucket of water," he said, pointing to a clean tin bucket Willa now saw for the first time on the counter. "Enough to wash a bit in anyway." Then he left.

Willa wondered if he would return. He hadn't said, and she resisted the impulse to run after him and ask. She wasn't about to do such a thing. What Jack did or didn't do wasn't her business, just as what she did wasn't any of his. She finished her coffee, then plunked the cup down on the table.

Holding Molly on her hip, she dipped a pan into the pail of water and set it on a burner on the stove. Her gaze fell to the glass coffee pot Jack had brought. Would he return for it? She heard his truck start.

Firmly keeping her gaze from the window, Willa walked into Molly's bedroom to gather her daughter's clothes for the day. She pulled a pair of pink overalls from the drawer, then hurriedly set Molly on the floor, threw the overalls aside and ran back to the kitchen window, standing well back so he wouldn't see her looking.

She searched the drive for the truck whose engine she still heard. Amazement stole over her.

Jack had moved his camper off to the side at the end of the drive, near the pasture fence. He was unhitching it from his truck. Apparently he was going to leave it there. On her property, without asking.

Well, Willa considered as she watched him finish unhitching the trailer, I'm not about to go out there and ask him what he's doing. She wasn't going to make a big deal out of it, to act as if it meant something to her.

He got back into the pickup and drove away. Willa stood back and closed her eyes. Jack had a daughter to get to know, and she herself had extended the invitation for him to come around and see Molly whenever he wished. She would simply have to put aside her feelings for Molly's sake. She'd have to see Jack, be often in his company, though it hurt beyond belief.

The hurt will pass, she told herself. Everything does sooner or later.

"Mama...I's 'ungry," Molly said, coming into the room, dragging George beside her.

"I guess you are, sweetheart." The water on the stove bubbled. "How 'bout some warm oatmeal? With apples?" She smiled, lifted Molly and kissed her soft cheek. She hoped it would work out between Molly and Jack, and knew she herself would have a great deal to do with the success of their relationship.

The workmen from the electric company showed up not long after Jack had left.

"Hey, Willa!" Jody Miller called out, waving his bright yellow workman's hat in the air. "We'll have you some juice in a few minutes."

"Oh, I sure would appreciate it!" Willa called back from where she stood on the back step. "I can't take a bath without electricity!"

"Looks like you were lucky," Jody called again, not moving any closer. "The Conrads lost their barn and their garage. Deloris said she wanted new ones anyway. Guess you and the Conrads were the only ones hit—storm wasn't too big."

"Big enough," Willa called back. Jody answered with a grin and a wave.

The air reverberated with the sound of the men's shouts, the rumble of truck engines, the whine of the bright yellow boom lifting men into working position. In no time they had run a temporary line for power to the house.

The first thing Willa did was turn on the faucet and watch the beautiful well water run into the sink. Filling a glass, she drank with relish. It seemed the only time a person became truly thirsty was in the absence of fresh water.

The next thing she really wanted to do was take a shower; she still wore the jeans and sweater she'd put on the night before. But both she and Molly wanted to see the goings-on outside and to discover in the bright light of day the exact extent of the storm's fury. Slipping into sweaters, they stepped outside.

The sky was a clear blue, the air crisp with a northerly breeze. It promised to be another beautiful day, belying the previous stormy night, as if Mother Nature delighted in confusing everyone.

Taking care to stay out of the workmen's way, Willa held Molly on her hip and walked out to take a good look at the drilling rig. It stood solidly beneath a bright sun, exactly as it had the previous day. The only telltale sign that there'd ever been a storm was where the tall grasses surrounding the vehicle's wheels had been bent over by the pounding rain.

Suddenly, to Willa's and Molly's delight, a trio of mallard ducks waddled out from under the drilling rig. Apparently they'd managed to escape the storm and had taken refuge beneath the heavy machine.

"Ducks," Willa said, pointing. "Just like in your book—ducks."

"'Ucks," Molly said, clapping her hands. Willa set her on the ground, and she ran after the ducks, who honked and waddled well ahead.

Tiring of her futile pursuit, Molly ran back to Willa and, hand in hand, they again skirted the workmen to walk down the drive and inspect the damage to the house.

The big limb from the old elm remained as it was, fractured from the trunk and angled over the driveway, resting atop the roof. The black charring where it had burned was easily visible. Willa walked over to the great tree to look at the heart carved into its trunk. Within the heart was carved *J.C. loves W.L.*

An eternity ago Jack had carved that, she thought, remembering her delight when he'd showed her. Her heart squeezed as if a vise had hold of it.

Well, she had learned a few lessons, she thought. One was never to rely on another person for her happiness the way she had on Jack. Another person couldn't give you happiness. That had to come first from inside. And it was simply easier and safer all the way around not to get in a position of tying your life to someone else's.

Willa again bent and held Molly's hand. They walked out to the back of the yard. The air smelled of damp earth and crushed grasses. Beneath the morning sun, all growth looked a rich emerald green, as if it had absorbed the night's rain with relish.

Looking over at the orchard, Willa saw that one of the dwarf apricot trees had been broken off at the ground. Out across the pasture, she saw some debris that could be the tree. Well, she considered, one tree out of twenty wasn't so much to lose.

The only chickens in sight were two dead ones lying like limp rags on the ground. What had been the chicken enclosure was swept clean; not even a single blade of grass stuck from the ground. Boards and tree limbs lay scattered here and there. There was no way of telling if the boards had been from her chicken house or from the Conrads' buildings the tornado had hit earlier.

Walking across the yard, Willa thought she could trace the path of the storm, which must have been small in diameter and touched down like a bouncing ball. It looked as if it had missed the corner of the barn by inches, and Willa breathed a silent thanks.

After a second's debate, Willa bent to retrieve the dead chickens. They didn't look at all appealing, battered into the ground, with mud-splattered feathers, but dressed out she figured they'd look and taste as delicious as any chicken.

The telephone was ringing when she and Molly got to the back door. Rushing inside, she tossed the chickens into the sink, set Molly on the floor, then reached for the phone.

"Willa?" It was Mitchell. "You sound like you've been running."

"I had dead chickens in one hand and Molly in the other," she said, chuckling at the picture her words provoked.

"At least the storm left you dinner," Mitchell quipped.

"Oh, two dinners, at least."

"Maybe you'll invite me to one."

"Maybe," Willa allowed coyly. She thought of Jack, then impatiently pushed his image aside. She would ask Mitchell to dinner soon. She felt she owed him for all he'd done on her behalf concerning the auction. And she didn't want to owe him in any way.

"Well, what I wanted to tell you was that I called Ace Barker this morning, and he says he's free to fix your roof and will even take care of the tree limb. He said he'd drop by your place this afternoon after church to give you an estimate. He's a good man, well respected by the insurance companies, too."

His words hit Willa like a snapped suspender. He had called Ace Barker about her roof?

"Thank you, Mitchell." Her tone came out ultrasweet with the attempt to keep the irritation from her voice. "I'll certainly take your advice into consideration. I do appreciate your help, but the roof is not your problem. I can handle it."

"You're right," Mitchell said after a moment's pause, briskly and good-naturedly. "You let me know if you need anything."

"You know I will, Mitchell . . . and thanks."

"Sure." He cleared his throat. "Is Jack still there? I'll need to talk with him about his inheritance, the papers and things to get the acreage legally put into his name."

"He's not here now," Willa said slowly. "I have no idea where he is." Then she admitted, "He did leave his trailer here, so I guess he's coming back. I'm sure he knows he needs to see you before long."

"Yes, I'm sure he does."

The conversation had turned awkward. Willa bit back the urge to explain about herself and Jack. To do so would give undue place to Mitchell in her life.

They said goodbye, and Willa slowly replaced the receiver. Mitchell was a good, reliable man, and handsome enough to make your teeth ache. She liked the way he laughed, and if he still kissed the same, she liked that, too. She knew he cared for her. Though he'd not said it straight out in words, she knew by his actions. And she was fond of him. She could probably love him if she so chose.

But she hadn't so chosen, and she didn't know at the moment if she ever would. She needed to keep the distance between them, not allow Mitchell to think them anything other than good friends.

She had gained a measure of independence, and she liked it, even clung to it. Her independence was her security. If she didn't need others, she wouldn't have to deal with the hurt of losing them.

When she'd married Jack at the early age of seventeen, she'd been mature enough, but in many ways she'd simply exchanged Hoppy's shoulder for Jack's. Finding Jack to love, to love her, she'd put all of herself into the relationship and had had very little life apart from her marriage.

Then it had all crumbled. She'd felt like a crystal vase thrown against a brick wall, shattered, never to be whole again. Finding herself, gaining strength, had been a long, hard struggle. She didn't want to jeopardize that in any way. If it meant being a little lonely at times, perhaps that was the price she would have to pay to attain a life of peaceful contentment.

Chapter Six

Taking Molly with her into the shower, Willa bathed them both. Afterward, she took several minutes to choose her clothes, settling on old but still nice-looking corduroy pleated slacks and a newer cotton sweater. They were finer clothes than she'd normally wear to do the cleaning needed in Hoppy's bedroom and elsewhere about the farm, but work or no work, she wasn't about to let Jack see her looking shabby and unkempt, a woman who had no pride in herself.

She dried and brushed her hair, then pulled the front up and back, fastening it with a clip. She even put a bit of blush on her cheeks and brushed her skin with powder, deciding there was no need to go to more trouble. She just wanted to look presentable. And pretty, she admitted to her image in the mirror. She wouldn't have him glad he'd lost her, after all.

Pausing before the mirror, she had the whimsical image of him looking after her, wistfully, like a hound pup gazing at a bone that was just out of reach. She wanted Jack to be sorry he couldn't have her. For a split second she wished it ruined the rest of his life.

"Oh, Willa," she said in a loud whisper, "you don't wish such a thing!" How very awful of her! Looking at her reflection, she scolded herself for her uncharitable thoughts. Her heart gave a tug. She didn't want any of that for Jack—not really. She didn't want him unhappy.

Besides, she reminded herself firmly, she didn't care what he thought of her. She didn't need to care. She wished him the very best. She had a good life, and she wished for him to have the same.

Then she realized she was frittering away time in front of the mirror while her daughter ran around the house nude. At least with the furnace working again the house was quite warm.

Willa took the same care in choosing Molly's clothes as she had her own. She wouldn't have Jack think her less than a capable and caring mother. Molly insisted on wearing frilly panties instead of a diaper. "'ike Mama," she said, her face screwed up to defend her point. Willa agreed readily enough; it wouldn't do to dampen her daughter's endeavors.

By early afternoon, the electric company workers finished with their preliminary efforts on the new pole, though they said they would need to return the following week to complete the job. Willa spoke to her insurance man and arranged for a settlement. Ace Barker showed up, looked at the roof inside and out and named a price that sounded reasonable. Willa told him to begin on Monday morning.

Feeling once again in control of her life, she concentrated on clearing the broken limbs and roof debris from Hoppy's bedroom by pitching it all out the open window to the yard below. She was unaware of Jack's arrival until his deep voice boomed out from below.

"Hey! There's a person down here!"

Willa poked her head through the open window. Her eyebrows puckered as if she were about to tell him to get the hell out of the way. She looked exceedingly young with her hair pulled away from her face. Her gaze fell to the enormous box he carried.

"Come on down," he said. "I brought my daughter a surprise!"

With Molly sitting on Willa's lap, both of them watching his every move, Jack assembled the spring horse he'd bought. It was large—big enough for Molly to grow into—and made a galloping sound when it moved. When reared way back, it made a loud whinny, like the real thing.

Molly's wide blue eyes stared at first, more in curiosity than fear. When Jack reached over to pluck her from Willa's lap, she didn't protest. His heart gave a powerful twinge as he held his daughter. She was warm and, oh, so small in his big hands. He noted her burnished curls and soft round cheeks. Setting her atop the horse, he held her steady while gently bouncing it up and down. Her eyes grew wider, and she looked to Willa for reassurance.

"Oh, my! Molly's riding a horsey," Willa said, smiling and coming to kneel closer, though she didn't reach to touch Molly. Jack was grateful she allowed him to be in charge of helping Molly get to know the new toy.

Speaking softly, he showed Molly the handles to hold. For a moment, her pudgy little hand rested in his own. His daughter. The thought would never wear out. He stayed bent beside the horse a very long time, ignoring his aching knees and back. Molly began to giggle, her eyes sparkling at him. And Willa's eyes held a warmth, too. Jack felt pretty darn good, positioned as he was between the two females in his life, or at least the two females he wanted in his life.

Reluctantly he realized if he ever intended to walk straight again, he had to stand and stretch the kinks from his body. He lifted Molly from the horse's back. She regarded him uncertainly but didn't pull away. Jack looked with pride to Willa. She returned an amused smile.

"Would you like a glass of iced tea?" she said.

"Sure would." Pride and joy nearly split him wide open.

Willa turned quickly to the cabinet to get the glasses. She didn't want Jack to see her face. He looked so joyous, standing there with Molly in his arms. She was happy for him, and for Molly. Ecstatically so. But she felt left out and wished in that instant that it could be different. That they could be a real family.

Foolish, foolish, she scolded herself as she took the glasses from the cabinet and plunked them onto the counter. Her gaze strayed to the window and then beyond to Jack's pickup. Lumber protruded from the rear of the pickup bed.

"Jack, what's that lumber in your truck?"

Still holding Molly, he stepped beside Willa. "Materials to repair the roof."

Willa whirled to face him. "My roof?"

"Yes," he answered, watching a blaze kindle in her eyes and crimson steal across her face.

"You and Mitchell," she said, confusing him, though he appreciated the implication that she wasn't too happy with Mitchell. She raised her hand in an angry motion. "It is my house. My roof. You didn't talk to me about it. What if I don't want to pay for the materials you bought?"

"I don't expect you to."

"You don't..." She looked ready to explode. "I repeat. This is my roof. I intend to see to getting it fixed the way I want."

"Look, Willa, I'm here. I can do the work. There's no sense in you hiring anyone. Take the check the insurance company gives you and come out ahead."

"Why not ask me what I want?" She swept her silky hair behind her ear. "Ask me if I would like you to do the work—don't just assume. And I don't want you to do the work," she said, her jaw as sharp as a saw blade.

Jack thought better of pointing out her foolishness. "Let's not argue in front of Molly," he said instead, pleased as punch at his clever maneuver.

"I'm not arguing, I'm telling," Willa said firmly. "This is not your house, Jack—Molly or no."

"Okay," he agreed, forcing an easiness into his voice. "But I already bought most of the stuff you'll need to fix it—out of the money that belongs to Molly, anyway."

Willa studied him. "Give me the bill." She moved around him to the refrigerator and pulled out a pitcher of tea. "It's fresh," she said, filling the glasses. "I made it an hour ago." Without his saying a word, she pulled out a container of lemon juice and squeezed a bit into his glass.

She'd remembered he liked lemon juice in his tea, just as she had remembered the milk for his coffee. Her hand brushed his when she passed him the glass. He stared knowingly at her. A fresh blush swept across her cheeks, and she jerked her gaze away.

He ran his eyes down her hair to the creamy skin of her neck. A wanting grew in him. He wanted to touch her, to kiss her, to make love to his wife. It came as a powerful hurt to know she would reject him. Anger cut through him like a blade as he watched her movements. Then she turned around and caught him looking. He didn't shift his gaze.

It remained, he saw in that instant. She wanted him; at least he thought he saw evidence of desire in her hazel eyes before she blinked and averted her gaze to her glass.

If he were to reach for her, stroke her neck with his finger, a gesture that used to set her on fire, would she resist?

Just as he made to move toward her, Willa stepped away to gather Molly up into her arms. "Molly missed her regular nap," she said, not looking at him. "I'm going to lie down with her now. You can see yourself out." Her manner had turned as frosty as a January morning.

He stood there and watched her walk away. He considered going after her, making her face her feelings. What he *thought* were her feelings, he reminded himself. How could he really know?

He shook his head. No, it would do no good to push Willa. He'd have to give her time to see, to decide for herself. No one, but no one, pushed Willa. He hadn't lived with her for ten years without learning a little something.

After finishing his glass of iced tea, Jack toyed for a few seconds with the idea of stretching out on Willa's bed—the bed he used to share with her—or even on the couch. He decided against either. The couch was way too short for him, and there was no sense in chancing to annoy Willa further.

Returning to his trailer, he, too, laid down for a nap and managed to sleep for over an hour. It was early evening when he drove his pickup into the barn and began unloading the building supplies into its shelter. The sky was growing hazy. It wouldn't be good to let the lumber get wet if it rained again that night. He was wondering if Willa would invite him to dinner, or if he'd just invite himself, when Mitchell drove up.

Straightening and peeling off his leather gloves, Jack watched Mitchell alight from his car. As if sensing Jack's attention, Mitchell stopped and stared across the yard at him. Jack stared back. It was Mitchell who broke the gaze when he turned and strode into the house.

Watching Mitchell's tall, lean back disappear into the house, Jack cursed under his breath, jerked his gloves back on and bent to hoist a bundle of shingles from the pickup bed onto his shoulder. He tossed them onto the stack of lumber and debated about going to the house and simply barging in on Mitchell and Willa. Deciding definitely to do so, he tried to formulate exactly what to say. Just as he'd again pulled off his gloves, he heard the screen door squeak, then slam. Mitchell, walking with swift strides, came out, got into his car, circled it around the end of the drive and drove rapidly away toward the road.

Thoroughly pleased, Jack watched the brown sedan disappear into the distance. He wondered if Willa had sent Mitchell away because she intended to have dinner with him, alone.

That provocative idea evaporated into dust when the screen door again squeaked and Willa appeared, carrying Molly. He was surprised to see her dressed for going out— she wore a soft, hip-length sweater, a skirt that swirled past her knees and tall boots that encased her calves. Molly, too, wore a dress, a little-girl hat and a coat. Without looking his way, Willa walked straight to her pickup, fastened Molly into a child's car seat and drove away. She didn't look at him, didn't seem to be concerned with his whereabouts at all. She just left.

Jack watched her car disappear down the road in the opposite direction from that Mitchell had taken. Cursing under his breath, he jerked on his gloves once again and stalked to the toolshed at the corner of the barn, took up the chain saw in one hand and a ladder in the other and headed for the broken tree limb. He had to have something strenuous to do or he figured he might just burst. If Willa didn't appreciate his work, then that was tough.

She hadn't asked him to dinner. Hadn't said a word to him. Him, her very own husband! That was just plain rude!

It was dark when Willa returned. Her headlights played across the big elm. The broken limb had been removed. She stopped the truck and looked. Yes, it no longer lay across to the roof. Jack, she assumed, and managed mild irritation.

His pickup sat parked beside his trailer, and lights gleaming within gave evidence of his presence.

After nursing and rocking Molly to sleep, she stirred restlessly about the house, turned the radio on low and lit a fire in the fireplace. She'd run away again that afternoon—from the problems with the house, from Mitchell, from Jack, but mostly from her own feelings. She'd wanted time to get herself quieted down so she could figure herself out. It hadn't worked. She still had feelings she didn't understand.

She felt a terrible longing for Jack, a longing that had seemed to burrow its way under her skin, making her fairly tremble when around him. And that was plain stupid! He'd treated her abominably, thrown her away like a worthless trinket of which he'd tired. How could she still have feelings for him?

Heaven knew she couldn't afford to harbor such feelings with the situation as it was. He was going to be around of-

ten, visiting Molly. Willa couldn't continue to feel this way.
She just couldn't. Though she didn't find it admirable, she
found herself considering the possibility of setting aside
wisdom, practicalities, and dipping into the pleasure of
making love with Jack. She wouldn't have to think of to-
morrows, just now, today. Let tomorrow take care of itself.

The way he looked at her, as if he'd like to... Well, he had
no right to look at her in such a way! she thought hotly,
turning from the idea.

For an instant, an odd pleasure touched her. She was glad
he looked at her like that.

No! Of course she wasn't glad. She didn't care how he
looked at her, what he thought.

Heavens! she was a mess. And she didn't want to be.
She'd been this way when Jack had left, and she wouldn't
allow it to happen again. She wouldn't allow him to upset
her world again with his whims and wishes.

Taking Hoppy's bulky gray sweater from the hook behind the back door, Willa slipped it on and walked outside.
In the country everything was pitch dark at night, the sky
like a bolt of velvet with glitter spilled across it. The Milky
Way seemed to stretch right over her house, close enough to
raise a hand and touch. Willa looked at it and felt quite
small, insignificant.

"Stargazing?"

She started at the sound of Jack's low voice off to her
right. Suddenly she was very glad to have walked outside,
knew she'd wanted to see him. Her heart beat wildly, and
everything within her shouted caution as she peered into the
darkness, searching for him. His shadow appeared out of
the blackness as he came closer to the dim light from the
house.

"It's a good night for stars," he said.

"Yes."

He stopped beside her and looked upward. "Where'd you
go tonight?" he asked after a moment.

"Out to dinner with a friend, Carrie Spangler. You remember her?"

He nodded. "The lady who wears the baggy overalls and farms with a mule?"

Willa smiled. "Yes, that's her. We've become good friends. We had dinner at her house and then went to evening church."

"Oh."

"What did you do for dinner?" she ventured after a minute.

He looked down at her. "Drove down to Duncan for a hamburger. Beenie's—you remember?"

Yes, she remembered. They used to go there often.

"You cut away the limb," she said.

"It took me all of twenty minutes to get it off the roof and cut into firewood, Willa. Don't squawk about it."

Willa bristled. "I wasn't going to squawk. Thanks," she added after a moment.

She heard his boot scuff the ground, sensed his movement. Quite suddenly she was very aware of him; she could almost feel the warmth from his body. She wondered wildly if he'd bent toward her, and a split second later his hand moved onto her upper arm. Then he was turning her to face him, both his hands gripping her firmly by her upper arms and jerking her toward him. His breath fanned her cheek; his lips came down on hers.

At first she resisted, struggling to push him away. Then she let all resistance blow away with the wind and felt herself being enveloped by a heavenly, swirling warmth.

His lips were warm and smooth; his mustache tickled her nose. His tight hold turned to a wondrous embrace, and his kiss became gentler. He pulled back and seductively nibbled her lips, then again he was kissing her . . . taking her breath away. His body was like an enormous, hard rock to which she didn't want to stop clinging.

It was wonderful, breathtaking, and she allowed herself to flow away with the feeling. Just for now, just for these precious seconds, she told herself, savoring the feel of his lips against her own. Just this once couldn't hurt. But her body, having tasted a bit of heaven, clamored for more. And, involuntarily, she pressed against him.

Jack broke the kiss, and she felt his chest heaving as he gasped for breath. Or was it her own gasping? She couldn't look at him, though she sensed his eyes upon her. His hands stroking her back brought shivers. Frantically she tried to gather her frayed spirit. This couldn't go on, her pride insisted. She couldn't allow this to happen. Where was her self-respect? Her sense of dignity?

She opened her eyes and looked into his. They were dark and hot with desire.

No, Willa thought. No. It's wrong. It won't work. I will not give up what I've found for a few minutes of foolish pleasure. I won't let him back into my life.

As if he read her mind, his jaw tightened, his eyes glittered and he pressed her head toward him, trying to kiss her again.

"Willa...just let us—"

"*No!*" She struggled against him, pounding her fists at his massive chest. He released his hold, and she stepped away. "You can't come back and destroy my life, Jack!" she cried in a hoarse whisper. "I'm happy now. I don't need to play games. I don't need you!"

She whirled and disappeared into the house. Within her mind echoed all kinds of accusations of stupidity—against herself.

Jack stared at the porch for a second, then stomped toward his truck. Jerking open the door, he slipped behind the wheel and slammed the door closed.

He needed a cigarette, he thought, gunning the engine to life. He needed to feel the road beneath the wheels, needed to think of drilling and oil and football games.

What he didn't need was his offer of love thrown back in his face! he thought hotly, pressing the accelerator and sending the pickup racing down the drive.

It was an insane idea, thinking he could possibly change things, believing that Willa still loved him. He'd best give it up. What did he want her for? She was stubborn and hot-tempered and just plain ornery!

Willa listened to Jack's truck disappear down the road. It was best, she told herself. He'd probably be gone in the morning, or soon after. Perhaps they could arrange to meet for his visits with Molly. Willa could bring Molly to Jack in town.

The kiss hadn't been his fault, she told herself, tears slipping down her cheeks. She'd wanted him to kiss her. She'd wanted to make love with him. Some fools never learned, she guessed.

The matter had to be settled, she thought, gulping back the sobs. It would be better for both of them. Tomorrow she would call a lawyer. She would settle it once and for all.

Jack awoke early. He lay there for a minute listening to the birds' morning songs. Then he stretched and sat up. A half-empty cigarette pack lay on the shelf beside the bed. He'd enjoyed those smokes last night, but reaching out now, he crumpled the pack in his hand. A new day, and it was back to the gummy bears.

And back to his pursuit of his dream. Willa was stubborn and hot-tempered, he knew, but she was also loving and kind, and she had more life than any woman he'd ever known. He'd never met another woman who made him feel as she did. She was one of a kind. He loved her.

So thinking, Jack headed for the camper's tiny shower, his mind revolving with ideas of how to make his desires into reality.

Deciding against pressing matters with Willa that morning, he drove into town, directly to the bank.

He pulled into a parking spot out front. The building had been there since the twenties, the very bank begun by Mitchell Warner's great-grandfather. That it had survived the Great Depression and current hard times was a testament to the Warners' savvy. The Warner dynasty of bankers and lawyers was a powerful influence in several counties around about, but Mitchell had never acted superior when he and Jack had been friends in high school. No, Mitchell had been okay. The only thing he and Jack had ever clashed over had been their mutual desire for Willa. And they were about to do it again, Jack thought, slipping a gummy bear into his mouth.

Pushing gently through the modern glass doors, Jack walked over to the old-fashioned marble teller's window. "Like to open an account," he said, returning the smile of the pretty young woman behind the counter. He quickly filled out the forms she handed him and passed them back to her.

"Canada . . . Mr. Cashion?" she said, giving a flirtatious smile.

"Yes, ma'am. But I'm home now."

She stamped the forms, got his signature about a half dozen times and gave him all the respect due the amount of money he was having put into their bank.

Mitchell glanced out his inner office window, and his gaze fell on a big man at the teller's window. He recognized Jack Cashion immediately. Brenda, like all women who'd ever faced Jack, was eager to please. Why was it women's eyes invariably lit up as if they'd just found a diamond when they looked at Jack? It'd been that way even back all those years ago in junior high school.

That he himself did pretty well with the ladies crossed Mitchell's mind. He guessed he'd had his share and knew his current irritation stemmed from the old rivalry between himself and Jack. It was foolish, he told himself. He was on equal footing with big Jack Cashion now; he no longer needed to play second fiddle.

Jack turned from the teller and looked at him. As the big man walked forward with that self-confident saunter of his, Mitchell rose and stood behind his desk. He would have given a lot to roll a ball and knock Jack right off those sure-footed feet.

"'Morning, Mitch," Jack said. He folded his wallet and stuffed it into his back pocket. His big frame filled the doorway.

"Good morning, Jack. You had need of our services?"

"Yes. Just transferred my money from my bank in Canada."

"Oh? You staying around long enough for that?"

Jack looked at him, and Mitchell looked back.

"I'm glad to see you this morning," Mitchell said then. "I wanted to show you the papers giving you the three acres the Kinsey Oil well sets on. It's still pumping, by the way. Lease money, what little there is these days, will go to you." As he spoke, he bent to reach into a drawer and pull out a file, which he slapped onto his desk.

Jack stepped forward. "I stopped by and saw the well on my way in this morning."

Mitchell handed him a paper. As Jack studied it, Mitchell allowed himself to boldly study the big man. Were his suspicions about Jack's intentions correct? Did he possibly entertain the notion of making up with Willa? He wouldn't get anywhere, Mitchell told himself, though doubt was there.

"You want my signature at the bottom?" Jack asked, raising an eyebrow.

Mitchell nodded and handed him a pen. "And an address, too. I'll file this for you, and they'll start sending you the monthly checks."

Jack bent to the desk and scribbled the name. Mitchell watched him write Willa's address. When Jack handed him the paper, he stared for a moment at the address.

"What do I owe you, counselor?" Jack asked.

Mitchell raised his gaze. "Nothing. Consider it on the house." It was one small way to get at Jack.

Jack's eyes narrowed. "You know," he drawled, "it'd be awfully nice to step out back in the alley and have a go at it."

Mitchell gave a tight smile. "I'd like that, too, and I'll oblige if you feel it necessary."

Jack shook his head. "I guess we've outgrown that."

"Yes, I guess we have."

"But you'd like to punch me."

"Yes, I would. And I may still do it. Don't let this suit fool you."

"Oh, I don't," Jack said, his gaze slipping down Mitchell's frame, then back up to meet his eyes. "You're a fine man, Mitch, but Willa is still my wife. I want you to butt out and let us settle this thing by ourselves." He'd dropped his voice for the last.

"You worried about something?" Mitchell said after a moment. He hoped to see Jack squirm, but the big man just gave him a lazy look.

"I'm not worried. I just don't want the issue more confused than it is already. And I'm exercising my God-given right to protect my family."

"You should have thought more about Willa being your wife and Molly being your daughter during the past two years," Mitchell said.

Jack's eyes glittered. "I'm not denying I made a mistake, Mitchell. It's one I'm trying to rectify. Can you understand that?" His pale eyes bore into Mitchell.

"Yes," Mitchell allowed finally. "I can. But can you understand that I care for Willa? And that I'm not going to back off until she tells me to?"

Jack seemed to digest this information. "Okay," he said slowly, giving a thoughtful nod. "If it has to be that way, then."

Jack managed to keep his cool, to give a polite tip of his hat, to turn and saunter from the bank. Feeling Mitchell's eyes on his back, he kept it ramrod straight. But in the pickup, he cursed and gave the steering wheel a hard smack with his fist.

Willa had always had a liking for Mitchell. And Mitchell had a lot to offer. Money, security. He was handsome enough, and more; there was a settledness about Mitchell. And he'd never treated Willa as Jack had.

Again, shifting recklessly into reverse and backing quickly from the parking spot, Jack cursed his past stupidity. Lord, how he wanted to wipe it all away. But he couldn't, never would be able to. He'd just have to live with it. And he wasn't about to let the past wreck his future. Mitchell, or anyone—even his own mistakes—wouldn't take Willa and Molly from him without a fight.

Chapter Seven

We'll expect you at ten o'clock Thursday, then, Mrs. Cashion," the secretary said.

"Thank you," Willa replied faintly and replaced the receiver, allowing her hand to rest there as she stared out the window.

She'd called an attorney whose office she passed every time she drove into Duncan. She'd had no referral from anyone, had no idea of the attorney's reputation, but she didn't know anyone to ask. Except Mitchell, and no way could she speak of such a matter to him.

I should have done it a long time ago, she told the small accusing voice in her mind. It will be better for both of us to get it over with.

At that timely, or untimely, moment she heard a truck pull up the drive—Jack, returning from wherever he'd been that morning. Resolutely refusing to look for him, she turned from the window and went to the stove to stir the soup she'd been heating for her and Molly's lunch. Fool ishly she found herself listening for his footsteps. She jumped slightly when she heard his boots scrape the back step.

Should she tell him about making the appointment with the lawyer? Should she mention it? How?

With a cursory knock at the door, he poked his head inside and shot a smile from Molly to Willa. His gaze lingered on hers and seemed to be searching her face.

"Hello, Jack," she said. "Molly, look who's here. It's Jack. It's Daddy."

His eyebrows shot up at her words, but the pleasure was clearly visible on his face.

"Hi, Molly." He stepped inside, carrying a brown shopping bag. Opening the bag, he pulled out a box—a toy bear. "It talks. Have you seen these things, Willa? We never had things like this when we were kids."

Molly loved it, of course. She even sat on Jack's lap and let him show her the bear, whose mouth actually moved when he spoke. "Hi, I'm Wilbur Willoughby," the bear said in a squeaky tone. Molly giggled and put her finger in the bear's mouth. She looked so small, nestled in the crook of Jack's big arm. And Willa could see the resemblance between father and daughter—the shape of their eyes, the way both their smiles started slowly at the corners of their mouths. A resemblance Willa had recognized since Molly's birth but had tried to convince herself was all her imagination.

When she poured herself a cup of coffee, she automatically poured Jack one, too. Realizing what she'd done, she stared at the amber liquid a moment, then brought it to the table and set it in front of him. Her gaze fell to the dark hair at the base of his neck, and there came the strong urge to touch it, feel its silkiness.

Suddenly he looked up at her. His pale blue eyes were clear, and they seemed to see into the private places in her heart. She turned quickly away, grabbed the pile of dirty clothes and went into the adjoining laundry room. She hoped he hadn't been able to see what she was feeling. She couldn't let him know how he stirred her—she just couldn't.

"I see someone has begun work on the roof," Jack said when she returned.

"Yes," she answered, sparing him a quick glance. "Ace Barker and his son. They tore away the damaged parts this morning, then broke for lunch. Ace looked over the materials you'd bought and seemed pleased." She reached for the check she'd already written out. "Here's what I owe you." She laid it on the table beside his coffee cup.

He stared at it.

"One, two, three..." Wilbur, the bear, counted.

Willa didn't know what Jack was thinking. But it didn't matter. It was best this way—no strings between them.

Of course, she thought, her gaze falling to her daughter's burnished curls, there would always be one string between them—Molly. She considered telling him about the appointment with the lawyer but couldn't find the words.

Coward! she raged at herself as she lifted her daughter from Jack's knee. "Come on, Molly. You need to eat some lunch."

"Well," Jack drawled, "you'd better see about a change of clothes first."

Willa followed his gaze to the wet spot on his denim pants at the thigh—where Molly had been sitting.

"Guess you've just been initiated, Daddy," she said, chuckling.

Molly's bottom lip quivered.

"Hey, that's all right, Squirt." Jack grinned at his daughter. "You're growing fast enough. You go on with Mama, and I'll keep Wilbur safe with me."

Molly seemed to brighten, and Willa shot Jack a grateful glance, then turned and whisked Molly off to the bathroom.

The telephone rang.

After a moment's hesitation, Jack stepped over to answer it.

"Hello?"

"Jack?"

Jack recognized Mitchell's voice. "Yeah?"

"Where's Willa?"

Jack thought to say, *In bed, so goodbye*. But aloud he said, "Changing Molly."

"I need to talk to her."

"What is it, Mitch? I'll give her a message."

"I want to talk to Willa. Personally." Belligerence laced Mitchell's voice, causing Jack to answer in kind.

"Well, maybe you'd better call back at a more convenient time."

"I need to talk to her now."

Jack was on the verge of hanging up the phone when Willa stepped from the hallway.

"Who is it, Jack?" she said, straightening Molly's clothes as she came across the room.

"It's Mitchell." Reluctantly he held the receiver toward her.

"Hello, Mitchell," Willa said. Jack cast her a glance, then reached for Molly, talking softly to her.

"Willa, there's a problem—" Mitchell was saying, but Willa was motioning to Jack to get Molly's soup and crackers and missed everything between the beginning and the ending "—court order tying up everything."

"I'm sorry, Mitchell, I didn't catch it all."

Mitchell gave a patient sigh and began again. "As of late this morning, all the profits from the auction are frozen. Darlene's contesting the will."

She'd done it, then, Willa thought, telling herself she shouldn't be surprised. Still, she felt as if she were slipping into a sinkhole.

Willa rubbed her forehead. "She said she was going to do it . . . at the auction, Saturday."

"Why didn't you tell me?"

"Could you have done something to stop her?"

"Aw . . . I don't know." He took a breath, and Willa pictured his golden-brown eyebrows meeting in a V as they did when he was troubled. "No, legally there's nothing we could have done. And I doubt we could have talked her out of it." He paused, and then his voice became firm. "The bank received the court order freezing all money considered to be Hoppy's assets late this morning. As the executor of Hoppy's will, I received further papers informing me that the entire inheritance—the house, the land and the royalties from the well on the acres Jack inherited—is under contest.''

Willa didn't say anything for a long moment. She felt threatened, a threat that grew in her mind by leaps and bounds. The land, the house, was a part of her blood, a heritage to which she clung. Darlene wanted to take it from her. How could she fight back, when Darlene had taken away a good deal of the money Willa would need to fight with?

''How can she do this, Mitchell? Is there something wrong with the will?''

''No, it's perfectly legal. Just because Darlene is contesting doesn't mean she'll get anywhere. But by law, she has a right to be heard.''

''Heard? What has she got to say? How can she get more than what Hoppy left her?''

''Willa—'' Mitchell's voice dropped ''—she's claiming Hoppy was incompetent.'' He sighed. ''And she's saying you used undue influence.''

Incompetent. Undue influence. The words sounded so ugly.

''What does this mean for me and Molly?'' Willa asked, trembling with anger and trying hard to listen to what Mitchell said.

''As far as the house and land is concerned, you can still live there, can still use the land and the equipment. But you can't touch any profits from the auction. And you can't sell anything else.''

''Darlene wants the land, Mitchell.'' The panic in her voice embarrassed her.

''What she wants and what she's going to get are two different things, Willa. We'll get it straightened out. Don't worry.''

After assuring Mitchell she wouldn't worry, she replaced the receiver. She gazed out the window to the rig, thinking of her grandfather. He most certainly would have been roaring mad over this turn of events. I'm doing my best, Hoppy, she told him silently. If she'd been alone, she might have let out an ear-piercing scream. She felt as if she were blindfolded and trying to find her way through a maze. She simply didn't know which was the right way to turn.

Jack stared at Willa's back. Her shoulders slumped, and she suddenly looked very small, as if she were shriveling within herself.

"What is it?" he asked, prodding her with his voice to look at him.

She took a breath and pushed her hair behind her left ear. "Darlene, Hoppy's sister, is contesting the will." She looked so forlorn and lost that Jack's heart squeezed.

"On what grounds?" He set Molly on her booster in a chair and put two crackers in front of her.

"On the grounds of being a mean bitch, that's what," Willa said, fairly spitting out the words. She blinked, and her jawline tightened. "She's saying Hoppy was incompetent and that I used undue influence." She tossed her hands into the air, then let them fall. "Everything from the sale— and your inheritance, as well—is frozen. We can't touch anything."

Jack digested the information. He'd never met Darlene but had understood there hadn't been a lot of love lost between brother and sister. He also knew Darlene and Willa had never gotten on well.

He looked at Willa, seeing the hurt and frustration on her face and in the set of her shoulders.

"Mitchell did the will?" he asked.

Willa, eyes focused on the counter, nodded absently.

Jack took her by the arms and forced her to look at him. "Then it's a good will. Mitchell knows his stuff. He'll handle this."

She raised wondering eyes to his. "You don't like Mitchell."

"No," Jack said slowly, "but that doesn't mean I'm blind to his abilities. He's a right good lawyer. And it could be Hoppy had an inkling there could be trouble over this, which is why he made Mitchell executor of the will instead of you. So you wouldn't have to deal with Darlene directly."

"He never said anything." Her eyes searched his, as if straining to see some truth.

"Hoppy wouldn't."

She began to nod. "No, he wouldn't. He never talked much about Darlene. Once he said that maybe he'd failed her...but he never elaborated."

"Mitchell can handle it, Willa. This place is yours—and Molly's. No one's going to take it."

A crooked smile crossed her face, and for the very first time since he'd returned, a real warmth lit her eyes—for him.

His hands burned into her upper arms. She saw the expectancy in his eyes, the questioning. And she wanted to throw herself against the wide expanse of his chest, to thank him for his confident words, to take comfort in his strength.

But it would be asking for trouble, would be letting him think something that was just impossible. She simply couldn't take the risk of letting Jack back into her life.

When she gave a slight tug away, he immediately released her. She averted her eyes from his, unwilling to let him read the confusion boiling within her.

Willa fixed Jack a sandwich, and the three of them sat down for lunch. She and Jack said little to each other. It was all strained politeness.

"Thank you for the sandwich."

"You're welcome."

His knee brushed hers. "Oh, I'm sorry."

"That's fine." Willa spared him only fleeting glances. It was easier all around for both of them to keep their attention on Molly. It was nervousness on her part, embarrassment at revealing even a bit of vulnerability. She sensed for Jack it was anger.

He didn't tarry but hurriedly ate his sandwich, teased a few spoonfuls of soup into Molly's mouth, then left.

Willa listened to his heavy tread on the porch and the squeak and bang of the screen door. She wanted to call him back but wasn't at all certain of what she had to say. That she was sorry? That she wondered if maybe...

Molly's breaking into an angry squall brought Willa back from her thoughts. She found Molly rubbing her eyes with her tiny, pudgy fingers.

"Oh, Squirrel, don't rub your eyes." Willa reached for a wet cloth. "You have salt on your hands from the crackers. Yes... I know it burns... here... shush, darlin'." Molly's tears cleaned her eyes, and Willa wiped her fingers.

Pulling the shades in Molly's room, Willa sat in the rocker and held Molly to her breast. The chair gave a gentle creak as she rocked. She hummed and patted Molly's bottom rhythmically.

She thought of Jack. She pictured his pale blue eyes, the soft curl of his lips beneath his thick mustache when he smiled.

She thought about her future, Molly's future. She prayed the farm would remain hers and Molly's. She wondered what it would be like if Jack stayed.

In a flash of pure honesty, she admitted, almost angrily, that she wanted to feel his massive chest against her own, to feel his hands caress her body, to taste his lips. She chewed her bottom lip with the thought, and her gaze flowed around the room, lighting on Wilbur the bear, George's scruffy ear, the cotton-string throw rug, as if by doing so she could wriggle away from the fact.

It isn't any good, she thought. Not at all. What will it bring but heartache?

She thought about divorce with dread. It's the best choice, she told herself, though a small inner voice objected. Yes, she insisted to the voice, it is for the best. It would be easier between them then—no confusion, no wondering where each one stood. They would see each other often because of Molly. In the years to come, Willa wanted Jack to feel free to come and visit his daughter. There should be no strain between them. And probably he'd want to marry again. The thought sent a pain slicing into her heart.

Jack sat in the one comfortable chair in his camper, a half-finished bottle of beer dangling from his hand. He listened to the alternate pounding of hammers and the sharp whir of an electric saw. The men working on the roof. The sound annoyed him immensely. He felt totally useless. Why couldn't Willa have allowed him to fix the roof? Allowed him that one thing?

She didn't need him.

The realization hurt like hell. How could he make a place in her life again when she had found a way of living that completely cut him out?

He took a long drink from the beer and toyed with the idea of driving into town. But where he really wanted to be was with Willa.

Finishing the beer in a gulp, he rose to throw the bottle away. Then he pressed his hands on the tiny kitchen counter. He took a deep breath and tried to relax the knot inside him.

How he wanted to hold her, to savor her body, her love. He wanted to gaze into her eyes and see the passion there, the wanting, for him.

But she wasn't having any of it.

She was feeling the same! he thought, angry heat spurting through him like pressured oil through a pipeline. Willa wanted it whether or not she would admit it. The knowledge brought him satisfaction but not ease.

Would the past always stand between them?

Persistence, he reminded himself, angrily and sarcastically.

Unable to stand the confines of the camper another minute, he wandered outside. He spent half an hour at the woodpile, splitting firewood that had already been split. He spent another twenty minutes talking with Ace Barker about the roof and the probability of an early summer. Then he got into his pickup and drove to town, intending to stay late.

He could catch a hamburger and beer at the Corral; maybe Cy would want to play poker.

Jack couldn't face an evening in his camper, knowing Willa was within reach yet so far away. And he wouldn't go to her, couldn't go to her. A man could handle just so much of feeling a fool.

During the following three days the sun shone and the wind blew unusually warm from the south. The roof was completely repaired, and Ace Barker and his son came inside to finish up the interior of the attic bedroom. A new permanent pole was set in the ground by the electric company repairmen, and the remaining equipment sold at the auction was picked up by the various new owners.

And Jack remained at the farm.

He just seemed to be there, every time Willa turned around, jangling her nerves with his presence. Constantly she looked at his wide shoulders, his twinkling pale blue eyes, heard his deep voice and caught his scent.

He spoiled Molly outrageously with his constant attention. He brought her more presents: a clown, a bouquet of helium balloons, and then a redbone hound pup.

"Jack," Willa protested when he presented the pup. "Molly isn't even a year and a half old yet. She doesn't need a puppy."

"Every girl needs a dog," he countered, smiling as Molly squealed in delight and tried to cuddle the pup.

"That's *boy*—every *boy* needs a dog."

"Well, it fits for girls, too."

"And who's going to take care of it?" Willa folded her arms and tapped her foot. "Who's going to feed it and clean up after its messes? And the fleas, Jack." When the pup began scurrying around the kitchen, Willa yelled, "Get it out of my house! If we have a dog, it will be outside!"

"It's a he, and he's only eight weeks old, Willa," Jack protested, chuckling.

"He's a dog. You brought him home—you take care of him."

He pretended to look properly chastened, his eyes as playfully begging as the hound's. Willa refused to smile.

That afternoon he began building a doghouse for the puppy. Willa felt she'd been railroaded but could hardly remain angry. Jack and Molly were so happy, Molly already calling the puppy Doc and trying her best to run after it. Again and again both baby human and baby dog tumbled over on the ground. Willa rummaged around and found an old blanket for Doc's bed and handed it to Jack without comment.

After a few days it seemed easier between herself and Jack, though they watched each other closely and Willa took care not to let any part of her body brush his. She kept her distance with a carefully erected reserve.

They never spoke of a divorce, and Willa mentally chastised both herself and Jack for such behavior. Wasn't he concerned about it? Didn't he want matters between them settled? They couldn't simply ignore it as they had the past twenty-two months. It was time to take steps to straighten out both their lives. Still, she couldn't bring herself to talk to him about it.

She did keep the appointment with the attorney, yet in the end walked from his office without making any move toward divorce at all. She simply couldn't do it. And deep inside she found herself leaning toward trying again with Jack. The one reason she dwelled on was Molly. It would give Molly her real father, all the time, not just at certain times of the year. Perhaps it was worth a try.

That afternoon Willa's mind was taken from these dark, confusing thoughts by her first call about a drilling job. She'd been recommended by W.D. Moses, bless his soul, to a couple who'd recently bought five acres and were building a house.

She knew the land the man spoke of, knew it would be an easy job. After agreeing to begin work the very next day, she hung up, then immediately called the Spangler home. She paced from the sink to the counter, waiting for Carrie to answer.

"Oh, Willa," Carrie said after Willa had explained about the drilling job, "Thomas has driven up to Salisaw with Ben. Ben's running a horse this weekend. Thomas tried to call you this morning when it came up, but he couldn't reach you."

"I was in town," Willa said. "It's okay, Carrie. I'm sure I can get one of the other men who used to work for Hoppy. Just for this time. I'll still count on Thomas for future work."

Looking through Hoppy's battered old address book, Carrie began calling several of the men who'd worked for them in the past. Two calls later, she began to get worried. After the fifth call, she realized she had a real problem. She could find no one to work for her. Two of the men who'd worked with Hoppy had moved; the remaining three were employed elsewhere now and couldn't get away.

Willa considered calling Carrie back and asking for Temple, but Temple's abilities didn't run in the direction of heavy manual labor. If he could think the hole down, it would be fine, but with his hands he was clumsy and inept. Besides, he wouldn't even want to do it.

After checking on Molly napping in her bed, Willa wandered out toward the rig. She wondered in irritation if the angels were trying to disarrange her life, were plotting against her. There really was one person left she could ask, one person perfect for the job. And she didn't want to ask him. Not one little bit!

She tried her best to think of someone else to call on as she stepped through the grass around the rig. She ran her hand over the rough step in the back. The grooves on the step were still filled with dried mud. She'd stood many a time on that step and guided the pipe sections dangling from the cable into place for Hoppy to hook it to pipe already in the hole. She'd shared with Hoppy the anticipation as they'd studied the soil and the water they'd pumped from the hole for the first sign they'd drilled far enough.

Walking all the way around the rig, she stopped and stared at the company logo painted upon the door, the paint now faded and peeling. Coyote Drilling, Established 1898. Willa opened the door and hauled herself up into the cab. She gazed out the dusty windshield, searching her mind for an answer.

Though the rig was considered a one-man operation, it was plain foolish for even a man to work alone. There was always a certain amount of danger—ground cave-in, pipes going awry as they were put into place, or a dozen other unexpected things.

And for Willa the facts were plain. She was five foot five and one hundred and twenty pounds. She would have a hard time drilling alone. Hard? Nearly impossible!

Reluctantly she came to the conclusion that Jack was the only man available. It was either swallow her pride and ask him or call and cancel the job.

She needed the job, not only for the money, but to begin building a reputation. W.D. Moses had recommended her for this job. After she drilled this well, the couple would recommend her to other people they knew, and so it would go, word of mouth building her reputation and business, just as Coyote Drilling had been built in the first place.

So Willa swallowed her pride as much as she could and met Jack as soon as he pulled his pickup to a stop beside his camper a half hour later.

"I'll give you a third of the profit," she said after explaining her situation. "I know the area—it's just twenty minutes from here. We may run into some shale, but I don't think we'll have any problems. With an early start we should be finished by afternoon."

She tried to keep her face impassive, neither anxious nor reluctant, though she felt both, and a strange excitement as well.

"You just hired yourself a hand," Jack said, a slow grin stretching his thick mustache.

Willa's heart fluttered as her gaze slipped from his pale eyes to his velvety bottom lip. Immediately she stepped away toward the house, saying, "We'll leave about seven in the morning." She felt his gaze on her back.

When almost to the porch, she stopped and turned. Jack was at the camper door. "Jack," she called. "Would you like to have dinner with us?"

Why had she done such a thing?

"What is it?" he asked with a grin.

Willa almost told him dog bones. "Chili." She'd already prepared it, knowing full well it was his favorite.

"You bet!"

As the sun peeked over the horizon the following morning, Willa handed a sleepy Molly into Carrie's arms.

"Thanks, Carrie." Willa's gaze lingered on Molly's tearful eyes.

"Go on now." Carrie cuddled Molly. "We'll be fine."

"I'll try to get back by midafternoon. She likes to nurse before her nap."

Carrie nodded and urged Willa off the porch, repeating, "We'll be fine."

Fifteen minutes later Willa drove the support truck down the county blacktop into the rising sun. Jack followed with the rig.

A thousand doubts revolved in Willa's mind. Not about drilling the well—she'd done enough of that with Hoppy to feel secure—but her thoughts bounced back and forth between Molly and Jack. She hated leaving her daughter, worried that Molly would cry for her, would need her, though she knew very well that Carrie was fully capable and wonderfully caring. And then Jack—she would be working with him, for hours. They would be close; he would rely on her and she on him. It gave her an unsettled feeling.

When Willa reached the well site, however, the unsettled feeling passed, and her mind turned to the business at hand. She greeted the customer and learned where he wanted the well. When Jack had backed the rig into place, she set the rig supports and worked the lever that lifted the tower slowly into place. She stared upward, watching the massive steel tower rise up toward the clear, pale blue sky. In less than fifteen minutes they were ready to begin drilling, and Willa felt a familiar eagerness touch her spirit.

She smiled at Jack and saw in his eyes the same sort of anticipation that she felt. They were going to drill. For now the awkward situation between them was forgotten.

The sun was well above the horizon when Willa hooked the first of the pipe to the cable. Jack looked up and watched her sure movements as she guided the pipe through the air and down into place. The morning sunlight played golden on her small, oval face. The rest of her, every bit of skin, was covered by clothes: faded overalls, long-sleeved blue chambray shirt buttoned at the wrists, hands encased in leather work gloves, a wide-brimmed straw hat upon her head. Unusual attire for so feminine a woman, but necessary protection from the sun.

She smiled at him, and he sensed her vibrancy, something he himself felt, shared with her for that instant. He took the pipe and tightened the bit on it with the tool. Then he moved the lever, lowering the bit to dig into the ground.

The man whose well they were digging stood across from the rig, watching with interest. He stole numerous looks at Willa, and Jack thought he caught several curious glances at himself. No doubt the guy had a good bit to wonder about, Jack thought. It was unusual enough for a woman to be a well driller, but standing on the big rig, Willa seemed even smaller than she really was, the baggy, worn clothes in sharp contrast to her feminine movements.

The big engine rumbled, and the bit spun into the earth, biting through the sandy topsoil and eating into sandstone. Jack worked the lever that turned off the drill when it was time to connect the pipe Willa fed him.

It felt good to be drilling again, as if he were stretching muscles too long unused. Drilling a water well was about the same as drilling for oil, except not as deep, so without the peculiar complications and danger. Though water didn't bring the riches of oil, the search for it held its own challenges and excitement. It was also a heady feeling to know these people depended on him and Willa to find them water. They were too far from town to hook up to municipal water supplies; their only source would be a well.

He watched the rotating pipe, kept an ear tuned for the variations in sound from the engine, the pipe, the bit, even the earth itself. He couldn't describe what he listened for; his instincts were simply attuned for changes.

After half an hour Willa jumped down beside him. Her eyes sparkled.

"Feel good?" he asked, raising his voice slightly over the noise.

"Yes." Willa nodded, finding herself more concerned with the way Jack regarded her than with the drilling. Self-conscious, she looked down and pulled off her gloves. She watched the pipe twirl. It seemed to be having no trouble.

Their customer, who'd been watching so avidly, stepped up to them. "I hope we picked the right place."

Willa smiled at him. "It'll be fine. This area is known for a plentiful supply of good water not too far down. Besides, we'll believe it there."

It had been what Hoppy used to say. He'd never drilled a dry well and said it was because he believed the water there. Willa privately thought it due more to the fact that Hoppy never gave up; he would have put a hole to the center of the earth if necessary.

Willa looked at Jack and saw memory reflecting from his eyes. He grinned and winked. "Get back into place, boss," he said. "We're 'bout ready for more pipe."

Circling the hole, Willa hoisted herself up onto the step. She tugged on her gloves and reached for the hook to snare a section of pipe. With a twist of the lever the cable lifted the pipe, while Willa guided it with her hands to where it would hook onto the rotating sections. Jack stopped the drill and reached for the pipe Willa lowered. He set it into place, then tightened it down, his muscles straining beneath his shirt. Slowly he lowered the lever, and again the pipe began to rotate, twisting the bit into the earth. As the pipe drove the bit deeper, the process was repeated, inch by inch, foot by foot.

"Stop," Willa said, waving her hand to Jack when the bit reached a depth of fifty feet.

The pipe slowly stopped rotating, and Jack raised a questioning eyebrow.

"Let's hook up the water truck."

Jack shook his head, his gaze on the hole where moist soil pushed out at the top. "We don't need water, Willa. We can finish without it."

Willa hopped to the ground, looked at the hole, then looked at Jack. "Hook up the water," she said, placing her hands on her hips.

"Look at that soil, Willa. There's plenty of moisture there for drilling."

"That may be, but we're fixin' to hit rock." Willa bent, scooped up a handful of wet soil they'd pumped from the hole and held it out to him. "Look I want to flush the cuttings out."

He shook his head. "That's just a bit of gypsum. The water's right there."

Willa glared at him. Hadn't she done enough drilling to be able to tell when or when not to use water or air?

"Hook up the water," she said, keeping her voice and manner in check. She didn't care to lose her temper in front of her customer.

Jack looked at her and blinked. After a moment he walked away to attach the hoses from the water truck to the rig. Willa moved to help him, a token action. While the hoses were heavy, Jack was more than strong enough to handle them.

Once the hoses were connected, Jack turned the lever, starting the drilling again. Another lever allowed the water to flow through the pipe and down the hole. This water would aid in drilling as well as send the ground cuttings up to the surface.

Willa had been right about the rock, but it was thin enough for the drill bit to punch right through it—probably without the aid of water, she conceded to herself but not to Jack.

The job was easy, just as Willa had predicted, and they stopped drilling at a depth of one hundred feet, having brought out a wealth of water. With a pleased customer looking on, Jack began lifting the pipe, section by section, out of the hole. He'd disconnect each piece, and Willa would hook it to the cable that lifted it away while she guided it back into the waiting pipe tray.

The last section of pipe knocked against the front rail of the tray and lay there at an angle. Willa looked at it with disgust. She was beginning to get tired. Her arm muscles, no longer accustomed to the work, felt weak and trembly. With an angry jerk, she tried to settle it in place on top of the other pipes.

"Willa!" Jack called. "Here, let me. You're liable to squeeze your fingers in those pipes doing it like that."

Grateful for his help, she moved aside while he settled the pipe into place with his stronger arms.

"It's nearly noon," Jack said. "Let's break for that lunch you packed. We can case and gravel pack afterward."

Willa was more than willing to agree. She was starved. And with the good time they'd made, she should be able to get Molly in time for her afternoon nap. She chuckled at the thought. Sitting in the rocker and singing lullabies to her baby daughter provided a stark contrast to her activity of the moment. But both suited her fine.

After getting a check and bidding goodbye to her first satisfied customer, Willa strode to the water truck for the small lunch basket and cooler of soft drinks. Jack followed close behind.

"Tell you what," he said as Willa handed him the lunch basket, "you have lunch with me, and I'll stay to case the well while you take the rig on home. It's really only a one-man job anyway."

Willa shook her head.

Jack raked a hand through his hair. "You *are* paying me for this work. You'd have anyone else you hired do the casing."

"Maybe on another job, but not on this well. I want to do it all this time."

Jack's lips curved into a smile beneath his mustache. His eyes held an understanding light. Then Willa looked away, for there was a dangerous warmth there as well.

They sat in the shade of a large elm. Jack was acutely aware of being alone with Willa. He didn't bother to appear not to enjoy it; in fact, he gave himself over to looking at her.

She'd tossed aside her hat and opened the top buttons of her shirt, revealing the slim line of her neck. Even in those baggy clothes, there was a womanly quality about her. Her hair was pulled back, but stray wisps escaped and curled about her face. She didn't like him staring, he could tell. She wouldn't fully look at him, only sent him fleeting glances.

They didn't say anything to each other. It didn't bother Jack, though he did notice the silence seemed rather loud.

"You should feel pretty good," he said. "You've just given a man water for his home."

"And got paid fairly well for it," she said with a chuckle.

"Ah, nobility is not what it seems."

She laughed, and he liked the sound. She liked being here with him. If he were wrong about that conjecture, the moon would turn black.

"Thank you for your help today, Jack," she said after a moment, her eyes boldly meeting his.

"You're welcome."

She nervously shifted her gaze away. "I think I'll go get the casing from the truck. I'd like to finish as early as we can." She rewrapped her half-eaten sandwich. "You stay and finish your lunch. I don't need help."

Jack rose, anyway, and extended a hand to help her up. He wanted to touch her, if only in that small way. Then her hand was in his, and she was standing in front of him. It came as a natural reaction to pull her to him.

Willa's breath caught in her throat as she found herself gazing into Jack's eyes only inches from hers.

His eyelids lowered seductively. "It's okay, Willa," he murmured, his face bending toward hers. "We're married."

Chapter Eight

Jack's lips pressed, hard, demanding, and his arms crushed her against him.

Willa didn't resist. She couldn't. The sweetness of his lips, the warmth of his strong arms, were too exciting to turn away from.

His hair was soft and sleek beneath her fingers. He smelled of sweat and sunshine and spring air. And for many long seconds nothing else mattered but touching him, kissing him.

His hands stroked her hips and pressed her against him. Feeling the hard swell of him against her, Willa froze.

With all the strength she possessed, she jerked her face away and pulled from his embrace.

"No, Jack." She gasped and stared at him. "I'm not up to playing games."

"Well, I'm not, either, woman," Jack returned. The hot desire and anger burning in his eyes made her want to run. "You can't kiss me like that and still deny something remains between us," he demanded, his voice husky.

"I never denied it."

Jack didn't know how to respond to that. He studied the stubborn set of her jaw. "Willa, do you still care for me?"

"How would I know?" She brushed her hair quickly behind her ear. "I don't know you anymore. Two years and a lot of hurtful words stand between us."

"You know me more than you think. And the ten years we had together can't just be brushed away like they never existed."

She shook her head and looked away. Neither of them said anything for a long minute. Jack studied the pulse in her throat and the wisp of hair that fluttered at her temple.

"Do you want a divorce?" he asked finally.

Her eyes flashed. "I never wanted a divorce, Jack. I wasn't the one who left."

Her words stabbed him. "Willa," he said quietly, "I came back to our apartment two weeks later."

"You came back?" Her eyes grew into round saucers.

"Yes. I was sorry. I wanted..." He flinched. "Well, you were gone."

"You knew where I was." Her eyes demanded an explanation.

"Yes," he said. How could he explain actions and feelings he himself didn't fully understand? It had been pride, and hurt, and a tugging of the world. "And you knew where I was. I always made sure of that."

"You were the one who left. Who said he didn't want to be married anymore." Her hazel eyes glimmered with accusation. "I wasn't about to chase after someone who didn't want me."

"I was confused, Willa," Jack protested, raising his voice and giving a wave of his hand, wishing he could dismiss all that had happened. "I don't know exactly what was wrong with me, except I got lost. I loved you then... I love you now."

She looked away from him. "I don't know about a divorce, Jack," she said. "And I sure don't know about trying to make our marriage work." Slowly she returned her gaze to him. "I could tell you yes, let's try again. I'd like to tell you that. I could promise to do my best to forgive and forget, but I'm not sure my best will ever be good enough. And what if we don't make it? Not only would we get hurt, but Molly would, too."

"I'm thinking about Molly, too. I'm thinking the best thing is for her to have a complete set of parents." Couldn't she see the truth in what he said?

"The best thing for Molly is for us to be happy. And together we may not be happy."

"So what are you saying? Do you want us to go ahead with a divorce now?" Anger propelled him to do what he hadn't wanted—force the issue. The instant the words left his mouth, he wanted to recall them. He watched her, dread in his heart.

"I don't want to go ahead with a divorce." Her voice came softly as she shook her head, looked down and then back up at him. "I can't make that decision right now, but neither can I join my life with yours. I can't give you a reason, and I'm not intending to lead you on by not making a decision. I simply can't, that's all. If you want to go ahead and file for divorce, fine. I certainly understand. I'll go along with anything you decide." She bent to toss the papers and empty bottles into the basket. "Now, I'd like to finish the well so I can get back to Molly as soon as possible."

Willa's insides shook as she picked up the basket and reached for the small cooler. Stiffly, she headed back toward the well site. She felt Jack's gaze but refused to look at him. It was taking all she had not to burst into tears. And tears wouldn't solve anything—wouldn't get the well finished, get her home to Molly, get her heart to do what it simply couldn't at that moment.

She did have the consolation that at last she'd been honest about her uncertainty, with Jack as well as with herself. It was up to him now. If her answer was unsatisfactory to him, he could get the divorce. If not, he could stay around and wait to see what happened. Just as she was doing.

A lump rose in her throat as she thought of him leaving, deciding in favor of a divorce. His steps were very close behind her, and she kept her face forward, trying to get her emotions under control. With a longing so deep it reached down to her toes, she wished she could have given him the answer he wanted, wished she could accept him back into her heart with open arms. But she simply couldn't.

It was strained, working side by side, and Willa was glad it didn't take too long. First the well casing, six-inch diameter pipe, went down into the hole. The casing at the bottom ten feet contained wide slits that would allow the water to flow through and into the hole. Around the outside of the casing they shoveled gravel. It would provide a filter system through which the ground water would flow before it seeped through the slits in the casing, then gathered within it. Here a submersible pump would push the water up a hose to the surface. On top of the gravel, to an approximate depth of twelve feet, Jack shook powdered concrete from a bag. When wet, the concrete would harden and form a seal to help protect the water from surface impurities.

Then they were on their way home, Willa once again leading in the support truck. Her shoulders were stiff, and grit coated her face, but she felt supreme satisfaction at her first completed job. It had gone well, despite the huge problem between herself and Jack, she thought. An easy well to begin with, and that was a blessing. Some wells could take days and hundreds of feet.

Her mind sped ahead to the future. She would hire two or three men to work for her. That would leave her free to direct and not to do the actual labor unless she wished. Unless she simply couldn't keep her hands off, she thought with a grin. The business would never make her rich, but it would provide nicely for her and Molly. They had a home, orchard and vegetable garden, plenty of land to help bring in money. There should be no problem about financing Molly's college education.

But what was she going to do about Jack? Willa thought. She saw all her assets: the business, the house and the land.

And it all seemed empty. Without Jack there remained a gaping hole in her life. Was he truly serious? And dare she try to join her life with his? The questions remained.

It felt so good to cuddle Molly to her that the nagging problem between herself and Jack evaporated into thin air. Molly nursed and smiled up at her. Willa sang softly and smiled back, giving silent thanks for having been born a woman. After Molly had fallen asleep, Willa lay with her on her small bed and promptly fell asleep herself.

It was dim in the room when she awoke. Night coming on, she realized. Light shone from the kitchen, and there were the sounds of someone moving around. Carefully, so as not to wake Molly, Willa rose and walked stiffly from the room.

Jack leaned against the kitchen counter, tipping a bottle of beer to his lips. He wore a crisp shirt, and his hair was freshly combed, she saw at a glance.

Catching her movement, he looked at her. Willa put a hand to her head. Her hair flew helter-skelter, and she couldn't seem to get her eyes open. The same clothes she'd worn for doing the drilling felt damp against her skin.

Jack smiled. "I went into town and got a pizza," he said, nodding at the flat box on the table. "I didn't think you'd feel much like cooking, you being the head of a fast growing business and all." His grin widened with his teasing words, "It's still warm."

Willa fingered a button on her shirt. "I'd like to take a shower first," she said uncertainly. Then she flew into motion, calling over her shoulder, "I'll be just a few minutes."

He was still here. Her mind whirled with the thought. Her heart kept expecting him to leave, and he kept staying. And doing gentle things for her.

She paused to look in the bathroom mirror. "Maybe, Willa," she murmured. "Maybe."

The strain and awkwardness that continually returned to plague them was absent while they shared the pizza and glasses of iced tea in the quiet kitchen. Molly slept on, having begun her nap late.

It was as if Jack had decided, like herself, to put aside the question between them for the time being. Willa was glad, because she thoroughly enjoyed being able to talk to him, even if it was in a cautious way. They discussed drilling, the different approaches and problems, and Willa's plans for the future. Considering Jack something of an expert, Willa leaped at the chance to ask his advice. Which he never hesitated to give, she thought, keeping her amusement hidden.

Molly awoke and joined them, managing to spread as much pizza on her shirt as she got into her mouth. Willa had allowed Doc to enter the kitchen and pretended not to notice the bits of pizza Molly slyly passed down to the hound. Laughter seemed easy for them all.

Later Willa lit a fire, though they had to open the windows to allow the cool night air into the room. While Willa worked at the first of her bookkeeping, Jack and Molly played on the floor in front of the fireplace.

Jack read stories to Molly and played with Wilbur Willoughby. He dragged the large springhorse into the living room and helped Molly ride until Willa was convinced he would be permanently disabled from bending over; he refused to let go of his small daughter for very long. He hovered, Willa thought with a smile.

She watched them discreetly. There was something between them, she realized, as if Molly recognized her connection to Jack. When he read to her, Molly lay peacefully against him, belonging there. And she exhibited perfect trust in him to hold her securely on the horse as, ever bolder, she bounced on the seat.

Once Jack glanced up from where he stretched on the rug in front of the fire, stacking blocks for Molly to knock down. His gaze locked with Willa's. Her eyes, above the light of the desk lamp, were shadowed. He wondered what she was thinking, sensed her reserve and hated it.

The telephone rang. Willa reached for it, and Jack looked back at Molly, laughing with her as she knocked down the tower of blocks he had stacked.

"Oh, hello, Mitchell." Willa's soft greeting floated across the room.

Jack kept his gaze on Molly.

"'gin," Molly said, her eyes pleading with Jack to restack the blocks. He gave her a smile and complied.

"A," he said, showing her the letter on the block. She looked at him and blinked. Willa was doing more listening than talking to Mitchell. Jack had the urge to cut the telephone cord.

Willa gave a low chuckle.

Jack stood up and reached down for Molly. "Come on into the kitchen, Squirt, and Daddy will get you a cookie."

"A-fer," Molly said, hugging him around the neck.

Willa was speaking into the receiver as Jack left the room. He purposefully tried not to hear what she said, though it would have been difficult, anyway, since she'd lowered her voice. He wondered what she had to say that necessitated such an action. His insides felt like a whirlpool.

In the kitchen, he took a cookie from the jar, but Molly shook her head and said again, "A-fer... a-fer."

When she kicked her legs and practically lunged from his arms toward a cabinet, he stepped over and opened the door, looking inside. He ran his gaze over the cabinet's contents, trying to match something with the word "a-fer."

"Ah—one of these?" he asked, pulling out a box of vanilla wafers. Molly smiled, and her eyes lit up with satisfaction. He gave her two, saying, "One for each hand," then set her atop her booster in a chair.

From his jacket hanging on the back of a chair, he pulled a small bag of gummy bears. Digging one from the bag, he popped it into his mouth, then turned to pour himself a cup of coffee. Cup in hand, he leaned against the counter and absently reached for another gummy bear. His thoughts remained on Willa in the living room.

Should he force the issue? Should he tell her to either get a divorce or accept him back into her life? He gave a dry inner chuckle. There was no way he could force her to do either. The only options he had were to hang around, hoping he could win her back, or chalk it up as a loss and get a divorce. He liked neither choice.

Suddenly he realized Molly was sitting on the edge of her chair and staring up at him. As she held half a vanilla wafer in her hand, her deep blue eyes were focused on his mouth. He was sucking on a gummy bear—his third, he recalled then. Obviously she'd seen him putting them into his mouth.

Smiling, he reached into the small white bag and pulled out a yellow candy. "Gummy bear," he said, holding it toward her.

She looked at the candy with an expression of serious deliberation. Slowly she reached to take it. Her gaze on him, she slipped it into her mouth. He watched her mouth move as she rolled it around inside. She grinned, and a bit of yellow juice seeped from the corner of her mouth.

Jack watched her with enjoyment. "Pretty good stuff, huh?"

Her grin widened, and her hand came up to hold the candy inside her mouth. She sucked inward. The next instant her eyes grew as round as saucers. She gave a small raspy sound that sounded like a squeezed off cough.

Good Lord, she was choking!

Immediately he bent toward her, went to smack her on the back, then stopped his hand in midair. Should he do it? Should he press her diaphragm? Wasn't she too small for such an action? He didn't know what to do!

"Willa!" he called, pulling Molly into his arms. *"Willa!"* He shook Molly gently. She made a sound something like a rooster crowing.

Willa rushed from the hallway. "What..." She knew by the sound of Jack's voice that something was very wrong. Seeing Molly in his arms, the distraught look on his face and the angle of Molly's head and throat, she realized the problem at once.

She took Molly from Jack. With swift, sure movements, she laid Molly face down against her thighs and leveled three sharp blows between Molly's shoulder blades.

Molly coughed loudly and let out a cry as something fell from her mouth to the floor. Willa cuddled Molly to her, but after a moment she realized Molly's crying was from anger, not hurt or fear. Jack bent to the floor and lifted a tiny yellow object.

"I gave her a gummy bear," he said, holding it up for her to see, remorse written across his face. "Is she all right?" He hovered at her shoulder.

"Sure, she's fine," Willa said, experiencing the wild urge to comfort him as well as Molly. "She just wants another gummy bear."

Jack didn't look reassured.

"It's okay, Jack. She's just never had a small piece of candy before. Kids can often choke on things. It was an accident, that's all." She looked to Molly. "Now, if Daddy gives you another candy, will you be careful?"

Molly gulped back her sobs and nodded her head, her eyes fastened on Jack. In an exceedingly reluctant motion, he gave her a fresh gummy bear, and slowly she put it into her mouth. A hint of a smile crossed her face.

Jack was close enough to Willa for his arm to brush hers. She felt his tension, knew he'd much rather not have given Molly the candy and was ready to spring into action should she start to choke again.

"She's fine, Jack," Willa told him, holding back her chuckle. "Drink your coffee."

Seeing her amusement, Jack glared at her. He'd just lost ten years off his life, and she thought it so all-fired funny. She should have been in the kitchen with him and Molly instead of yakking on the telephone with Mitchell.

"What did Mitchell have to say?"

She looked up sharply. "He has some papers he needs me to sign and some things he'd like to discuss. I'm going in to have lunch with him tomorrow."

"He could have come out here."

"He wanted to talk to me—alone."

She looked at Molly, as if she couldn't meet his gaze. Jack stared at her until she glanced back up at him.

"I'll take care of Molly, then," he said.

"I..."

"You did want to talk to Mitchell *alone*," he said, allowing an acid tone to color his words.

She flushed, and her jaw tightened. "It won't be but for about two hours. I can leave Molly with Carrie Spangler. Molly knows her and—"

"I'm her father. She knows me fine. I'll take care of her."

Willa looked uncertain for a moment, then nodded. "All right. I'll be home to get her down for a nap."

Willa lay awake and stared at the moonlight making patterns on the wall. Her body had steadily become more stiff and achy.

She put a hand out and felt the empty expanse beside her. The bed had never before seemed so big.

She thought of Jack in his trailer. He was so close—and yet so far away. The saying had never seemed more true to her.

Thinking of him, a tenderness welled up within her. How much it must have taken for him to come back to Wensler, to her. Then to find out about Molly, to face what he'd missed and to not hold resentment. And here he stayed.

He was waiting, she thought with awe. Waiting for her to accept him. If she would.

Willa tried to harness her thoughts and delve deep into her heart. When she was around Jack, she felt something she couldn't quite put into words. Giddy...unpredictable...an added sense of life, of awareness of herself. Desire. Strong and hot. At the thought of love, her heart squeezed.

But... The word stood there, big and bright in her mind.

She'd learned to live without him. She'd lose her independence if she chose to join her life with his again. And the risk would be so great; it fairly stopped her breath just to think about it.

What if she and Jack tried and failed, as they had before? She squeezed her eyes shut and turned into her pillow, wanting to escape the gnawing fear. She couldn't stand the thought of his leaving her again.

After a moment, she rolled onto her back and took a deep breath. There was another emotion at work here, too. Resentment, lingering in a tiny place in her heart, like a rough-edged stone. She didn't like it. Resentment made her feel weak and fearful and tired. She wanted to completely forgive and forget, but it wasn't coming easy. And that seemed terribly unfair.

Willa rolled her head to the side, and her earring pressed into her soft flesh just behind her ear—as it must every night—caught her attention, bringing into her mind a flood of memories. What a surprise it had been when Jack had given her the earrings. And his face when she'd opened the box—he'd looked at her with such love. The earrings hadn't been the only gift he'd given her like that, for no special occasion, but simply because he'd wanted to.

Flinging back the blankets, she went to the dresser and turned on the lamp. She stared into the mirror. She touched her hair. Once it had fallen almost to her waist. The second day after Jack had left she'd taken the kitchen scissors and whacked it off, crudely, crying all the time. It had been an act of angry self-hatred. She'd been so hurt, so wounded.

She closed her eyes, then opened them. In her mind, she saw another picture: Jack standing behind her. He used to like to do that, hold her in front of the mirror and look at their reflection. Again she touched her hair. He used to like to brush it, when it had been long.

Often at night he'd hold her in his arms in bed and talk endlessly about his work. Most of the time she found it fascinating; at other times she didn't understand and wanted only to go to sleep, but she'd pretend to listen to every word to please him. He loved his work, was a man meant to dig into the earth, to seek out its secrets and surprises—like Hoppy, like herself, for that matter. They'd always had that in common.

Willa stared at herself again for a long minute. Then she turned to the bed, picked up her thick velour robe and slipped it on, tying it tightly around her. She went to the closet for her fuzzy slippers. She stepped through the bathroom to Molly's room. Molly slept soundly, one leg thrown free of the covers. After tucking Molly's little leg beneath the blanket, Willa walked to the back door.

The night coolness hit her immediately as she stepped out onto the back porch and looked over at Jack's trailer. It was shadowy silver in the light from both the tall pole lamp and the full moon.

She paused and hugged herself.

Should she go out and talk to him? They hadn't talked, not really. There were things that needed to be said. Things she needed to say.

Once, an eternity ago, they used to talk. Willa had been able to tell Jack more of her inner thoughts than she had ever told anyone. And he'd talked to her—until that last year, when he'd pulled away, become a man she didn't know....

Willa stopped the painful memory. Slowly extending a hand, she touched the cool wood frame of the screen door, pushing it open.

It was only when he heard a hard rapping at the trailer door that Jack realized he'd finally dozed off. He jumped, then stiffened, wondering if he'd dreamed the knocking. It came again.

"Jack?" It was Willa's voice.

He moved fast then, scrambling from the bed. His sweat pants seemed to grab at the covers, hampering his efforts, and he gave a low curse as he rose too high and hit his head. He wasn't wearing a shirt and was barefoot.

Willa's knock sounded again. "Jack? Are you awake?"

He flipped on the light above the stove as he passed, then opened the door. Blinking in the unaccustomed light, he looked down at her. Her eyes were wide, her face shadowed in the moonlight. She looked so small, and scared, like a rabbit ready to run. Her gaze skittered down to his waist, then back up to meet his eyes.

"I'm sorry to wake you ..." She pushed her hair behind her ear and turned as if to leave.

"I'm awake now," Jack said. "I wasn't truly asleep. Just dozing." He held her gaze. "I've been having trouble sleeping."

She blinked, her eyes round in her pale face. Jack longed to touch her cheek.

"Come on in," he said, stepping back.

She came inside and stood looking around his small living area. "It's really nice," she said, appreciation echoing in her voice.

"It serves me well." He stared at her, waiting.

Her gaze fell to the counter, and she reached out to stroke the Formica. "I..." She wet her lips. Jack's eyes strayed to where her robe made a V at her neck, a quite proper neckline yet still revealing the creaminess of her skin. He remembered what the skin looked like below. "I can't sleep very well, either," she said. Her gaze came up to meet his. Her eyes were luminous, frightened and glisteningly beautiful. "I thought we ought to talk."

He nodded. "Sit down." He switched on the lamp on the corner table. "Coffee?"

"Yes, thanks." She curled up at the end of the couch, tucking her feet beneath her.

As Jack prepared the coffee maker, he felt her eyes on his back. It was damned unnerving. He wanted to grab her and hustle her into bed, lay her back, and ...

"Thank you for helping me today," she said, stopping his thoughts. "I would have had to turn the job down if you hadn't."

He shrugged and nodded toward the check she'd already given him, which lay on the counter. "You've already paid me." He walked into the living area. She seemed to pull back against the couch. Taking the chair opposite, he sprawled his big frame on the cushion.

She looked at him for a long moment; he looked back.

"I still pout sometimes," she said.

He didn't know what to say to that. He wondered if she'd slept with Mitchell, if she'd slept with anyone. Her gaze flitted past him and down the small hall.

"It must be handy, carrying your bedroom with you," she said and immediately blushed, yet her eyes held the same question he'd been silently asking seconds before.

"It could be, I guess." He took a deep breath. "I've slept with a few women, Willa, but all that stuff about men having to have sex is sort of blown up...." He stumbled over the words. "At least for me...and I guess I had sex those times, just making time. I haven't made love since I left." The coffee maker gurgled its last, and Willa was gaping at him. "I'll get the coffee," he said, pushing himself out of the chair.

He poured two cups and brought her one. He handed it to her; she carefully didn't touch him as she took it. He sat down again.

"There's some things I thought you ought to know—" her eyes flitted up to his and remained there "—if you were still thinking about us getting back together." She took a sharp breath. "Like I said, I still pout. Hoppy said it's my worst trait. And I guess I have a pretty good temper sometimes."

"You still have that temper, huh?" he said after a moment. He couldn't hide a smile. "Well, I'm still stubborn about getting my own way. And I've never learned to pick up after myself."

She blinked and looked at him. "Why do you want us to get back together?"

He looked into his coffee, then back up into her eyes. They were so serious, so intense, it pierced his heart.

"No one should choose life alone—if they have a choice," he said after a minute of groping for words. "Life is meant to be shared, and I want to share mine with you. We had something special, and I did value it, Willa. I know I acted like I didn't, but I was just so mixed up. And now there's Molly. She's an added reason, and I don't know why she shouldn't be considered a reason as strong as any other.''

Jack had never been a man who found speaking his heart an easy matter, and Willa knew his words to her in the last five minutes had been difficult for him. She looked into his eyes, feeling warmth well up in her heart.

"Jack, it's a good thought—us getting back together.'' She spoke softly and with all the earnestness she possessed. "But it may not be what you imagine. You've only been here a few days. We don't know each other anymore. Along with occasionally pouting and having a pretty good temper, I'm independent now. I do what I want, when I want and how I want.'' She paused.

"And, Jack, this farm is my home. I...'' She searched for words to explain. "I'm building a business; I have a good start with the equipment. I love it here, I belong here. I'm never going to leave again.''

Not for you, not for anyone, she thought, leaving the words left unsaid but knowing they were visible in her eyes.

He shifted forward, rested his arms on his knees and held his cup with both hands. "Maybe we don't know each other very well anymore, but I believe there's enough left to build on. I can give you the space you need, Willa.''

"What about your work? There's precious little oil drilling going on around here.''

"I'd make a good partner for Coyote Drilling.'' He gave a wry smile. "I do know a bit about drilling. And a bit about farming.''

A sweet sadness touched her. She searched his face, wondering at it all. Would he truly be happy without the extreme challenges and rewards that oil drilling brought him? Then she sat back, ran a hand over her hair and looked down. She just didn't know about the whole idea. Doubts were crowding out her capacity to believe. Yet she wanted to.

"Willa..."

She looked up.

"I can make you happy. I can be a good husband to you and a good father to Molly. It can be good for us."

A lump rose in her throat. "Oh, Jack, I know you'd be a good husband and father." Seeing his confusion, she took a shallow breath and let it out. "You were a good husband to me. For those ten years you were a wonderful husband. But now—so much stands between us. And I don't know if I can do all it will take to put things back together again. And if I tie you down here, I may just be responsible for making you terribly unhappy."

"You're not hog-tying me, Willa. I want to stay here. I'm not going to leave again," he said as if reading her mind.

She bit her lip, trying to keep the tears from her eyes. They stared at each other. Willa's mind flitted to the bed she knew was only ten feet away in the front of the trailer. She saw Jack's wide expanse of chest. He would hold her. And for a few minutes at least she wouldn't have to weigh the choices, wouldn't have to think, but could satisfy her body's clamoring for release.

Yet thoughts of how she would feel afterward kept her riveted to the couch. Making love would seem to promise the commitment she simply couldn't give.

Jack shifted, stood, took a step and knelt in front of her. She sucked in a breath. Her gaze remained on his wide, bare chest. His hands came up, rested on her cheeks and tilted her face upward until she met his eyes. They filled with heat and determination.

"You feel it. I know you do," he said through gritted teeth. "You want me."

She nodded. "Yes," she managed at last. "But we need time for thinking this out. It's no good heading in a direction that could turn out wrong. It'll only hurt all the more then." She searched his eyes for understanding and found anger.

He dropped his hands from her face. "Then why'd you come out here?"

"To talk. There were things that needed saying."

"Sure," he said, giving an angry snort. "To talk! You in your nightgown and robe, wanting to talk in the middle of the night." He rose and looked down at her.

Jerking her feet from beneath her, Willa slapped them to the floor and stood, too. Her chest almost brushed his. Tilting her head upward, she glared at him.

"I came out here to communicate...maybe not only with words, but not by jumping into bed, either! And, yes, I do want to. But that isn't the answer to everything in the world, mule-head!"

"Look who's calling the kettle black." He stood in front of her, as if to intimidate her by his size.

Stubbornness emanating from him, Jack refused to move. The only way past him was to slide sideways, which Willa did, then tromped to the door. She stepped from the trailer and controlled herself enough to close the door quietly behind her.

She felt as if there was more to be said but realized there really wasn't. She'd told him where she stood, and she felt she'd done the right thing. Now he could think about it, change his mind if he wished. And she, too, had to decide. If he stayed.

And still, her body ached for him. But she wasn't about to let it rule her head. Once, she'd done that. It had gotten her what she wanted, at that moment and later, when Jack had taken her as his wife. But this time she intended to control her desire. To think about this, to let him think about it. They each had to make a decision free from all strings.

Chapter Nine

To her amazement, Willa awoke to find she'd slept
soundly, hadn't even dreamed. It was later than usual, the
sun already peeking above the horizon.

Jack was her first thought. Flinging back her covers, she
hurried into the kitchen to look out the window. An incom-
prehensible action, she thought even as she peered through
the glass, wondering if his trailer would still be there.

It was, of course, as it had to be, she reasoned. It was still
early, and even if Jack planned to go, he wouldn't leave
without a word to Molly. She knew this all perfectly well,
but something inside her eased as she gazed at the trailer.
Willa felt joy flowing throughout her body. Oh, she
thought, don't get carried away. Don't think that just because he's still here things can work out. The world isn't a
fairyland.

Still, her heart seemed to take wing. She began to hum as
she turned from the window and hurried to dress. She was
still humming a half hour later when Jack came to the back
door, inviting himself for coffee and breakfast. Apparently

he'd decided against leaving, even after what she'd told him the previous night.

He smiled and talked as if they'd parted lovingly the night before, or as if they hadn't parted at all. His gaze remained heavy upon her, and, feeling it, she became all jangled, dropping things—an egg to the floor, the whisk into the bowl of eggs, a cup into the sink. She felt he was looking at her as if... as if he were seeing her nude!

And he knew it! she fumed, tossing an eggshell into the sink. He knew it and was quite pleased with himself!

With determination, Willa calmed herself. It was really silly to have such a reaction. And she would not give him such satisfaction. It was too humiliating.

After complimenting her on the breakfast and teasing Molly, Jack left, saying he had maintenance to do on his truck. He didn't say if he still intended to watch Molly while Willa went for her lunch meeting with Mitchell, and Willa didn't ask. Later in the morning, she took a shower and dressed for her trip into town. She readied Molly, too. If Jack didn't say anything about keeping her, Willa would call Carrie and ask her to mind Molly. She would not ask Jack.

He appeared at eleven-thirty. As soon as he entered the house, Molly ran to him and held up her arms to be picked up. Jack complied, obviously pleased at his daughter's reaction. His grin widened, nearly splitting his face in two, when she said, "Da-ddy!"

"Yes, it is, Squirt." He turned an excited face to Willa. "Did you hear that? She said it!"

"Yes, I heard. It's the candy." With a teasing smile, she inclined her head to where Molly was intently looking in his pocket.

He chuckled, then looked back up at Willa. His eyes held hers for a long second, then skimmed boldly down her body. "You about ready for your lunch with Mitchell?"

"Yes." She'd been in the middle of brushing her hair; she still held the brush in her hand.

"Well, you'd better wear a sweater or coat. The air's turning cool. Weatherman says we have a hard cold front coming in." He paused, his gaze intense. "Molly and I will be just fine."

Willa nodded. "I know. But if you need me, I'll be at the café. And I'll be home no later than one-thirty."

His gaze again moved up and down her body. Self-conscious, Willa turned away to get her coat from the closet. How odd everything was all of a sudden. Her leaving Molly, with Jack, to go have lunch with Mitchell. Where was the guilt coming from? she thought, slamming the closet door.

She kissed Molly's cheek, and Jack held his out for her, his eyes twinkling with daring. "See you later," she said. At the last second before she passed, she stopped and pecked his cheek, then whirled away out the door.

Jack carried Molly to the door and watched Willa get into her car. "Mama," Molly said, pointing, her lower lip trembling.

"Yes, that's Mama all right." He watched Willa drive away. "How would you like to go into town in a bit and have a nice milk shake?" he said to Molly. She showed him four teeth in a bright grin.

Willa met Mitchell at the bank. He looked extremely handsome in a yellow shirt, striped tie and western-styled suit of tweedy brown. His obvious pleasure at seeing her touched Willa's heart with joy. The next instant the joy was replaced by the burden of worry. He shouldn't be so glad she thought, guilt heaping upon guilt, and I don't need this confusion.

He ushered her into his office, indicated a chair facing his desk, then closed the door behind them. It was hardly private, though, since three walls of the office were windows.

"How's Molly?" Mitchell asked as he sat behind his desk.

"Fine. Jack's keeping her." Now, why had she said that?

Mitchell's head came up quickly, and he raised an eyebrow. Willa bit back further comment about Jack and Molly and how well they were getting on. Poor Mitchell. He'd tried to make friends with Molly, had brought her gifts just as Jack had. But Molly remained distant from him, al lowing him only on rare occasion to hold her, and she never advanced toward him. Whereas, in only a few short days, Molly had become completely captivated by Jack. Then the sharp thought came into her mind: of course, he was her father.

Mitchell cleared his throat and scanned the papers on his desk. Not wanting Willa to know of his jealousy, he didn't look up until he could do so with a calm expression.

"You know pretty much what's in these papers—the final accounting for the auction. The costs of holding it and what was finally cleared." Not wanting to be so far from her, he rose and came around his desk, sitting on the corner. He passed the papers to Willa. "I need you to look them over and then sign at the bottom of the second page."

He stared at her rich, dark hair as she looked down at the papers he'd given her. He caught her sweet scent. It was hardly the place to be thinking what he was thinking.

After taking barely long enough to read one paragraph, let alone two pages, she laid the second page on the desk, saying, "Can I borrow a pen?"

"You should look at it better than that," he scolded her mildly, handing her a pen.

She flashed him a smile. "I trust you. Besides, we don't want to hold up everyone's Saturday. It's time for the bank to close, or haven't you realized that, Mr. Boss?"

Again he studied her dark head while she signed. His mind was miles away from figures and wills when she looked up at him and extended his pen.

"Well, that's one more thing out of the way," he said, rousing himself. "I've gotten some information together concerning Darlene's suit, but it'll be a while until the hearing. The courts are busy, and Darlene's lawyers will want time to prepare their case, so they'll take as long as allowed."

"What can we do?" Willa's eyebrows knitted over her luminous hazel eyes.

"We don't do anything," Mitchell said. "The burden of proof is on Darlene and her lawyers. She has to show to the judge's satisfaction that Hoppy was not in his right mind and was under duress. Granted, Hoppy was a bit unusual, but I don't know how Darlene can prove him unstable. I don't have a lot of worries about arguing whatever nonsense she trumps up. The plain fact is that, by Oklahoma law, the mere fact of mentioning her in his will is sufficient. He didn't have to leave her a cent.''

"What about...'' Willa's gaze flickered nervously away, then back to him. "What about the fact that my father never legally married my mother?''

"Makes no difference,'' Mitchell said. "Hoppy claimed you for all these years as his grandchild. That's sufficient.''

Willa took a breath and thought about it. Mitchell was so calm and assured about the entire matter. But then, it wasn't his property at risk.

"Do you know anything about Darlene's lawyers?''

"They're a relatively big firm out of Dallas,'' he said. "And they're good. 'Course if they were all that great at law, they would've told Darlene she didn't have a snowball's chance in hell. But maybe they did, and she insisted they try, anyway. And they get paid, just like everyone else.''

Willa nodded, imagining Darlene insisting. Darlene did that a lot. And, she told herself darkly, many a will had been changed. The law could be fickle.

"Willa...'' Mitchell's voice brought her attention back to him. "I had Jean prepare us a lunch out at my house. I hope that's okay.''

"Oh.'' She didn't know what to say; she thought of Jack at the farm. But Mitchell looked so hopeful, she just couldn't disappoint him. Something told her he had other things to talk about—and she had a few things to say herself. She couldn't duck it any longer. The Township Café wasn't exactly the most private place for talking.

"I think that'd be fine.'' She hesitated. "But I need to call Jack. I told him I'd be at the café if he should have an emergency with Molly.''

Mitchell wasn't pleased, though he hid the fact well, and Willa was grateful, knowing his tact was out of consideration for her. He nodded toward his telephone. "Go ahead."

Willa dialed, then turned her back to Mitchell. Guilt raised its head again. How very silly, she thought. Yes, Jack and I are married, but not . . . well, not like for real. That statement made no sense at all. Lord, it was getting confusing, and she needed to straighten it out.

When the fifth ring came and Jack hadn't answered, Willa's heart picked up tempo. She hung up on the eighth ring.

"No answer," she said to Mitchell, wondering where Jack was.

"They could be outside," Mitchell offered.

"It's gotten too cold." Willa nibbled her bottom lip.

"Maybe Jack took Molly over to his trailer."

"Yes, that's probably so," Willa agreed, feeling more secure at the idea. She smiled at Mitchell and firmly put foolish worries aside.

Mitchell smiled, his deep blue eyes lighting with pleasure. "We can take my car."

His hand pressed her back as they walked out to his car. He opened the door for her and closed it after her. She watched him walk around the front of the sedan, so tall and straight and broad-shouldered. There came a stirring in her stomach, faintly, and she thought, he is a damned handsome man. He slipped behind the steering wheel and smiled at her. Willa thought it could be good with him, pleasant, secure.

The Warner mansion, as it was termed, sat on the main street at the edge of town, its lawn stretching far back from the road. Willa had never been inside. She was surprised now to find it much more comfortable and inviting than she ever would have thought. It was an elegant yet much lived-in home.

As Mitchell led her down the great hall and out onto a glassed-in porch, she kept an eye out for his mother, a housekeeper, someone, but apparently they were alone in the house. Their lunch had already been spread out on a lovely table.

"If the weather had cooperated, it would have been really beautiful out here," Mitchell said, giving a self-conscious grin and looking suddenly boyish.

"It is beautiful," Willa replied.

She went to the window and looked out at the carefully manicured lawn and the woods beyond. A sea of yellow daffodils filled the flowerbed immediately outside the window. Mitchell came to stand behind her, obviously delighted with her appreciation. Suddenly, it seemed to Willa they were standing too close. With a discreet step, she shifted away.

"Hoppy did the big well for our water supply that keeps all this green in the summer," Mitchell said.

"Oh, yes, I remember now. He'd done that before I came to live with him." She smiled broadly and looked up at him. "I had my first drilling job yesterday."

His eyebrows rose in surprise, and then he smiled in return, but Willa thought she caught a flicker of sadness in his features. She couldn't be certain, and she didn't want to believe it had been there. She waited for a comment.

"I guess it went well, judging by the look on your face."

Willa couldn't stop her wide grin. "Yes, it did." She shook her head. "But it was a very easy well. You know, over there near W.D. Moses's ranch. There's never any problem drilling and getting water there, so I can't really feel we've done something exceptional. Still, it's a start." She squared her shoulders.

"You are exceptional," Mitchell said, his gaze studiously on hers.

She shrugged her shoulders and looked away. "No, I'm just a woman who needs to make a living. I'd be a fool to do other than what I know."

"Did Thomas help?" Looking at her, his eyebrows rose. "You didn't do it alone? I don't care how easy the job was...." He looked thoroughly disapproving.

"No, no," Willa hurried to say. She had to force herself to meet his eyes. "Thomas wasn't available—he was off with Ben Wheatley." She stuffed her hands into the pockets of her skirt. "Jack helped me."

"I see.... Well, I'm glad you didn't try it alone."

"I know I can't do that."

He chuckled then. "I wouldn't put it past you." He stepped toward the table. "Hope you're hungry. Jean made enough for an army."

"I'm starved." She was glad for the ease that settled between them again.

Jean, who was apparently the housekeeper, had indeed prepared a feast. There was chicken salad, fresh greens, strawberries and peaches, rolls and iced tea. Sitting opposite her, Mitchell poured her a glass of tea from the crystal pitcher. She looked at his strong, finely tapered fingers. His hands were clean, free from scrapes and calluses, in stark contrast to Jack's big rough ones. Willa thought of the fact that she and Mitchell were in the house alone again.

Over lunch they made small comments about things going on in town, talked a bit about Hoppy and discussed Darlene's motives and what could happen at the hearing on the will.

"I could get another lawyer," Willa told Mitchell. "You shouldn't have to bother with this. You have a bank to run."

Mitchell waved his fork. "I'm already involved. It's not so much to handle." He looked her in the eye. "I'd like to finish it."

She nodded. "But I will pay you whatever is the going fee for a lawyer on such a case. It's only fair." At his expression, she said softly, "I can afford it, Mitchell."

His lips twitched. "One well and the lady is in big business."

"I'll get other jobs."

"Okay." The agreement came reluctantly. "We'll talk fee when this is all over."

It wasn't exactly what Willa wanted to hear, but she knew it would have to do. Lifting her glass of iced tea, she looked into it. She had to do something to straighten out her life. She had to take a step in some direction. Clearing things up with Mitchell would be a start.

"Willa," Mitchell said quietly.

She looked up at him.

"Jack came to see me Monday."

"He did?" Why was he staring at her so? Her heartbeat became thready. "Why?"

"He told me to stay away from you."

Mitchell's words echoed in her mind. Anger flared at Jack's audacity, and a bit of joy flickered, too.

"Jack wants you and him to get back together," Mitchell said with a raised eyebrow. It was half question, half statement.

Willa nodded. "Yes, he does." She studied his face, noting the sadness and, yes, the warmth, too.

"I told him I'd stay away when you told me to," he said then, his jaw tight.

"Oh." She averted her eyes to the table.

"Willa, I want you to know how I feel about you," he said. She looked up quickly, meeting his gaze. "I don't want to lose you, to miss out on what we could have together because of a misunderstanding. I love you, Willa. I think I could make you happy. And I'd love Molly as my own."

His words plunged into her heart. She'd known it all along.

It would be so easy with him, she thought as she gazed into his deep blue eyes. It would be good, safe, secure. Always certain about him being with her—at least as certain as a woman could ever be.

But...

Gazing at him a long moment, she prayed for wisdom. Then, feeling the need for space, she pushed her chair back from the table. She ran her hand along its smooth armrest.

"I know you'd be wonderful for Molly, Mitchell, and I have no doubt you could make me happy," she said, forcing herself to meet his gaze. "I'm not blind. And I feel . . . have felt . . . when we've been together . . ." She took a deep breath. "I care for you, Mitchell . . . but I couldn't make you happy. I'm not in love with you." She said it as gently as possible. And a small part of her heart shriveled, knowing what she was giving up.

The light in his eyes turned to a hard glitter. His gaze flickered downward, then back up. Willa wished none of this had to be.

"Are you in love with Jack?" he asked.

"I don't know the answer to that. Nor if we'll get back together." She met his gaze. "But we have to settle it between ourselves."

"Willa, I'm a patient man."

Willa shook her head. "Mitchell, there is something between you and me, but it's not enough to build a life on, even if Jack weren't around." She leaned over and touched his hand. "And my choice isn't between you and Jack, but a choice between living my life with Jack or without him." She searched his face for understanding.

A muscle in his cheek twitched. "He left you once—traipsing off halfway around the world. He won't stay, Willa. I will. I'll be here every day for you, to take care of you and Molly."

Willa shook her head, averted her eyes. It hurt to see his anger, knowing she was the cause of his hurt. And his accusations stung, for she feared their truth.

"Okay," he said at last and breathed a heavy sigh. "I just didn't want to regret that I never told you." His eyes burned into hers.

"I thank you for that, Mitchell."

They gazed at each other. Willa saw the heavy weight of disappointment in his face, in the set of his shoulders, through eyes blurred by tears. She wouldn't cry, she told herself. She wouldn't do that to him.

"I'll still handle the will," he said firmly. He looked away, his jaw tight.

Willa nodded. She couldn't get the words *thank you* past the lump in her throat, and she had the idea they would hurt him, anyway.

Well, she told herself, she'd taken one big step toward cleaning up the confusion in her life. Now, how in the world would she ever force another bite of peaches and strawberries past that lump in her throat?

Molly didn't fully comprehend the action needed to drink through a straw. Besides, the milk shake was too thick, so Jack spooned it into her mouth. Not having had a lot of practice, he got a great deal of it on the front of her blouse. He took a napkin and wiped Molly's chin and wondered what Willa would say about the chocolate stain.

And he fumed, wondering where in hell she and Mitchell were, anyway. They'd never shown up at the Township Café, where he and Molly waited in a back booth.

Jack had intended to come upon Willa and Mitchell when they'd already begun talking over their meal. Just to make his presence known. He was going to stop at their table and say hello, then carry Molly on to a back booth for the promised milk shake.

After Willa had left, he'd searched around for Molly's coat, then had driven to town and killed some time at the drugstore, buying Molly a lollipop before coming over to the café. When he'd walked in and not found Willa and Mitchell, he'd become powerfully curious. And mad. Where in the world had they gone? Together. In Mitchell's car, too—Willa's white pickup was parked across the street at the bank.

What kind of thing was that for a mother to do, he fumed, going away and leaving her child without telling anyone where she was? When he saw her, he'd certainly tell her what he thought of it!

"Well, hi, Jack!" came a call from across the room. It was Cy Stanfell. In long strides Cy crossed the café and slipped into the seat opposite Jack. "Well, she sure gets cuter every day, Jack. And you're doing pretty good, Daddy," Cy teased. He shook his head. "Never would have pictured you takin' care of your daughter."

"Hope I meet with your approval," Jack said as he tried to wipe a chocolate smear from Molly's cheek. Getting tired and fussy, she whined and tried to twist away.

"You can wipe harder than that, Jack," Cy advised. "And hold her head. She ain't made of glass."

"Spoken like the father of five," Jack said, trying Cy's suggestion.

"Yeah—and it ain't so bad. 'Course, I can't sit here jawin'—I got to grab a quick bite, then get back to the garage and make money to feed those five." He waved to the waitress, then turned back to Jack. "No need to hurry off—I've heard kids cry before."

Jack glanced at Molly, her pouty mouth tugging at his heart. "I've got to get her home for a nap. Good to see you, Cy." He buttoned Molly's coat high around her neck and tied her hood over her hair, his big fingers clumsy at the job.

"Heard we're going to be seeing a lot more of you." Cy gave a wicked and curious grin. "Heard you opened a pretty good account at the bank. And that you're living out at Willa's farm. In the trailer some say—in the house is others' opinion."

"You heard right," Jack said, responding with a wicked grin of his own and refusing to end speculation as to his sleeping arrangements. He settled his Stetson at a jaunty angle. "Small towns never change."

"Not much." Cy waved. "Good luck, buddy. The poker is at my house, Wednesday nights when the wife and kids are at church."

"Thanks," Jack sent over his shoulder as he left.

Immediately after closing the café door behind him, he looked across the street and spied Willa getting out of Mitchell's car. She stopped and stared at him. Jack looked away and walked to his pickup, opened the door and slid Molly, who hadn't seen Willa, inside, then slipped onto the seat himself. As he closed the door, the brisk air swirled inside the pickup, cold enough to bite at his ears.

He rolled down the window, caught Willa's image in the sideview mirror and heard her footsteps on the pavement as she approached.

When she stopped beside the truck, her gaze flitted from him to Molly, then back to him again. She looked ready to explode.

"What are you doing here?" She pinned him with her stare.

"Mama...maama..." Molly wriggled over to lean against Jack's shoulder.

"Where were you?" he countered.

Molly let out a small whimper.

"You came here to spy on me," Willa accused.

"You weren't here. What if I'd needed you? What kind of thing is it to go off with some man, leaving your daughter without word of where you intend to be? More accurately, lying about where you'd be."

Molly's whimpers grew louder.

"I did not lie!" Willa drew herself up straight and jammed a hand onto her hip. "And I tried to call to inform you of the change in plans, but you weren't home."

"Where did you and Mitchell go?"

Molly began to cry softly. "Maamaaa..."

Willa stared at Jack, then answered finally, "We went to Mitchell's house for lunch." Her expression dared him to make something of it.

Jack bit back the angry words that wanted to spew forth. Staring at her, he tried to keep his thoughts from showing on his face. But the words *at Mitchell's house* echoed through his brain.

Willa's eyes narrowed. "And it's a good thing we went there, because obviously we wouldn't have been able to have any kind of talk with you watching me like you were my...my keeper! And you have no right, Jack Cashion—no right!" She looked past him to Molly. "It's okay, sweetheart. Mama will get you home. Open the door, Jack, and let me have Molly."

Molly dozed on the fifteen-minute drive home, but when Willa stopped the pickup behind the house, the child roused. When Willa had to set her down in the house to remove both their coats and put them away, Molly followed her around, a finger in her mouth, crying and whining. Willa was already so tense, she balled her hands into fists to keep from screaming at her daughter.

She hurried to get Molly ready for a nap, doing everything automatically, her mind on Jack and his outrageous gall.

Finally, knowing Molly's fussing had a lot to do with her lack of attention, Willa pushed the furious thoughts away, sat in the rocker and pressed Molly to her breast. Leaning her head against the back of the chair, she slowly rocked, patted Molly's bottom and began singing a lullaby. The actions gave Willa as much comfort as they seemed to give her daughter.

Soon Molly had fallen into a deep sleep, and Willa transferred her to the bed. In her own bedroom, she stripped off her skirt and blouse and slipped into denim jeans and a heavy ivory-colored sweater. The house had grown cool, so she turned up the furnace. A misty rain had begun outside. Willa stared out the living room window, wondering where Jack was. He hadn't followed them out from town.

She shouldn't have gotten so mad, she thought. She pressed her forehead against the cool glass. She'd warned him she still had that flaring temper.

But how silly of her to be mad at his attention. She chuckled softly. He was jealous. The thought warmed her. He cared enough to be jealous. How awful it would be if he didn't care at all. And he did have a right, she thought, to be interested in what went on between herself and Mitchell. She shouldn't have told him he had no right.

Still, she wasn't too happy about his following her, prying. It was a perfect example of the erosion of her independence with him in her life. And if the big lughead had simply stayed home, he would have known where she was all the time!

Just as she turned from the window, she heard a vehicle
pulling up the drive. It was Jack, she saw as she pivoted to
look. She was the curious one now.

Hurrying into the kitchen, she watched out the window
as he alighted from the pickup carrying a brown paper bag.
He disappeared into the barn and returned seconds later
minus the bag. As Willa chewed her bottom lip, hesitating,
she was amazed to see him head for the old tractor he'd
purchased for her at the auction. He actually started it up.

Willa plucked her coat from the nearby rack, shrugged it
on and hurried out across the yard after him. He had to have
seen her, but he paid no mind. He simply drove the old
tractor into the barn.

Willa followed into the dim, high-ceilinged barn. It
smelled of wet dirt, hay and grease. The chugging tractor
engine seemed to echo, then all was quiet when Jack
switched it off. Without looking at her, he hopped to the
ground.

"What are you doing?" Willa asked, quaking at his stern
profile.

Slowly he faced her. "This old tractor needs an overhaul
if you're going to cut that hay Hoppy planted. Carbure-
tor's shot. Thought I'd take it apart." He nodded toward
several cans and packages on the nearby workbench.
"Picked up some cleaner and parts in town. Stuff cost eight
dollars and fifteen cents, if you plan on paying me for it."
His last words cut through the air.

"I appreciate your doing this," Willa managed after a
moment.

He shrugged and turned his back to her as he began digging through Hoppy's old toolbox. It was so like him, Willa
thought. Any time Jack had things weighing on his mind, he
liked to tinker and to do something that got his hands dirty.

She clenched her own hands, which were stuffed into her
coat pockets. "It's awfully cool and damp out here.
Couldn't it wait?"

"Good a time as any." He didn't look at her.

"Jack..."

"Willa..."

They both spoke at the same time and stopped, each waiting for the other. Giving a half grin, Jack inclined his head. "Ladies first."

"I wanted to apologize for getting so angry before, in town. I'm sorry..." She thought quickly. She wasn't sorry for going to talk to Mitchell, nor for being alone with him at his house. She wasn't sorry Jack couldn't find her—she had called home. "I'm sorry for the misunderstanding," she said at last.

He nodded. "I'm sorry for butting into your business." He reached for a tool from the bench.

Willa took a deep breath. "Mitchell has no part in my life, Jack. He knows that now. And there never has been anything between us."

She saw Jack's shoulders tense beneath his denim jacket. He raised his head to look at her.

"And you do have a right to know that," she said. She wondered if he still cared.

He studied her, no expression on his face. She gazed into his eyes, pale pinpoints in the dimly lit barn. She made him no promises, other than what she'd just said. She couldn't tell what he was thinking.

Jack stayed. At times, he thought he should have his head examined. Trying to deal with a woman as stubborn and mule-headed as Willa was taking years off his life. But he always came back to the decision that it was worth it. No one ever said digging for oil, so-called black gold, was easy—and what he was after was worth far more.

For the next week the heavy spring rains and violent storms came mostly at night, leaving the days clear and warm. Twice Jack hurried Willa and Molly into the shelter. And once they feared the threat of a tornado, but it either passed high in the air or dissolved before reaching the farm.

Jack readied the tractor for cutting hay, strung new fencing and began building a new chicken house to replace the one the tornado had taken out. Willa worked with him every

step of the way, like a shadow, her pride refusing to allow
him to do anything totally for her. Like a fool, she had to
prove herself capable of doing everything she needed to do

Having her so near wasn't all that easy at times, and Jack
began to plot various ways of getting her into bed. More
than once he quite seriously considered the soft, greening
grass.

But she seemed to guess exactly when he was having such
thoughts and kept herself just beyond reach. At those times
she didn't look at him. Several times he saw her skin seem
to quiver, as if she were waiting for him to touch her, but
when he'd steel himself to reach for her, she would move
quickly away.

He watched her dealing with the demons inside herself
and it hurt more than a knife slicing into his gut to know she
watched and waited, wondering if he were going to leave—
again.

Would his past mistakes always stand between them?

He tried not to dwell on that possibility. He pursued his
goal with determination, and he didn't consider bribery too
low a tactic. He bought Molly a tricycle, two dolls and a
goose. The goose proved to be a mistake, though, in his
quest to please Willa.

"A goose, Jack?" she railed. "We already have a
hound!"

The pup tumbled along the ground, practically tripping
on its ears as it tried to chase the large goose.

"They'll be playmates." Jack chuckled. "And Molly likes
it."

"You're spoiling her."

"I know. I can 'cause I'm her father." He stared at her
until she blushed and looked away.

He figured bribery was good for Willa, too, and concentrated on the two things he knew she had a fondness for
flowers and work gloves. He brought her two rosebushes,
a bouquet of flowers and a pair of the softest leather work
gloves he could find. He took every opportunity to make

coffee for her, and once she agreed to drive down to Duncan for a steak dinner.

Jack told himself he was making progress, however slowly.

Thursday afternoon he met Carrie Spangler and her twin sons, Thomas and Temple. Thomas's attention was immediately drawn to the rig and discussing with Willa the well she and Jack had drilled. That the young man was knowledgeable and plainly liked Willa didn't help the foolish jealousy tugging at Jack. Nor did he care for Temple's easy relationship with Molly. The guy used the same easy charm on Jack's daughter that he probably used on adult females.

He did, however, like Carrie Spangler immediately. She was a brisk and blunt woman who laughed easily.

"Don't let my boys make you uneasy," she said when she and Jack stood alone, watching Willa and Thomas at the rig and Temple push Molly on the swing.

Jack looked at her with a raised eyebrow, intending to ask what she meant. He didn't speak, knowing she'd know perfectly well he lied.

Carrie crossed her arms. "Thomas is a good man, but too young for your Willa. And Molly will have many friends besides Temple, but only one father." She smiled at Jack. "And any fool can see both females are crazy about you."

Few people made Jack speechless, but Carrie did at that moment. Digging into his shirt pocket, he slipped out a gummy bear and put it into his mouth.

Stuffing her hands in her baggy overalls, she fixed Jack with a speculative eye. "So, you think you're strong enough to win her again?"

"Guess I'm betting on it," he answered after a minute. They grinned at each other.

"Do you know Willa's the one who found Hoppy dead?" she said then and inclined her head toward the grape arbor. "Over there, at the corner. Looking out from Molly's bedroom window, she saw him drop to the ground."

Jack frowned and shook his head. He hadn't talked to Willa much about Hoppy. Every time he brought up the old man's name, Willa sort of seemed to freeze.

"Well, she did," Carrie said. "And she lost the only person who'd always been there for her." Her expression gentled. "Be patient with her, and just maybe you can replace that only person, can be the one she relies on."

Jack's respect for the woman grew; she was a rare friend. He was also gratified to discover he had found an ally.

"Now..." Carrie turned brisk. "Go on over there and butt in with Willa and Thomas. I'm figuring you're going to be right in there on all future jobs. Get to know my son. You'll like him."

Jack felt like a kid, being bossed around in such a way, but he did as she said. He warmed when Willa fixed him with a welcoming smile and immediately asked him a question about the rig's hydraulics. And exactly as Carrie had said, after a few minutes he found that he just might like Thomas Spangler.

Later, after the Spanglers had left, Jack thought to ask Willa about Hoppy but shied away from it, unable to figure out how to approach the subject. Besides, she was happy, more at ease with him that day than she'd been since he arrived. He didn't want to take a chance on ruining that.

Chapter Ten

When Willa returned home after church Sunday afternoon, she saw Jack standing on a block and bending over the engine of the drilling rig. He wore faded denims; his upper torso was bare. He'd put on a bit of fat in the time he'd been away, but most of his added weight was hard, thick muscle. He'd become a fully mature man.

She tore her eyes away and reached for Molly, then slipped from the truck seat. Her nerves felt as tight as a banjo string. She'd found the church services a haven in more than one way that day. She'd needed to get away from the farm. Away from the close proximity of Jack.

Whenever he was around her, he looked at her so intently, never bothering to hide his stares, never bothering to hide the thoughts inside his head.

Willa knew she had to decide something soon, but the weight of fear and indecision held her back. If she decided to allow Jack back into her life, she would put her life so much into his hands—and out of her own. What about the drilling business? How would they work that? She certainly didn't want to give it up. She'd told him she would never leave the farm. What if that caused problems in the future?

All those questions were valid, she knew, but not ones that couldn't be answered in some way. The biggest question of all remained: *Was Jack back for good, never, ever to leave her again?*

Would she be a fool if she joined her life with his again?

And what if she opted to sever the marriage once and for all? The idea hurt beyond belief, causing her to search for a middle road, a way she could have her marriage with Jack and still retain the secure independence she'd gained.

Immediately, when Willa set her on the grass, Molly ran across the yard toward Jack, calling, "Dadddyyy...dadddyy!"

Willa raised her hand to shield her eyes from the bright sun and watched Jack step down from the block and bend to talk to his daughter while he wiped his hands on a rag.

She saw quite suddenly something she'd overlooked in all the questions, questions that had concerned only her. What would be the best thing for Molly? And an even deeper question: *What about the best thing for Jack?* If she refused to accept him into her life, that meant he'd lose much of his daughter's life, too. But if he stayed, would he find himself unhappy in the future? Was he seeing things now as he wished they could be, not as they really were? Would she be able to give him all the things he needed?

With the wind tugging at her skirt, Willa walked over to them.

Jack rose from where he crouched and gave her a careful look. "Been to services?" He wasn't thinking about church, and she knew it.

"Yes." She nodded, though she, too, wasn't thinking about church. Her eyes lingered on his chest, and when she saw a knowing grin slip across his face, heat crept into her cheeks.

"You find something wrong with the rig?" she asked, averting her eyes to the big machine. Just like him to tear into it. Asking her wouldn't enter his mind. She couldn't be angry; he was simply tinkering as he liked to do. He'd been too idle at the farm as it was.

"Nothin' really wrong," Jack said, allowing his gaze to rest on Willa's lips. "Just noticed it running rough the other day. Thought an oil change and tune-up would be a good idea." He saw the pulse in her neck begin to throb. He grinned. "No charge. I wasn't doing anything else, anyway."

Molly touched his pant leg. "'Ummy ber."

Jack grinned. "Willa, will you get the bag of gummy bears out of my pocket?" He held up his hands, showing the grease.

Willa looked around for his shirt. "Where's your shirt?"

"The bag's in my back pants pocket." His grin broadened, and his blue eyes twinkled.

She hesitated. It was dangerous to touch him. But at his visual dare she stepped over and slipped her hand into his back pocket, pulling out the bag as if the pocket were on fire. "Aren't you afraid you'll sit on them?" She gave him a satisfied look.

"I'm not sitting down."

Pulling a yellow gummy bear from the bag, Willa handed it to Molly.

"Hey, what about me?" Jack opened his mouth.

Willa hesitated. Then, scolding herself for being silly, pulled a green gummy bear from the bag and slipped it into his mouth. Quickly, he clamped her fingers between his lips. For only a fraction of a second he held her, just long enough to lick her fingertips with his tongue.

She jerked her hand away. "Come on, Molly. It's nap time." In swift motion, she lifted Molly into her arms and pivoted away.

Watching Willa stride away, Jack felt his resolve harden. He had to hurry this whole thing along. He'd about stretched his patience to the limit.

He had to get her to make love. Surely that would decide the matter. Maybe, if he could possibly get her pregnant, that would cement the relationship. He wasn't certain of his ability in this area; it'd sure taken him a long time to father Molly. But maybe now things were different. Maybe, if he could just lie with her once...

The idea caused a throbbing in his loins. "Lord, I need a bit of help," he muttered.

Forty-five minutes later, as he was gathering up his tools, he heard the back porch screen door squeak and then slam. Turning his head, he saw Willa, a trowel swinging from her hand, head for the flower bed that stretched around the corner of the house. She wore slim-fitting denims and a pale pink sleeveless summer blouse. While he continued to return his tools to the toolbox, he watched her drop to her knees and begin attacking the weeds.

He smiled as he watched her round bottom. It could be, he admitted to himself, that he had too big an ego, but he'd be willing to bet cash money that Willa had come outside in order to see him. He wiped his hands and carried the toolbox back into the barn. Then he headed for the outdoor faucet at the corner of the pump house, a bare three yards away from Willa.

She looked up and met his gaze. Her eyes were large and round in her pale face.

"Spring is here at last," he called to her.

She nodded. "Yes." She returned to her weeding.

Jack turned his back to her, bent and pulled up the handle of the faucet. He sensed her eyes on him. The water gurgled as it came up the line, then rushed from the faucet. He splashed it over his chest and shoulders, shivering at the cold shock it gave his hot skin.

He heard her footsteps approach, but, his back to her, he didn't turn around.

"You could take a full shower inside," she said.

He didn't know to which inside she referred—his trailer or the house. "I like it like this. Feels fresh." He ducked his head beneath the cold water, then shook his head and raked his fingers through his wet hair.

"You're sunburned," she said. "You should have put your shirt on."

He rubbed his shirt over his wet hair and turned to speak, but before he could say a word, or even look her in the eye, Willa walked quickly away toward the porch.

His gaze slipped down her back and rested on her nicely curved hips. Surprised, he saw her turn.

"Come inside, and I'll put some aloe on your sunburn," she said. There was absolutely no expression on her face.

Willa didn't wait for him to answer. Feeling her face grow warm, she turned, opened the screen door and entered the house.

Why had she allowed herself to get carried away? she raged at herself as she tossed the trowel into the sink. Jerking open a drawer, she got out a knife and neatly sliced off a thick shoot from the green aloe plant sitting on the windowsill. She didn't want to think, she fumed angrily while she peeled the aloe down to its gelatinous interior. She didn't want to analyze. It was, after all, the polite thing to offer to help ease his sunburn. Hearing the screen door squeak, Willa stiffened.

Jack stepped into the kitchen, stopped and looked at her. Holding up the aloe, she motioned him over. Stepping close, he turned his back. She gently touched the moist aloe to his reddened skin, standing on tiptoe to reach his shoulders.

He flinched. "That's cold!"

"It's supposed to be, to cool the burn."

She opened more of the aloe spear and continued to rub the healing plant over Jack's back. She saw his muscles twitch. His skin was smooth and hot beneath her hand. He smelled of sweat and warm spring air.

"You're getting fat," she said, trying to turn her mind away from other things.

"It's the candy," he answered. "Guess I can't win. Candy and cigarettes both strain the heart."

She chuckled softly. Pictures suddenly flashed through her mind, one after another, of their times together: sharing the shower and washing each other's back, her massaging him after he'd had a particularly bad day, stretching out together on a blanket in the sun.

"All done?" Jack asked, glancing over his shoulder.

Foolishly, Willa realized she stood with her hand in the air. "Yes ... by morning that sunburn should be tan."

Jack turned to lean against the counter. Willa reached for the remaining bits of aloe lying on the counter, aware of his stare as she did so. But she didn't look up at him. Her arm brushed his. She froze. He didn't move, either.

Slowly her gaze moved to the coarse hairs on his arm, then to the sleeker skin of his biceps, and upward to his face and his pale blue eyes. The heat she saw there set her heart to pounding. She couldn't tear her own eyes away. Then he was lowering his head toward her. Her gaze fell to his thick mustache and velvet bottom lip only an instant before he kissed her.

Immediately she made to step back, but, as if anticipating her move, he wrapped his arms around her. She told herself to turn away, to protest. His lips were wonderful against hers. No, she thought, pushing at his chest and tearing her lips from his.

"Jack ... no ..."

"Willa ..." His voice was deep and soft. His hands played over her back, and again he tried to capture her lips.

"This isn't the answer," she managed to say, her voice breathless. She was fighting both Jack and herself—and it wasn't fair!

"Quit thinking, Willa."

Twisting to capture her against the counter, he kissed the sensitive skin of her neck, sending shivers throughout her body. She couldn't seem to get her breath.

"Just for right now, quit thinking," he murmured into her ear. "Right now is all I'm asking for."

The raw emotion in his voice seemed to turn her legs to liquid. She leaned against him and lifted her face, searching for his lips. The stubble of his beard scratched her cheek. She tasted the saltiness of his skin, smelled the earthy smell of him.

She loved him then, more purely than at any other time she could remember. Practicalities and concerns over their differences melted away in the heat that burned between them. The all-consuming craving to merge with him swept over her. She had to have him, had to love him, had to receive his love or she felt she would break into a million pieces.

Willa melting against him, turning soft and pliable in his arms, sent the blood pumping hot through Jack's veins like oil gushing out of control up a well hole. Then his hands discovered she wasn't wearing a bra. And her skin was so warm, and soft, like satin. Jack thought he would explode with wanting.

Her soft groan sounded in his ear. He kissed her, forced her lips to part and accept him. His head was pounding, yet somewhere something spoke to him, telling him to ease up. He stroked downward, and she quivered against him. For a fraction of a second he stilled his hands and drew in a deep breath. For some insane reason, he was almost afraid to move, fearing to let go of the passion that possessed him.

Willa reached up to cup his face in her hands and gaze at him. Her eyes were glazed with burning desire and glowed with pure love. The look caused his pulse to beat so loudly in his ears that it drowned out all other sounds. She bent her head to kiss a trail across his chest.

"Willa..." He choked out her name. Spanning her waist with his hands, he lifted her and pressed her against his throbbing groin. For the briefest of moments he felt relief, only to have the pulsing need return with a force that was actually painful.

He lifted her onto the counter and pressed himself between her legs. Her lips were like velvet fire, her skin quivering beneath his touch. Working the few buttons free, he sought to pull the blouse from her shoulders.

"Please, Willa, let me look ... it's been so long...."

Eyes closed, she stilled her hands upon his shoulders while he gazed at her. Her skin was creamy, her breasts full and round, looking as if they awaited his touch. Feeling emotion welling up in his throat, he lowered his head to love her skin with his lips.

His woman, he thought. He loved her so powerfully, it seemed to be drowning him.

Her fingernails cut into his shoulders, and her breath fanned the top of his head. He hugged her to him, trying to slow the demanding need coursing through his veins. He didn't want to scare her, was afraid of hurting her. She was so much smaller than himself, so fragile in his arms.

With a low growl, he swept her up and carried her toward the bedroom. He wouldn't take her on the counter, or on the floor, as he truly wished. He would have her in their bed, the bed they'd slept in for ten years. And he would give her all he could.

In the bed, lying with her naked body a bare inch from his own, Jack explored every inch of her, taking in the womanly differences that had come to her body. The slight swell of her stomach from producing their child, her pleasantly fuller hips. He lingered long over her much heavier breasts, and his tongue caught a bit of moisture there. He caressed them tenderly, aware of her sensitivity. A miracle, he thought, wondering at her body, how she fit so neatly next to him, how she had borne a child and could satisfy a man.

Willa looked up into Jack's eyes. The glow there sent a shaft of joy deep into her heart and an immediate urgency to her body. She pressed against him, raked her fingers into his hair and met the hard, demanding kiss he gave.

Suddenly she couldn't stop quivering. Then his skin was hot against hers, and the most wonderful sensations a body can experience were washing over her in waves from her head to her toes. Her body pulsed with life, with desire.

As naturally as breathing, she met his need with her own. Again she was his... and he was hers. As man and wife.

Willa awoke with a start, surprised that she'd dozed off. She jerked up, finding she'd been lying on Jack's arm, his body curved around her. He gave her a lazy smile. Willa felt her cheeks grow warm at his intent gaze.

"Jack! We've got to get dressed. Molly could wake up anytime." She clutched the sheet about her and inched away, but a dawning awareness that she'd have to get up from the bed stark naked before she could get a robe held her where she was.

Jack gave a low chuckle. "So what if she does?" He shifted toward her and reached for her arm.

She pulled away. "It will confuse her, Jack, to see us...like this."

"What's confusing about seeing her parents in the same bed?" He looked genuinely puzzled; then his eyes narrowed as he observed her.

"Jack..." She paused, uncertain of what to say. "We've made love. That doesn't solve everything. It doesn't change everything."

"You make love to me like that and try to say you don't want me to come back here to live with you?" His voice was low and sharp.

"It was an...an accident that never should have happened," Willa said. "It isn't the answer to the problems between us."

"Maybe not, but it's a hell of a start." He shifted into a sitting position, revealing his wide, bare chest. "You wanted it, Willa. Your mind may be saying no, but you certainly showed me what you really want."

Willa didn't like the remark. "Oh?" She raised an eyebrow. "And the other women you've made love to—after they'd given themselves to you, didn't that prove they wanted you forever? How could you leave them?"

"This is different, and you know it! And I'm not proud of what I've done, but it's over with. That time has nothing to do with you, with us."

"You off with who knows what woman, enjoying yourself, while I'm here with your daughter, sleeping alone, has nothing to do with me?" Her voice rose. Yet even as jealousy raged through her, she knew the argument truly did have nothing to do with what Jack had done while he was away. It had to do with here and now and her fear of being hurt again.

He stared at her, then turned and flung his legs over the edge of the bed. Standing up, regally naked, he bent to gather his clothes.

"I thought you wanted me, Willa. I thought I'd proved how much I want you—not only just now, but in the last weeks." He jerked on his shorts and picked up his jeans. "I don't know what else I can do to show you." His jaw tightened. "And I'm getting tired of trying."

As Willa watched, he pulled on his jeans, zipped them up and fastened the button. Not bothering to put on his boots, he grabbed them and stalked from the room.

Willa's heart constricted, and her mind whirled frantically, an emotional war raging within her. Suddenly she realized her need for him was greater than her need for independence or her fear of the future. Hardly realizing what she was doing, she jumped from the bed, dragging the sheet with her, and ran after him.

Dear God, give her the words, give her the wisdom.

"Jack!" Her soft call caught him as he reached the kitchen. He stopped, took a breath and turned to face her. He thought he'd given up but knew deep inside he never would.

"I'm trying, Jack," Willa said in a small voice.

She clutched that stupid sheet around her. The look on her face melted his heart.

"You may not believe it," she continued, "but I am thinking of you and Molly." She took a shaky breath, and her bottom lip quivered. "I'm as doubtful about me as I am about you. I'm doubtful about us and afraid we'll all end up getting hurt again. What if we don't make it, Jack?" The last came out in a bare whisper.

Pain sliced through him like a knife. With two long strides he reached her and held her to him. He felt her tears on his chest, and his own eyes misted.

"I don't know," he said, his voice hoarse. "But I know it'd be wrong not to try. I know I love you." He waited, his heart aching for her answer.

The need to tell him welled up in her like a powerful spring. "I love you, too, Jack," she said, her voice surprisingly clear and loud.

Relief burst into her heart like a south wind across the land. At last she'd said it; at last she'd admitted her feelings. And when she looked into Jack's eyes, her heart swelled.

She held her breath and focused on the torrent of love pouring from the hidden spring and surrounding them. An inner instinct told her she would need it for times to come.

Jack parked his trailer on the far side of the barn and hauled his chest of drawers in from where it had been stored in the barn. Willa cleaned out half of the closet for his clothes, and within days the house became more fully theirs. Jack's small portable television sat on her dresser, his boots were at the foot of the bed, his clothes invariably lay scattered around the house. The hook on the back of the bathroom door held both his robe and hers, and two different bars of soap sat on the edge of the bathtub. After several nights, Willa learned to sleep with someone else in the bed again. And to like it.

Two days after Jack had moved back in, Willa left Molly with him and drove over to Duncan. To grocery shop, with a side trip to the doctor, though she didn't tell Jack. It was *her* body, she reasoned, and she chose to use birth control. There was no need to discuss it. She felt a nagging guilt, yet for some odd reason that she didn't want to fathom, she would not tell Jack.

In the first weeks they got little sleep. It was early mornings mostly, before the sun peeked over the horizon, when Willa would groggily feel Jack's hands playing across her body. The air was cool and fragrant, and both of them, fresh from sleep, were ready to indulge in each other.

Most of the time during those weeks of bright, beautiful moments, Willa was happy, enjoyed having Jack home and knew she'd done the right thing. He was one special man; he made her feel as she knew no one else could. And above all, there was Molly, who readily accepted Jack's living with them and seemed to bloom under his attention, perhaps growing slightly spoiled, but not in a serious way.

Then there were the dark times. Times Willa struggled with insecurity.

Before, when she'd had only herself to rely on, at least she always knew where she stood. It might have been lonely and at times difficult, but she wasn't always questioning herself or wondering what another person was going to do that might affect her life, as she did with Jack. Before, she'd accepted her exclusion from his life. Now she lived with the recurring question of whether one day he would leave again.

She found herself watching, waiting, wondering. His slightest grumpy word could set her heart racing. When he went into town to play poker Wednesday nights with Cy, she prowled the house restlessly, finding herself continually gazing out the window. When the telephone rang, her heart leaped into her throat as she imagined it was Jack, telling her he wasn't coming back. It was nonsense, and she knew it, but the insecurity remained. When Jack did come home, she pretended to be asleep already. She didn't want him to know how she felt—it would hurt him terribly.

At every turn she hid her distrust, her fear. It wouldn't do either of them any good to talk it over, she'd decide. She would have to deal with it. Only time would build trust between them again, just as only time would enable them to understand each other. They seemed so far apart, but they were loving each other simply in the act of trying.

Over the weeks, they cut and baled the acres of hay Hoppy had planted before his death. The barn filled to overflowing. Willa worked right along with Jack, feeling she needed to do so in order to keep a handle on her own life. During this labor the understanding between them seemed to flow readily, but when it came to drilling another well, tempers flared.

The job was twenty miles away and proved more difficult than the first they'd had. The water was well over two hundred feet down, and they hit more than one level of sand, which caused the hole to cave in. They ended up abandoning one hole and drilling another.

Jack was for continuing with the first hole; Willa was against. Jack was for using air; Willa was for using water. Jack was for adding gel to hold back the sand at seventy feet; Willa felt it safer to do so at fifty, then again at eighty. She began to feel her every decision was subject to his approval, even though she was the recognized boss, she had the license and the company was technically hers. This would have to change, she knew, but her pride rebelled.

Since it took three full days to drill the well, Willa was grateful that Thomas was working with them. At least they were both inhibited enough by Thomas's presence to keep their arguing to a minimum. She was also grateful for Carrie, who brought Molly out to the well site each afternoon so Willa could nurse her and play with her. Holding Molly seemed to give her strength.

"Do you want me to work with you in the company?" Jack asked that night as they lay in bed. He hadn't touched her; she felt his anger.

"Do you want to?"

"I asked you a question," he snapped. "I expected an answer, not another question."

Willa's first impulse was to snap back and to hide her true feelings. Then a small voice stilled her words. Jack had a right to be annoyed. Any man would have been. Their situation with the business went against each of their personalities. And she had to risk telling the truth now. She hid too many of her feelings from him, and it wasn't good that way.

"Yes, I want you in the company," she said slowly, frightened the whole time that he might throw her feelings back in her face. "I want to be partners."

He answered after a long second. "It's not working too well so far."

She grinned in the darkness. "Well, you and I are pretty opinionated people."

"It's your temper."

Willa bristled. "My temper—"

"I was joking, Willa." He laid a hand on her thigh. The moment was a good one, if fleeting.

"I know how you feel about drilling, Jack. You're good. You could find work in the oil business. And it would definitely bring you a lot more money." It was very hard to say, but to keep him, she knew he must feel free. "I told you from the start that I wouldn't leave the farm. I can't, Jack. But I can always be here for you when you come home."

He shook his head. "I don't want that. Not now." He paused. "I like the water drilling business, Willa. I like it a lot, and I have some ideas." The bed moved as he raked a hand through his hair. "But we're going to have to work it equally. I'll get my license. We'll discuss the jobs."

"I think I'll like that," she said. Then she couldn't resist adding, "As long as you see things my way, big Jack Cashion."

He grabbed her and pulled her across his chest. "I'll show you who's boss."

And she let him.

How would they ever work it out? she thought as she drifted into a troubled sleep. How would either of them ever bend enough to find a happy medium?

She tried; Jack tried. She worked on taming her temper. Jack worked on taming his stubbornness. The days passed, some shining bright, others clouded with hurt feelings and love only by will.

But love did grow, settling deep into her heart as she discovered all over again the man she'd fallen in love with at the age of fifteen. He was more patient now, more giving, didn't take himself quite as seriously. He was thoughtful about the little things, like having coffee not only made for her in the mornings but waiting on the table in her favorite cup. And whether she was freshly showered and dressed in a flimsy nightgown, or hot and sweaty from working beside him, he had a way of looking at her that left little doubt as to his earthy thoughts. He made her feel distinctly a woman.

He was also, however, still as stubborn as a half-blind mule, just going ahead and doing whatever he wanted, whether or not she agreed with him. A prime example was when a truckload of cows showed up one morning. Willa had told Jack she didn't want cattle and had thought the matter settled. She told herself she should have suspected differently when he'd just smiled and dropped the subject.

Glaring at the truck, she forgot all about Molly and strode out across the yard to where they were unloading the cattle into the pasture.

She jammed a hand onto her hip. "Jack, what is this?"

"Last time I heard, they were called cows." He flicked her a glance as he supervised the unloading and gave her a sweet smile.

Willa watched a small cow clamber down the ramp from the truck and run out across the pasture. Pivoting, she marched to the house, unwilling to have the truck driver be privy to the argument.

In the kitchen she jerked open a cabinet door, reached in for a glass and slammed the door closed. As she stuck the glass under the faucet, Molly entered the kitchen. Her panties and shorts were down around her ankles.

"Potty, Mama," she said, a beaming smile on her face.

"Okay, honey."

Willa automatically reached to pick Molly up and carry her into the bathroom, her thoughts on what she intended to say to Jack about his high-handed manner.

Molly began kicking and hollering. "No! No! Molly potty...self."

It dawned on Willa that Molly had gone to the bathroom all by herself, and the look on Molly's face was one of supreme pride. Bathing Molly in all the glowing words of praise she could think of, Willa straightened her clothes and was getting her a glass of juice when Jack stepped in the kitchen door.

Handing Molly the glass, Willa leaned against the counter and took a deep breath. She didn't want to fight—but she was mad!

While Molly told her daddy about her recent accomplishment and he praised her, Willa stared at the refrigerator.

"Okay," Jack said, rising from where he'd been talking to Molly, "let's get it over with."

Willa didn't speak, didn't trust herself to speak for fear she'd say something she'd regret.

"Ten more cows are coming tomorrow," he said. "And a bull on Friday."

Willa let go then. "Ten more! We decided no cattle, Jack. You said—"

"*You* decided," he broke in.

"You agreed."

"No, I just didn't say anything."

"A rotten thing to do, and you know it." She jabbed the air as she spoke.

He took off his hat and reached for a nearby towel to wipe his forehead. "Look, you have the land. It's stupid to let it lie fallow. The price of cattle is down, and we got a good deal." His eyes narrowed. "*I* got a good deal, if you prefer to think of it like that. I had the money, and my wife had the land. It's a good investment."

She looked into his pale blue eyes. She hadn't known exactly why she hadn't wanted to invest in cattle, just that it had something to do with wondering what would happen if Jack left in a few months. And she couldn't say that to him, halfway didn't admit it to herself.

"So you just did what you wanted," she said.

"Guess that's about the size of it." He made no apologies.

Willa stared at him. "Fine," she said finally, then strode from the room.

That evening, silence stretched thick and heavy over the dinner table. Once Willa dared to glance over and meet Jack's gaze. The anger fairly crackled in the air between them. Molly, sensing the tension, looked from Jack to Willa and remained inordinately quiet.

Afterward, Jack kissed Molly and left the house. Willa rose and watched him walk out toward the barn. He was retreating to tinker. He probably thought he'd give her time to cool down and everything would be fine. But she didn't want to cool down.

She carried the plates to the counter and plunked them down on it. Then she stopped and stared at them, remembering Jack's face earlier that afternoon. Even knowing he had a fight ahead of him, he'd been excited. She'd seen it. And it was an investment of his own.

Her heart suddenly felt weighted with iron. She so hated the strain between them. Grudgingly she admitted the purchase of cattle was a good idea—providing Jack cared for them. He had the money. And wasn't it a sign of his thoughts of permanence?

Willa tried to cool her anger with loving thoughts, such as that she should accept Jack exactly as he was. A stubborn mule, that's what he was, she mused hotly, tossing silverware into the sink. To buy the cattle behind her back, when he knew she was against it, as if her opinion didn't count for so much as a dime!

The thought made her angry all over again. She wasn't about to go out there and apologize! As if to cement her righteous indignation, the bawling of a cow filled the summer air.

It was nearly eleven o'clock when Jack turned out the light in the barn and headed back for the house. He'd cooled down, at least some, and he hoped Willa had, too. He knew he'd been wrong in buying those cows like he had. But he knew it was a good idea, and Willa's attitude had galled him.

Veering off to the grape arbor, he paused to stand, look at the stars and suck on a couple of gummy bears. The urge to smoke was strong for the first time in weeks.

An invisible breach remained between him and Willa. It wasn't something he could explain; sometimes he wondered if he imagined it. But he felt Willa kept herself behind a barrier, one he didn't know how to break down. He was rushing things, he told himself. And maybe he kept himself behind a barrier, too. They each watched the other closely, as if ready to run from the possibility of more pain.

Their first time together all those months ago had been one he'd never forget, just like the time he'd taken her virginity in the seat of his pickup. She'd been his, totally without reserve. But not so much since. Jack sensed it, didn't like it. When he'd discovered how warmly responsive she was in the first light of morning, he'd begun deliberately waking up early, stroking her to a groggy but, oh, so hot passion. She forgot her reserve then, and it was good between them.

Thinking of this, Jack spit out the remains of a piece of candy and strode toward the house. The sooner they dealt with the disagreement and put it behind them, the better it would be.

The house was quiet; the light burned above the kitchen sink. Looking for Willa, Jack checked Molly's room, then moved on into the dimly lit living room. Willa sat there in her chair, her arms wrapped around herself.

When he realized she was crying, his heart leaped to his throat.

Chapter Eleven

Alarm hammering in his heart, Jack crouched on his haunches before Willa. He'd never felt more clumsy and inept. Why'd she have to go and cry?

"Aw, Willa, don't...." He put a hand on her leg, the other up to stroke her arm. "I'm sorry, honey. I didn't mean to hurt you by buying those cows."

She shook her head and squeezed her eyes closed. Tears seeped through her eyelids, soaked her long lashes and streamed down her face. Still shaking her head, she rubbed the back of her hand across her cheeks.

"It's not... that...." A loud sob broke from her.

"It's not?" Jack searched her face and dared to try to wipe away the tears with his thumbs. The tears kept coming, and he only succeeded in dirtying her face. He cursed himself for not washing up the minute he came into the house. "Well," he practically demanded, "what's the matter?"

"Molly... fell asleep... growing up..." She sucked in a ragged breath, then tried again, but her words weren't any more decipherable. "You...those stupid...cows bawl-ing...Hoppy...and then...the water!" She broke into fresh sobs hard enough to shake her entire body.

Jack remained crouching before her, puzzling over her words, trying to decide what, if anything, to do. Then, gently taking her upper arms, he pulled her from the chair down into his lap.

"It's okay, Willa," he crooned. "It's okay, honey." Sit-ting on the floor, he cuddled her in his lap like a small child. Repeatedly he stroked her silken hair and shaking arms, forgetting about his dirty hands. Her trembling body was hot against his, and her tears soaked his shirt. He held her firmly until at last she began to quiet.

"I need a tissue," she mumbled softly and pushed her-self away from his chest.

"Here." He handed her the tail of his work shirt. "Sniff and wipe your eyes with this."

She half chuckled, half sobbed and did as he told her.

"Now," Jack said, searching her face, "you feel bet-ter?"

She nodded, shyly averting her eyes.

"What was that all about?"

"Molly..." Her lower lip started to quiver. "Molly fell asleep all on her own tonight, not nursing or anything...." Her voice broke as the tears started afresh.

Jack tried to understand the significance of Molly's go-ing to sleep. At night. "Molly went to sleep?"

Willa nodded, sniffed and sat up straighter. "She's growing up, Jack. She doesn't need to nurse anymore. It's time I weaned her, anyway, I guess." Her reluctance plainly showed. "Tonight was a signal that she's ready."

"Oh." Jack nodded in understanding, light dawning on the situation, if dimly. Willa was a mother experiencing the lonesomeness of losing her tiny baby. "She's not ready for college, Willa," he teased, trying to boost her spirits.

She smiled wanly, her thoughts clearly on Molly.

"What else was all that about—water, and the cows?"

"I . . . you were right about the cows, Jack," Willa said then, bluntly, clearly, yet her eyes dared him to agree with her. "Only you shouldn't have acted as if my opinion didn't count."

"It did count." He leaned back. Willa started to rise, and he pulled her back down to his lap. "It's just that you were wrong, and you weren't going to change your mind, and neither was I. What was I supposed to do?"

"We could have talked."

"We did."

"Oh, Jack!" A grudging amusement touched her. She couldn't be mad at him anymore, at least not in this minute. She felt close to him, as if a veil of understanding she couldn't begin to explain had reached out and wrapped around them both.

"You were crying about Hoppy, too, weren't you," he said in a gentle voice, changing the subject.

She nodded, her face growing somber again. "I miss him. He should be here to see Molly growing up."

"Maybe he is seeing her."

She gave a little smile.

"Now," Jack said, purposely dumping Willa off his legs and onto the floor, "I need a shower." He stood and stretched.

Willa scrambled up beside him. "You can need all you want, but that was the other thing I was crying about." Her bottom lip quivered. "We don't have any water."

"No water?" His eyebrows puckered.

With a sinking heart, Willa shook her head. "The well's caved in."

She felt the world piling up on her shoulders all over again as she told him about going to the bathtub and turning on the faucet. The water had spurted, then gurgled in the pipes, dribbled out for about one minute, then stopped altogether. It had been the last straw in an afternoon fit to try the strongest man's soul. The tears began to well in her eyes again. She was hot, her breasts were growing tender, she could hear the bawling reminders of Jack's stubbornness, and she wanted a bath!

"Are you sure it's caved in? Did you check the circuit breakers?" Jack asked.

"Of course. They're fine. I do know a little bit about this, Jack. I know by the sound of that old pump."

"You should have come and gotten me earlier," he said.

She looked at him, saw the reproach in his expression. She probably should have summoned him first thing, but she'd been so angry with him. And she wasn't used to sharing her problems with anyone else. Her first reaction was to handle them herself.

"Let's go have a look," he said with a sigh.

The well house was too small for both of them. Willa waited outside and looked up at the stars. She supposed it was natural for him to have to see for himself—though she'd already told him what had happened. The well itself was at least sixty years old; the casing had deteriorated and finally collapsed. She'd vaguely suspected trouble months before when the water pressure appeared weak and she'd found bits of sand in the water. But too many other concerns had crowded out worry over the well. Thinking of the problem now, her thirst increased.

Jack came out. He rubbed the back of his neck. "Looks like we're going to have another drilling job."

Willa nodded, and at the prospect of being without fresh water for a while, her mouth seemed to go as dry as cotton.

In the bedroom, Willa slowly removed her clothes. She'd had a glass of iced tea but really wanted water. When she'd thought to melt some ice, all she'd discovered in the freezer were five cubes, which she saved in case Jack should want an iced drink when he returned. He'd gone to get at least enough water for them to drink.

Brushing her hair up off her neck, Willa stood before the open window, enjoying the cool night air that played like soft fingers on her naked body. With only the darkened fields stretching away from the house, there was no need to worry about neighbors' prying eyes. She thought of closing windows and turning on the air conditioning, but the fresh night air with its heavenly scent of honeysuckle was too good to miss.

At the distant bawl of a cow, Willa thought of Jack, then of the stock pond a half mile away. Longing for the feel of water on her skin, she thought briefly of going to the pond for a swim but quickly discarded the idea. She couldn't leave Molly, and the idea of snakes and creepy-crawly things in the night didn't set too well with her, either.

She had just slipped on her nightgown when she heard Jack coming in the door. She hurried to the kitchen to find him bearing two large buckets, trying not to splash the water.

"Where'd you go?" she asked, gazing in surprise at the water and at his steady pace toward the bathroom.

"The pump at the south pasture," he said, huffing slightly. "Get your gown off." He leered at her, then poured a bucket of the water into the tub.

"I'm not getting into that water." Willa backed away. "It'll be like ice. And we need to save that water for drinking. Jack, don't pour it all in there!"

"I've got five more buckets in the truck. Now heat some up, and we'll get washed."

He grinned at her, and she grinned back. Whirling away, Willa went to heat some of the water he'd brought. In ten minutes she was peeling off her gown and settling into the bathtub filled with lukewarm but magnificently fresh water. Again and again she lifted her washcloth and dribbled the water over her shoulders and swelling breasts, giving thanks for the precious liquid, thinking how much she'd taken it for granted.

Jack came into the bathroom. She looked up to see his gaze roaming over her body, his eyes radiating a heat that made her blush. Then he smiled at her and began stripping off his shirt.

His grin took on a playfully wicked slant. "We'll have to share this bath."

"Oh, Jack, you're not going to fit—"

But he did.

They soaped each other thoroughly. Willa rubbed the washcloth over Jack's massive chest and felt the cocoon of understanding she'd experienced earlier that evening wrapping itself around them again. What a precious feeling it was, something elusive that she wished to hold forever in the palm of her hand.

Slowly she raised her head to look into his pale blue eyes. After a moment, with his gaze holding hers, he took her by the arms and hauled her up onto his lap, pressing her against his swollen organ. His eyes heavy with desire, he bent to kiss her, tenderly, sensuously. His skin was warm and moist beneath her fingers, and its scent tantalized her nostrils. She spun away into a bliss too heady to resist, forgetting about caved-in wells, babies growing into children and the aggravations of stubborn men.

He would have liked to make love to her there in the water, but his size and the confines of the bathtub prevented such a notion. Breaking off the kiss, he held her to his chest and relaxed against the back of the cool tub. Her hand caressing his shoulder had a drugging effect. The water surrounding them felt awfully good, and he was loathe to rise.

It was with a start that Jack realized he'd dozed off; Willa seemed asleep against him.

He shook her slightly. "Willa, honey, we need to get out of here."

The muscles of his buttocks seemed to have gone to sleep, and the water had grown cold.

Willa roused, lifted her head and gave him a smile. It was a darn sweet smile, sexy in its drowsiness. Jack felt his body begin to throb with wanting again. He helped her from the tub, and they dried each other off. Sweet heaven, what her hands did to him when she touched him! The tension inside him coiled even tighter as he observed her sleepy state.

"Jack, check Molly," she murmured, then tottered off to their bedroom.

She was sleeping lightly when he slipped beneath the sheet beside her. She hadn't even bothered to put on her nightgown.

Running a hand down her back, he felt her quiver. His spirit soared when she turned to him, her mouth searching for his. She was his, he thought. And he loved her. Thank God he hadn't lost her. For an instant he cursed the stubborn pride that had propelled him to buy the cows, to argue with her, and then all those nagging thoughts faded away, the pulsing of swelling passion taking their place.

He loved her... he loved....

Her mind numbed with grogginess, Willa felt warmth turn to sinuous flames within her body. Jack's hands caressed her with an insistent rhythm. How strong he was, yet how gentle, tender. The sweet heat glowing throughout her body intensified until she thought she would light the night like a thousand candles.

"Oh, Jack," she whispered against his shoulder. "Please..."

She welcomed him. She gave love, and received it gladly.

Willa awoke at the break of day. The first thing she was aware of was a dull ache in her breasts. She touched them. They were hot and hard. She shifted, intending to get up and trying to do so gently so as not to awaken Jack, when his arm snaked around her waist and pinned her to the bed.

"Good morning," he mumbled and nibbled her ear. She stroked his muscular shoulder, recalling wonderful bits of last night's lovemaking.

When his hand moved to her breast, she flinched and sucked in an involuntary breath.

His head came up off the pillow. "What is it?"

"It's nothing." Willa covered herself with the sheet. "Just that my body doesn't know yet that it's time to wean Molly. I'll be fine."

"You sure? What do you do? Does it hurt?"

How wonderful his concern was to her. "Yes, it hurts some. There's nothing to do. Nature takes care of itself. The milk will dry up on its own, and I won't have that much, because Molly only nursed a couple times a day. And yes, I'm sure. Now let me up to get some aspirin."

As she stood before the bathroom vanity shaking two aspirin into her palm, Jack, wearing only his shorts, came up behind her and encircled her with his arms.

"Mmm...you smell good." He nuzzled her neck and nibbled playfully at her earring.

"So do you," Willa murmured.

She pressed her face to his for a brief moment, enjoying the feel of his strong arms surrounding her. She knew she'd never tire of it, if allowed to experience his presence for the rest of her life.

Then she stretched to replace the aspirin bottle into the vanity drawer. For some odd reason her gaze fell to the flat blue case containing her diaphragm, and instinctively she knew Jack saw it, too. She felt his muscles stiffen.

His hand extended slowly, and he pulled the blue case from the drawer. "Is this—" He broke off as he opened the case and looked inside. It was as if a dark cloud settled over his face. Snapping the case closed, he tossed it aside. "Have you been using this? Without telling me?"

Willa picked up the case and replaced it in the drawer. She nodded. "Yes."

There'd been a few nights, like the previous one, when she hadn't taken precautions, but mostly she had. As she faced the accusation in his face, she also faced it in her own heart. But what, she thought with anguish, was she to do? She had her life to live, and if he left her with another child, what would she do?

"You got mad about those cows, about my going ahead without considering your opinion. What in hell is this? Didn't you think I had a say in using birth control or not?"

"This is hardly the same thing as buying cows. This is my body. I don't happen to want to get pregnant at this time."

He stared hard at her. "You're still worried I'm going to up and leave." His words were angry and blunt.

Lord, she didn't want to hurt him. She had to force herself to look him in the eye.

"Until we're sure this whole thing is going to work out, we don't need to think of bringing another child into the world."

His eyes seemed to shoot fire. "Damn it, Willa! People get married every day. They don't know if they're going to make it, but they don't put off buying homes, cars, furniture and starting families. They don't *plan* not to make it."

"I'm not planning not to—I'm not planning anything. I...I don't know what I'm doing, except that I'm not having a child right now. Not until I feel more stable."

He stared at her a second, then pivoted and strode back into the bedroom. Clutching the aspirin, Willa followed.

"Jack, maybe I should have told you, but I didn't want to argue. And I do feel this is my choice. I'm the one who has to carry the baby, deliver it, nurse it."

He didn't turn around. She watched the tight muscles of his shoulders as he jerked a T-shirt and jeans from a drawer. She started to say, I love you, but bit back the words. It seemed like a plea, or subtle coercion to get his approval, and she refused that.

Jack thought what Willa left unsaid: that she would also be the one to end up caring for the child should he leave. As he'd done before. He couldn't blame her. Trust was something a person earned—or uncarned. And it took time.

The knowledge hurt, and the hurt made him angry. The wrinkle this put in his own plans only added to his frustration. As the weeks had stretched into months, he'd held on to his idea of getting Willa pregnant. He believed carrying his child would be just the thing to bring her close to him again.

So, he thought wryly, he wasn't totally innocent of making plans without consulting her, either.

Slowly he turned to face her. "Is this birth control for now—or forever?"

"For now, Jack. I want other babies." Her eyes were wide, luminous. "Our babies."

He nodded. "Okay." He paused, then a faint smile twitched on his lips. "I'll give you those babies, Willa. Or die trying."

Purposely taking her by surprise, he reached out, grabbed her and pulled her against him, crushing her mouth beneath his. He felt her quivering body through the thin cotton of her nightgown, and she responded eagerly to his kiss. The next instant she pushed him away.

"Jack!" she said, trying to catch her breath. "You...you sneak!" He knew she wasn't protected! And Molly could awaken at any time.

He gave a self-satisfied smile. "Can't blame a guy for trying."

She loved him dearly in that second, a love welling up and spilling from her heart into every cell of her body.

"I love you, Jack," she whispered.

"I love you, Willa. And I'm never going to let you go. Someday you'll believe that."

She believed it in that instant, and she pressed the precious moment into her heart.

Though the ache in her breasts was mild enough, Willa felt herself growing tense and irritable. And the ache went clear through to her heart when Molly toddled into the kitchen all sleepy-eyed and tugged at Willa's shirt, mumbling, "Nap...Mama."

If Jack hadn't immediately reached to take Molly in his arms, Willa might have given up on the idea of weaning then and there.

"How about some fresh orange juice this morning, Squirt?" Jack sat Molly on his lap at the kitchen table. "You're growing into an awfully big girl—big enough for orange juice, I think. Even from a big glass. Here, if you give Daddy a kiss, I'll share my glass with you."

How hard it was to let go, Willa thought, gazing at Molly's shiny brown curls. You give them life, bear them and provide for all their needs, watch over them—and then you have to let them go. It didn't seem fair. And she wondered if sometime, so long ago that Willa had no conscious memory of it, her own mother had felt the same. A sadness of something denied engulfed her. She couldn't remember a mother's love. Her mother's interest had seemed a casual, offhand sort of thing.

Molly would have love, Willa thought, determined. She would know that her mother and her father loved her. In this way, Willa would make up for her own loss.

Jack looked at her over Molly's head. "You doing okay?"

She nodded and forced an encouraging smile.

"I'll go get us some more water in a few minutes," he said.

"I'll call Thomas," Willa said, "and tell him we have another job." She grinned.

Jack smiled in return. "If I had a wild imagination, I'd think you managed to cave in the well yourself—just so you could have an excuse to drill."

Willa laughed aloud. "I know we're hard up for work, but I'm not so desperate that I want to work for nothing." She slanted a glance at him. "You seem quite eager yourself, Mr. Cashion."

"Oh, I love to work up a sweat in the hot sun and get all dirty and not get paid for any of it." He plopped his hat on his head at a jaunty angle. "I just live for it." He was teasing, but she saw the gleam in his eye.

"This hole won't be easy, Jack." Rather than a threat, it was a promise.

He cocked an eyebrow and waited for her to elaborate.

"The well we did have was punched by Hoppy's father with a cable tool rig." She chewed her bottom lip. "I almost wish we had one to use now. It's a bit slower but would give us more control." She raised her eyes to his. "We're going to hit a lot of both sand and rock. And we're going to have to go deep to find enough water. I think the old well was nearly three hundred feet."

"We'll use what we have," Jack drawled. Then he winked. "And I think we might have us some fun. Now get on the phone to Thomas. You're not going to be working all that hard today. You'll supervise, boss."

She grinned. "Yes, sir!"

They chose to punch the new well not far from the old one. When the state was new Hoppy's father had made his living by dowsing, the act of divining where the water was beneath the ground using a willow branch, a stiff wire or plain intuition. The elder Lowe had been renowned for the ability, and Hoppy had possessed a bit of the intuition himself. Willa liked to believe the ability ran in her veins, too.

"Right here," she told Jack when they discussed where to site the well.

"You feel the water there?" he teased.

"Yes, I do," she replied emphatically, then lowered her voice. "Besides, Great-granddad's well was a good one. We're bound to find water if we stay close."

Holding Molly in her arms, Willa stood to the side while Thomas backed the rig into place. Jack pulled the support truck, filled with water from the well at the back pasture, nearby.

At the instrument panel at the rear of the rig, Thomas lowered the rig's supports, then raised the tower into place. Willa stared off to the west, where dark clouds were gathering.

Jack paused beside her. "We could be in for some storms."

Willa nodded. Already the heat was high; by afternoon they could have severe thunderstorms. If storms brought lightning, the drilling would have to stop, and the tower would have to be brought down. Sticking up in the air as it did, the tower was a perfect lightning rod. She hoped no storms would come, because she wanted water in the house again. Even at the thought, her mouth became dry.

"I'll get us some iced tea," she said. "Look after Molly for a minute."

When she returned with the cold drinks, the men had things ready to begin drilling. With an eager smile on his face, Thomas moved the lever to lower the bit and began the hole. Jack downed his iced tea in a few gulps, then tugged on gloves and stepped up onto the rig, ready to hoist pipe from the rack and connect it when needed. Willa brought a chair and sat with Molly beneath the shade of the apple tree. But she couldn't be still, so she took Molly in her arms and went to stand beside the rig, watching the pipe revolve and drill into the orange clay of the earth.

The day turned hot and muggy, with a heavy layer of clouds, but no storms. Willa went so far as to roll up the sleeves on her shirt and remove her wide-brimmed straw hat.

Thomas remained at the controls, taking occasional direction from either Willa or Jack. He was easygoing, not in the least bothered by instructions from two people, and at last it seemed that Willa and Jack were learning the art of working together. Willa left the pipe and speed of drilling to Jack; he left to her the monitoring of the cuttings that came up out of the hole. Willa recommended drilling with air first, and Jack readily agreed. It was a joint decision to change to water and then mud when they hit sand.

Willa divided her attention between the drilling and Molly and bringing cool drinks out for them all. Occasionally her breasts ached, but, as she'd suspected, not severely, because over the past months her nursing had tapered off, anyway. And after the first bad moments of the morning, she no longer felt such separation anxiety. And Molly still lifted her hands to be held, still often clung to Willa.

That day Willa felt more in her element than she had in a long time. It was a rare combination—being involved with the magic of drilling for the valued water and taking care of her family as any mother did.

Jack smiled at her often and came to drape an arm over her shoulders. Seeing him so happy made her happy. And he was a rare man, she thought. He, too, kept an eye out for Molly, and he, too, took a turn at bringing cold drinks and snacks from the kitchen.

It's going to work, she thought when he paused to give her a fleeting kiss. For a fraction of an instant his pale eyes held hers. She saw excitement there, and joy, and love—a mirror of all the things she herself felt.

Just after lunch, a hydraulic line broke, forcing a halt to the drilling for that day. While Jack and Thomas drove over to Duncan to purchase the needed repair parts, Willa and Molly took a nap.

That evening, after working long hours at repairing the rig, Jack again hauled the precious water in buckets from the south pasture. Willa bathed Molly, who thought it quite fun, in the wide kitchen sink. Willa then washed her own hair with several pitchers of water, and later she and Jack again shared a bath in the tub.

Lying in the darkened bedroom that night, Willa listened to Jack's even breathing beside her. The cicadas clicked loudly, and an occasional bawl came from one of Jack's cows, as she called them.

Her head resting in the crook of his arm, she heard his heart beating and realized with startling clarity that she loved Jack as much for his faults as for his sterling qualities. Without that stubborn streak that made him always insist on his own way, without his enjoyment of being pampered and served, without his bent toward sloppiness, he wouldn't be the same man. She didn't overlook his faults; she loved him the more because of them.

Turning onto her side, she rubbed her face on her pillow. Emotions welled up in her heart. She loved him so much it was frightening. Her love for him left her vulnerable.

She would handle it, she told herself. She would love him, savor his presence in her life, but she would keep her self-sufficiency. She would remain dependent only on herself. It would work very well for both of them that way.

The following day dawned bright and sunny and hot. Willa was careful to keep her sleeves buttoned to her wrists and her wide-brimmed hat on her head. Molly, too, was carefully protected from the drying effects of the Oklahoma sun and wind.

The drilling slowed, and Willa carefully monitored the cuttings blown up out of the hole. Having hit some hard rock, they used mostly air.

"We're not hitting much water," Willa told Jack that afternoon.

He nodded. "Hope we're not sealing it off as we go down."

Willa bent and scooped a handful of chips from the water-filled pan surrounding the hole in which the pipe turned. She rubbed her thumb over the grainy, white, rocky substance in her palm. The drill was at a depth of two hundred and twenty feet.

"We should have hit good water by now, Jack. For heaven's sake, we're only ten feet from the old well."

He raised an eyebrow. "You believing hard enough?"

"Guess I'll have to believe harder," she returned.

Jack looked thoughtful. "We need some hydrofracturing equipment."

Willa knew what he referred to. Widely used in the oil industry, beginning to be used more in drilling water wells, the equipment injected high-pressure fluids down the hole into the formations below to create fractures through which water could flow.

"Maybe we can afford it someday," she said, "but I'd sure like to have water in the house without waiting that long."

"I can get it for us," Jack said thoughtfully, "but not right away."

Willa sighed. "I'd give a hundred dollars for a full bathtub."

"Let's shut it down for today and begin again in the morning," Jack said with a chuckle. "And you concentrate on believing."

Willa nodded in agreement. Lifting Molly, she carried her into the house. She thought longingly of a shower.

When they began the following morning, the hydraulic system seemed to have a problem, but Thomas discovered the trouble in short order. Willa continually inspected what they blew from the hole. They hit more water, but Willa knew from experience it would pump out only about two to three gallons per minute—not nearly enough for their household needs.

Jack left right after lunch, stubbornly refusing to tell Willa where he was going. With a teasing grin, all he would say was "We'll have water when I get back."

Willa wanted to smack him but was amused at his self-satisfaction, knowing he enjoyed it so.

Together, she and Thomas kept the rig going, the bit drilling to nearly three hundred feet. They had reached three hundred and ten feet and seemed to be producing a bit more ground water when Jack returned, but Willa still didn't consider it adequate for their needs.

"What do you have?" she asked Jack when he stepped from his pickup carrying a small bundle in his hand.

He gave a smug grin. "I've got our hydrofracturing equipment."

Willa looked from his face to his hand and the bundle. Thomas, carrying Molly, joined them.

"Well?" Willa raised an eyebrow.

Slowly Jack opened his package. He held two sticks of dynamite.

Chapter Twelve

Willa's eyes grew as round as saucers. "Jack, you're not really considering blowing it?"

He'd known she wouldn't like the idea. "I've done it before Willa, with Dad." He stepped toward the rig. He grinned. "We'll have to get the pipe up and move the rig."

Willa followed and placed a hand on her hip. "Jack, it's dangerous. Hoppy did a couple of wells with dynamite, but he . . . well, he didn't think it was something you did unless there wasn't anything else *to* do. For one thing, we could cave in the well we've already dug."

"Did you and Thomas get any more water?" Jack asked.

Willa gave a reluctant shake of her head. Thomas still held Molly and looked at Jack. The boy was eager for the experience, Jack could tell. Youth, he thought, feeling wonderfully young himself.

He turned his gaze back to Willa. "I know what I'm doing, Willa. I'm trained in using dynamite. I know there's water at that level. We've just got to open it up."

"What about it being so deep?" Thomas asked.

"The hole is there, clear down to its bottom," Jack answered. He looked at Willa. "I do know about dynamite, Willa."

Willa didn't like it. All she could think of was Jack getting blown to bits as he lit the fuse. It was silly imagination on her part, but she just didn't like fooling with explosives. Yet the look on his face touched her. Something like this was part of the life of him.

After a long minute, she nodded and turned to take Molly from Thomas. "Let's get the pipe out of the hole," she said to Jack over her shoulder.

Working fast, Thomas and Jack removed the pipe section by section from the deep hole, then moved the rig and support truck back to their place beside the barn. For a brief moment, Jack paused and wiped his forehead with his bandanna. He touched Willa's shoulder, skimmed Molly's cheek lightly with the back of a knuckle.

"'Ummy ber," Molly said, and Jack dug into the bag of candies in his pocket, handed her one and slipped another into his mouth.

Willa gazed at him. She didn't say anything.

"You and Thomas move away." Jack pushed his hat back on his head and looked from Thomas to Willa. "I'd just as soon not have anyone around me while I do this."

They did as he said, moving away a good hundred feet. Willa clutched Molly to her and watched Jack's every move.

Please, God. Don't let anything go wrong.

There was always an edge of concern around working with explosives, but Jack was familiar with dynamite; he knew what he was doing. With sure hands, he trimmed the fuse to the length he wanted. He intended the dynamite to go off ten feet before the bottom of the hole.

Taking the box of matches from his pocket, he struck the head of a match against his boot and allowed it to flame. He lit the fuse, then carefully dropped the stick down the hole and hurriedly stepped back several feet.

Giving fervent thanks, Willa ran forward.

The dynamite exploded, rumbling deep in the earth. Bits of rock, red earth and water spewed from the hole, raining down on all four of them. After a moment's shock, Willa raised her eyes, swept the strands of muddy hair from her face and looked from Molly to the men. Jack's teeth showed extra white as he began to roar with laughter.

"You don't look so great yourself," she told him, breaking into chuckles.

"I'm billing you for a new hat," Thomas said as he swept off his cap and wrung it. "This was my favorite. And it *wasn't* orange."

"'gin'" Molly said with a giggle.

Willa brushed drops of mud from Molly's forehead. "No, sweetheart," she said with a shake of her head. "We don't want to do it again."

Jack rested a hand on his hip. "Willa, how about getting us something to drink while Thomas and I hook up the pump so we can see what we've got?"

Casting another look at the hole, Willa gave thanks for Jack's safety and prayed the dynamiting had worked. She didn't want him to try again. In the kitchen, as she filled glasses with ice, she longed to be able to run gallons of water from the faucet once again. She gazed at the amber tea as she poured it over the ice in the glasses. Water. Water made tea, water made soup, water made soft drinks. All she seemed to be able to think about was drinking.

Then, calling for Molly to follow, she carried the glasses outside to hear what Jack and Thomas had to say about the situation.

She watched as they finished hooking a hose to the pump, then held her breath as they lowered the submersible pump by its long cord. Would it go down three hundred feet? Or would it get stuck in sand that clogged the hole as a result of the dynamiting?

It went down, and Jack raised it a little bit. Within minutes they turned on the pump and were pumping good, fresh water at what Willa estimated to be over twenty-five gallons per minute.

Lifting Molly, Willa swung her around in the air. They were all laughing. With Molly still in her arms, she hugged Thomas, then turned to hug Jack.

Water! They had water! Thank God!

Jack beamed. "Let's get this well cased and gravel packed, then I'm treating us all to the best steak dinner in Duncan!"

Less than an hour later, Willa was cleaning up in one of their last two buckets of water. Jack had the other one. She found it no mean trick to wash both her body and her hair in the small amount of water.

Wrapping her wet hair in a towel, she flipped the towel back from her face. "We're done with you!" she said and tapped the empty bucket with her toe.

Rubbing her hair until it was only damp, Willa brushed it back from her face and left it loose. She'd looked anything but feminine the past three days, and she intended to remind Jack of what she could be when she put her mind to it. She chose a pink cotton sundress she'd rarely worn, slipped on summer sandals and received a low whistle of approval from Jack for her trouble.

Thomas returned from his trip home to clean up, and they all drove down to Duncan and lunched on T-bone steaks and salad at a nice restaurant. While waiting for their meal, Willa drank the entire glass of water the waitress had brought. Jack and Thomas each drank two, and even Molly polished off over half a glass.

Talk turned to purchasing hydrofracturing equipment. "I think we'd be the first driller in the area to have it," Willa said. "If we could afford it."

Jack stabbed at his steak. "I've got a bit of money," he said, then grinned. "Enough for a down payment. And I think I know where we can get what we need at a good price."

For some odd reason, Willa heard the word *we* louder than any other. She looked deep into Jack's pale blue eyes. They shone with love.

Immediately she looked back down at her plate. Her heart seemed to rise to her throat. *We.* Jack was thinking of them together. She wished she could believe in them again, but she couldn't help remembering that once before, so long ago, he'd thought and spoken the same way. And then he'd changed his mind.

Thomas finished off a steak the size of his plate and left, planning to stay on in town and visit with friends. Willa and Jack lingered over coffee, talking about business ideas, until Molly began to fret.

"Okay, sweetheart," Willa told her, "you've been patient long enough."

As they got up from the table, she couldn't resist drinking several more swallows of cool water. "I don't think I'll ever take water for granted again," she said, replacing the glass on the table. She found herself looking into Jack's eyes. They twinkled, then grew somber.

"No," he said, his voice dropping low, "we won't. Sometimes it takes doing without something necessary to our lives before we realize its value."

He held Willa's gaze for a long time, and it was as if his energy, alive and vibrating, were channeled to her. And she knew that Jack, like herself, was thinking of something besides water, something they'd lost and were working to find again. Willa hoped very sincerely that they dug and dug and found the wellspring of love they both needed. But playing at the edges of her mind was the realization that sometimes a person sunk his life savings into a well, only to have it come up dry.

In the late afternoon, they headed for home. Willa held a sleeping Molly in her lap and leaned back against the seat, dozing. Her thoughts lingered enjoyably on images of water spurting from the shower. And on Jack joining her there.

They'd found water. It seemed an almost magical thing, and certainly something beyond price. Now she understood how important her great-grandfather's endeavors had been all those years ago when settlers had first come to

Oklahoma. They'd found an often dry and forbidding land. No wonder her great-grandfather had been considered almost a mystic.

She thought again of the luxury of turning on faucets and having water run from the spigot.

"What are you smiling about?" Jack asked, a hint of a chuckle in his voice.

"Showers," Willa answered. "And baths and ice water and coffee and tea. Wet, wet water."

Water, she decided, was a much more valuable commodity than oil, and, eyes closed, she dwelled on this provocative thought until the pickup rocked, signaling Jack's turn into the driveway of their house.

Holding Molly tight against the rocking, Willa opened her eyes to see a powder-blue Lincoln Continental parked at the end of the drive beneath the old elm tree.

"Who is it?" Jack asked.

"Darlene and Ray," she answered, her heart constricting.

Jack slipped from the pickup, came around the front of the truck and took Molly, still asleep, from Willa. She followed him to the house, her gaze skimming the yard for Darlene and Ray. Then she saw the back door ajar, and her stomach lurched. Apparently Darlene still possessed a key to the house and felt perfectly free to use it.

When she and Jack stepped into the kitchen, they heard movement from upstairs. Jack raised an eyebrow.

"They're in Hoppy's bedroom," Willa murmured, amazed. Her heart began to pound. They had come right into her house and were up in one of her bedrooms!

"I'll put Molly to bed," Jack said, stepping toward the hall.

Willa nodded and moved toward the stairs. She shook with fury. How dare they enter her house as if they already owned the place! She felt invaded, violated.

She mounted the stairs with care, unwilling to have them hear her approach. When she reached the landing and stepped to the doorway, she saw that Darlene was alone in

Hoppy's room. Her back was toward Willa, her thin legs bent, her wide buttocks swaying back and forth as she dug through a dresser drawer. She would scarcely have heard a horse clomping up the stairs, Willa thought, so involved was she in her search.

Ransacking! Willa thought with a glance around the room so bright and clean with its new ceiling and paint—and now scattered with Hoppy's belongings. For some reason Darlene had torn the covers from the bed and pulled clothes from the drawers and piled them all on top of the mattress.

Oh, I'm sorry, Lord, but I'd like to snatch every red hair from her head!

"Looking for the family silver?" Willa spoke loud and clear, gratified at making Darlene give a little squeal, jump and drop the clothes she held.

Darlene stared at her, inhaled sharply and elevated her chin. "I'm just looking through my brother's things."

"You were more than welcome to see Hoppy's things. But you have no right to barge into the house—*my* house— without the common courtesy generally given to the owner." Willa was so angry that she felt as if she were seeing everything through a red haze.

"Just whose house this is will be decided by the courts," Darlene said easily. "Until then I have a perfect right to be here whenever I want. After all, I grew up here."

She stepped away from the dresser, and Willa saw the old, intricate brass picture frame that housed her favorite photo of Hoppy, the one she'd kept for herself.

She strode forward and snatched up the picture. "You've been through the desk downstairs!" She whirled on Darlene. "How dare you!"

A small, hard smile curved Darlene's lips. "You may have thought yourself sitting pretty here, but you aren't going to get everything, Missy." Her eyes glittered, and the smile disappeared. "Everyone thinks you're such an angel, the way you stuck by a grumpy old man. Angel, huh! You had nothin' until my brother took you in, and you knew a good thing when you fell into it. I know there's money around here, as well as his coin collection. Hoppy used to hide money under his mattress—he'd been through the Depression and didn't trust banks. And he'd collected those coins for thirty years."

Willa stared, shocked nearly speechless. Darlene really and truly believed what she said.

"There's no money, Darlene," Willa managed at last. "Hoppy didn't have any more than was in the bank. And the coins aren't worth more than three hundred dollars. He left them for Molly."

"You can play sweet all you want, but you can't fool me. Even twenty-five years ago my brother guarded those coins like they were diamonds. And I saw his money before I ever left. He had it stuck under his mattress—more than ten thousand dollars at that time." Her voice echoed with bitterness.

"And once our father died, and he was in charge of things, he wouldn't buy me hardly anything—only Mae did. Mae was a good woman. Too good to be his wife. When she'd ask him for money to get me things other girls got, he'd just say it was spoiling me." She gave a sharp chuckle. "He didn't think that for you, Willa, now, did he?"

Never before had Willa hated anyone, but she thought she hated Darlene at that moment. Yet almost equally, watching the woman move to the bed, she felt a deep, deep pity. Hoppy had, at times, been a hard man, Willa knew. She also knew he'd mellowed by the time she'd come to live with him. Losing Mae had changed him, a good many people had told her. Willa guessed he'd spoiled her on occasion, if it could be considered that. She'd never known Darlene harbored such jealousy, hadn't seen enough of Darlene to know much about her at all.

"If you think there's more money here," Jack said, his voice breaking into the tension, "you can bring that up at the hearing."

Willa looked over to see him standing in the doorway. Darlene glanced from Jack to Willa.

"You didn't wait long to bring another man into the house, now, did you, Willa?"

Willa's pity faded. The instant was perfect for a slap to Darlene's face, but she stood too far away. Willa settled for a firm command. "You can leave now, Darlene."

The older woman smirked. "I'll go...because I'm ready. But I'm telling you, you and your bastard daughter are not getting what rightfully belongs to me and mine."

Without thinking, Willa reached out, her hand closing around a small bottle of Hoppy's after-shave nearby on the dresser. Faster than she could blink, she sent the bottle sailing across the room at Darlene.

Jack's gaze followed the bottle's path through the air, saw Darlene, eyes wide as saucers, duck and scurry toward the door at the same time. The bottle hit the wall with a thump but, surprisingly, didn't break.

Jack moved out of Darlene's way and sucked in his stomach as she squeezed past. He thought it a grave mistake for her to stop at the top of the stairs. This was only the second time he'd ever seen Willa so mad—the first time was early in their marriage when he'd stayed out late with the guys and not phoned to tell her where he was. She'd put a dent in the door of the truck he'd had at the time.

Darlene looked back over her shoulder and opened her mouth but must have thought better of speaking, because the next instant Jack saw her scuttling down the stairs as fast as her skinny legs would carry her hefty body. Looking back at Willa, Jack saw what Darlene had seen—the blazing fire in Willa's eyes as she stalked forward. But instead of following Darlene, she jerked open the closet door and bent inside.

The next instant, Jack was dumbfounded to see her emerge with a shotgun—and she was loading it!

"Willa..." He put a hand on her arm. "You can't shoot her."

"No," she allowed seriously, "but I can sure scare the daylights out of her." She looked at him. "Allow me that, Jack."

He couldn't help chuckling. "Yes, I guess you can do that."

She hurried down the stairs, and he moved to the window to get a better view.

Darlene was halfway across the yard when Willa stepped out onto the porch.

"You can say what you want about me, but you'd better not be slandering my daughter ever again!" Willa called out.

The gun in her hand presented a stark contrast to her pale pink dress. But Willa herself was a woman of contrasts, Jack thought, and that was one of the reasons he loved her. She was certainly never boring.

Darlene stopped, her heavy breasts heaving, and turned to retort. When she spied Willa holding the gun, her mouth fell open, though she made no sound. Then she practically fell all over herself as she bolted for her car. Jack felt slightly guilty for the good time he was having watching, for the woman was definitely scared. Her skinny, shaking legs couldn't seem to propel her fast enough.

"And don't you come back here until you have papers proclaiming this place as your own, Darlene Woolard!"

The air reverberated with the blast of the shotgun Willa had pointed into the air. Jack looked from Darlene, who fumbled frantically with the handle on her car door, to Willa. She tilted her head upward toward him. Even from a distance he caught the look of satisfaction on her face.

Jack watched from the window as Darlene's powder-blue car circled the end of the drive, its spinning tires throwing up rocks and dust as it roared out. Then he walked down the stairs and into the kitchen.

The shotgun lay on the table. Willa was just coming out of Molly's room.

"I was afraid I'd awakened her, but she's still asleep. She must have been exhausted." She spoke in a low voice, her gaze straying to the shotgun.

"Feel better?" Jack asked, watching her closely.

A slow smile began on her lips. "Yes," she said with a deep breath, "I believe I do." She laughed, her eyes twinkling, all traces of anger gone. "Till the day I die, I'll be glad I did that."

"Well, I doubt she'll be back."

With a shake of her head, she picked up the gun and ran her hand down the stock. "I feel sorry for Darlene," she said. "It must be awful to carry around such hate."

She lifted her luminous golden brown eyes, and the hurt Jack saw there tore at his heart.

"She hates me so much, Jack, and maybe in her place I'd feel the same. Hoppy did give me so much more than he did her."

Jack stepped over and swept her into his arms. "You're not responsible for Darlene's twisted character, Willa. She's the one to determine how she's going to react to life. We all have to do that for ourselves."

"I know," she mumbled into his sleeve. Then she pulled away and looked up at him. "I sure hope everything goes as you and Mitchell think it will at that hearing. I don't want Darlene to get the new well we've dug." A small smile quirked her lips, but he sensed the seriousness deep within her.

The rest of that evening and late into the night, Jack and Willa worked on connecting the pump and pipes and getting water flowing into the house. As Jack had predicted, they had a good flow, even better than the old well had provided. It appeared there had been problems with the old well for some time.

Willa turned on the kitchen faucets and simply stared at the water pulsing into the enamel sink and swirling down the drain. Later she lingered in the shower, repeatedly cupping her hands to taste the precious, crystal liquid. At last Jack joined her, and he, too, seemed to find something so mundane quite a treat.

It was after midnight when they got into bed. Jack reached for her, kindling a warmth within her with his kisses and intimate caresses. Afterward, exhausted, he fell promptly to sleep. Nestled in the curve of his body, Willa fell asleep quickly herself, only to awaken forty-five minutes later, thoughts chasing each other through her mind like hounds after a raccoon.

Slipping from beneath Jack's heavy arm, she got up, put on her robe and walked out to the backyard. The moon was full, the air alive with the sounds of night creatures—hoot owls, whippoorwills, cicadas, crickets. A rustle came from one of the fruit trees, probably a visiting coon checking out the crop.

Willa stared toward the barn and the big drilling rig. The trucks looked somewhat eerie in the silvery moonlight. Scenes from the previous days of working the rig and making do with buckets of water flitted across her mind.

She recalled the often intense look on Jack's face, his smiles, his frowns. At his moody times it seemed as if a rope had been wrapped around her heart and tightened. Though she told herself she was being silly, she always wound up worrying whether she was the cause of his mood, whether he was unhappy with her.

She thought of his cows and his stubbornness in buying them and knew she'd been right to accept them. She thought of their lovemaking and wondered at the magic that happened between them. She thought of her choice in using birth control and felt confusion. She wasn't getting any younger, and she did want more children.

Looking out across the land beneath the moon, she thought of Darlene, and she shivered, feeling a distinct threat. She recalled the events of the afternoon, and her cheeks grew hot with shame.

Good heavens! Chasing her with a shotgun. How could she have done such an outlandish thing? True, she'd never have hurt the woman, but still, the act had been crude. It had brought her down to Darlene's level, she chided herself. And just when she'd begun to feel she could control her temper in any situation, she thought with a shake of her head.

Was she sorry? came a whisper into her brain. She tried to be—but couldn't quite make it. Darlene deserved to have the pants scared off her for speaking those ugly words about Molly, for her entire greedy nature.

The screen door squeaking behind her made her jump.

Jack stepped from the porch. "I missed you."

Willa turned back to gaze at the land, and he put his arms around her and nuzzled her neck. Immediately desire flickered and flamed in the pit of her stomach. Suddenly, as if to block out all the concerns plaguing her heart, she grasped him to her and returned his kiss with unaccustomed fierceness. The next instant, Jack scooped her up into his arms and headed out across the grass.

"Where are you going?" she asked, feathering kisses along his neck.

"To make love to you in the moonlight." His voice was husky.

Willa kicked her feet. "Oh, no, you don't! I don't like to lie naked on the grass!"

Jack pivoted and headed once again toward the house. Carrying her as if she were no more than a doll, he stalked inside to their bedroom, where Willa expected him to place her on the cool sheets. Her hands ran up and down his strong arms, and her imagination raced ahead, anticipating.

But instead of putting her on the bed, he shifted and threw her unceremoniously over his shoulder.

"Jack! How dare you!" Willa beat her fists against his bare back.

"Shush. You'll wake Molly."

"Let me down!" she demanded in a loud whisper. With surprise, and delight, she saw him jerking the sheet from the bed. "Jack, all the blood's rushing to my head. You'd better let me down."

He ignored her, padding softly back through the house and outside once more. Teasingly, Willa raked her fingernails over his back, then allowed herself to go limp, as if she'd fainted.

Jack stopped and lowered her gently to the ground. "Willa..." His voice was anxious, his palms scratchy against her cheeks. "Willa, are you all right?"

Opening her eyes, Willa made a face and stuck out her tongue. The next instant Jack let out a low growl and covered her lips with his in a rough, demanding kiss. Minutes later they lay upon the sheet with the silvery moonlight playing over their bodies. The air caressed her skin, cooling it even as Jack's touch heated it. The need rose like a flood within her, and she turned to wrap her legs around his.

She loved him with every part of her body, every movement, as she never had before. And when, afterward, she lay sated in his arms, she sensed that things within herself had taken a turn. While not exactly merging her life with Jack's, she knew she could allow their lives to exist side by side.

In the following days, Willa took two showers a day, just for enjoyment. She drank numerous glasses of water and twice stood at the kitchen sink, allowing the water to run while she stared at it, enthralled by how clear and abundant it was.

She and Jack, often with Molly's little hands joining them, built a new well house. In the heat of the day, Jack retired to the barn to work on the rig, making modifications to boost the engine's power. He was also scouting around among his many oil business acquaintances for affordable hydrofracturing equipment.

Eight days after the completion of their well, in the evening, they got two calls for drilling jobs. Willa knew the areas and agreed to the jobs over the phone. After the second call, Willa scooped Molly into her arms and ran out across the wide yard to meet Jack as he drove in from checking on his cows in the pasture.

"Jobs!" she said, gasping from running. "We have two jobs!" She was as excited as if someone had said Christmas was coming in July. "Mr. Henderson down at Henderson's Pump Supply recommended us for both of them."

Jack grinned. "Looks like word is finally getting around."

"Yes." She beamed. "Yes, maybe it is."

After those two drilling jobs, more followed. With his experience and background, Jack got his driller's license easily, and it seemed natural for a good deal of the responsibility to slip into his hands. Willa no longer had to be at the well site until the completion of each well, though she chose to be there most of the time. Carrie often cared for Molly, and practically as often Willa took Molly with her to the site.

Twice Jack received telephone calls from old acquaintances at oil companies, one from Texas, the other from Canada. The calls concerned questions about drilling. The Canadian company made a lucrative job offer, but Jack turned it down, helping the man with his problem for no charge on the telephone.

"Jack, you can go and see," Willa told him. "It sounds interesting. Molly and I will be fine until you return, and Thomas and I can keep the business going."

"I know you'll be fine, Willa," he replied in a curious tone. "I don't want to go. Not now."

Willa let the subject drop, but for the rest of the day she puzzled over his tone and expression when he'd told her he knew she'd be fine.

Though at times, with all the work, Willa wondered how she'd gotten into the whole mess, she never regretted going into the business of drilling wells. While demanding and at times revoltingly dirty and uncomfortable, it was fascinating and rewarded her with a feeling of extreme accomplishment. People needed this water, and she took pride in helping them get it. And it was something she could share with Jack; they were working well together.

It was the second week in June and late evening when Mitchell drove out. Willa was pushing Molly on the tree swing, Jack running water hoses to the fruit trees.

Immediately upon seeing Mitchell's car, Willa felt a gladness in her heart. Except for a couple of times they'd passed in town, she hadn't seen him lately, and she'd missed him. He was a friend, and a good one, and she'd like it so much if they could remain such. She'd like it even more if Mitchell and Jack could become friends again.

Some inner instinct told her Mitchell had come about the court hearing, and her heartbeat picked up tempo.

Mitchell stepped from his car and stood looking across the yard at Willa. She appeared slimmer than he'd remembered. She wore a pretty yellow sundress, fashionably long, almost to her ankles, and matching sandals. Molly, sitting in the tree swing, looked to have grown a foot taller.

Helping Molly from the swing, Willa bent and murmured something in the child's ear. Molly scampered across the yard toward the fruit trees. Glancing over, Mitchell saw Jack's big frame at the far row of trees.

Willa gracefully walked toward him, and it was hard to believe what he'd heard about her drilling wells. She was actually doing it, a hard, rough job. He still couldn't understand why it held such an attraction for her, yet he couldn't honestly picture her any other way but working out-of-doors, close to the land.

She came nearer, and her luminous hazel eyes met his. They held a warm welcome. Her skin appeared fair and smooth and, though a bit tawny, it wasn't the deep, dark tan of someone who spent days in the sun, as he'd heard she'd been doing. Her glossy hair brushed her shoulders, and the hand she extended to him was soft and smooth. He wondered if he'd ever truly get over loving her.

Chapter Thirteen

Hello, Mitchell." Willa took his hand, squeezed it and saw the welcome she felt reflected in his eyes.

"Hello, Willa." He stared at her a long minute. "You look well."

"I am, thanks. And you look pretty good yourself. You're so tanned."

"Spent a week fishing in the gulf," he said. His hand still held hers, and gently Willa tugged away. "Heard Coyote Drilling is back in business."

She nodded. "It's still slow, but we're getting more jobs all the time." Out of the corner of her eye, she saw Jack approaching with Molly in his arms.

"Molly has her father," Mitchell said, his voice dropping low.

"Yes."

"You're happy?" His deep blue eyes searched hers.

"Yes," she said again, meeting his gaze unflinchingly. Mostly she was happy, and she would never tell anyone about the times of doubt. She wished Mitchell had never cared for her; she hated feeling responsible for hurting him.

Jack joined them. "Mitchell." He gave a sharp nod, and Willa immediately felt tension swirl in the air.

"Jack," Mitchell responded with a small nod of his own. His gaze returned to Willa. "I drove out to tell you the court date. Just found out this afternoon. It'll be August seventh."

No one said anything for a moment.

"It still looks okay?" Willa asked.

Mitchell nodded. "I don't anticipate any problems. The laws are on our side, Willa. The will is legal. You wouldn't even have to be there, but I know you wouldn't miss it." He smiled at her.

"I sure wouldn't." She gazed into his eyes for an instant before looking away.

Mitchell turned to speak to Molly and to compliment her on how she'd grown. "Getting as pretty as Mommy," he told her.

To Willa's irritation, Jack didn't say anything else to Mitchell. He just seemed to wait quietly for him to leave.

"Would you like a beer, Mitchell?" Willa offered. "We've got some cold."

Mitchell glanced from her to Jack and back again. "No, thanks," he said, giving a shake of his head. "I've got to get back to town. Just wanted to tell you in person about the hearing date."

Willa's heart fell. She hated to give up hope on the men becoming friends again. She hated the entire situation. "Well, thank you for coming out to tell us, Mitchell."

He nodded. "I'll be in touch."

Willa stood beside Jack beneath the big elm and watched until Mitchell's car disappeared from sight.

"You could have been a bit more cordial to Mitchell," Willa said. "He's doing an awful lot for us."

Jack set Molly on the ground so that she could chase off after Doc. Then slowly he stood and faced her. "He's doing an awful lot for *you*."

"He's trying to make sure I keep the land, Jack."

"The land..." Jack said in a thoughtful tone. He looked pointedly at her. "Are you sorry about not choosing Mitchell?"

Startled, Willa stared at him. His expression was unreadable.

"No, I'm not, Jack," she said at last. "I love you." It was a hard thing to say because of the cold way he was looking at her.

His eyes narrowed as he searched her face. "I think you do, Willa, but you leave out a part. You don't let me love you."

They stared at each other for long minutes.

"What do you mean?" She had to force the question from her throat.

Jack took a deep breath. "I could leave again, right now, and you'd never even notice I was gone. You don't need me."

A horrible, cold chill swept down Willa's spine. Immediately she averted her eyes to the ground, unwilling for Jack to see her expression. Was he thinking of leaving again? Her heart hammered painfully at the possibility, but she refused to let her panic show.

"Are you considering leaving again?" she asked coolly. She couldn't meet his gaze.

"No!" He spoke vehemently. "That's not what I said, Willa. I said you don't need me."

She looked up at him then, confused. "You live here. We own and run a company together. What more do you want?"

He seemed to consider her words. His jaw muscle twitched. "I'd like to be more than the hired hand who sleeps with the boss."

Anger flashed through her. "I'm sorry you look at it that way. What do you want? Me to quit work altogether?"

"It's not the drilling, Willa." Jack shifted his big frame. "I'll admit, it bothered me at first, your calling out all those orders. But we've settled into a pretty good way of doing things, and I'm proud of you, proud of us. I feel I've contributed knowledge and money to the company.'' His chin tightened stubbornly. ''But you only let me get so close, and that's it. You won't let me in, Willa. The land and the drilling are everything to you. You rely on those things, not on me. The only time I've felt like you might care if I up and left was when I was handling that dynamite.''

His criticism stung. ''I told you I'd changed,'' she said. ''Maybe you don't like what you see anymore.''

''I think we've both changed,'' he said, pivoting away. ''I'm going out for a while.''

Jack drove away, leaving Willa, with Molly clinging to her leg, standing in the driveway. He called himself every kind of fool. But at last he'd put into words something that had been eating away at him.

He didn't have any answers. He wasn't even certain if part of his problem wasn't in his imagination. It was just something he felt; he couldn't actually lay the blame to actual disagreements with Willa. On the contrary, Willa seemed inordinately obliging most of the time. Too obliging. She remained uncertain of him. And that hurt like hell.

Jack considered going to see Mitchell. He had been rude, owed Mitchell an apology. But his pride wouldn't let him do it. He wondered if all his frustration at the moment was brought on by simple jealousy.

He ended up driving all the way to Duncan, getting a soft drink and the Oklahoma City newspaper, and turning around and going home.

Willa jumped when she heard the pickup pull into the drive. She'd been sitting in the darkened living room, waiting. After Jack had left her in the driveway, she'd brought Molly inside and put her to bed. Then she'd changed into her nightgown and dawdled around the house, straightening up an already clean kitchen, picking up Jack's clothes from the bedroom, attempting to read a magazine. But nothing held her attention; every fiber of her seemed to listen for Jack's return, to wonder if, indeed, he would come. Of course he would come, she told herself a number of times. All his belongings were at the house. Still, the unreasonable doubt remained.

Now her heart beat rapidly. At first she couldn't move. She listened as the pickup passed the house and stopped at the end of the drive. Then it shut off. The truck's door slammed, and seconds later the back door squeaked.

Willa rose and walked to the kitchen. Jack was in the act of setting a newspaper and his hat on the table. Hearing her, he turned. They stared at each other. It was the first time Willa had ever revealed that she was waiting up for him.

He opened his arms, and she went to him. "I'm trying, Jack," she said.

"Me, too," he murmured into the top of her head.

And so, she thought, they'd each have to dig a little deeper at the well of patience and love—and hope it didn't go dry.

When the day of the court hearing arrived, they were in the middle of a drilling job that was taking longer than they'd anticipated. Willa had agreed to the job on impulse in the first place, feeling the need to take every job they were offered. Jack had fumed when he'd found out, telling her she should have kept the week of the hearing open.

Feeling his criticism now justified, Willa told him there was no need to interrupt work on the well; she could go to court alone. But when the time came, he was there beside her, dressed in his best suit and tie, holding the pickup door open for her and Molly. "I shut the rig down for the afternoon," he told her.

"Shut it down?" Willa said, dismayed. "Jack, we have the customer to think of."

"Missing an afternoon of drilling on this well isn't going to make that much difference," Jack said. "If the customer doesn't like it, he can get another driller. He won't get one for the price we're charging him, and he knows it."

Willa nodded and slid onto the seat, holding Molly upon her lap. She saw Jack looking at the sky and followed his gaze. "Maybe we should have taken the tower down," he said. "I don't like the looks of those clouds. They're going to have lightning in them for sure."

"I think they'll stay to the south," Willa said. Right over the courthouse, she thought and didn't find the thought in the least reassuring.

After dropping Molly at Carrie's, they headed for the county courthouse, where they would meet Mitchell.

Questions reverberated in Willa's head. What if the judge decided Darlene had a case? Would she get the land right away, or could Willa fight? Why hadn't she asked this of Mitchell?

She'd felt sick from the moment she'd gotten out of bed that morning, and now her stomach seemed to tighten by the minute. She alternately wished she could eat and hated the thought of food. Again and again she smoothed her skirt. Of course, Darlene wouldn't get the land, Willa told herself firmly. This was just a stupid formality.

Jack encased her hand within his big one. "You're going to wear that skirt out," he said. "Worried?"

Willa nodded. "Sort of." She wanted to speak more of her fears, but the words choked in her throat.

"Tell me, Willa."

She glanced up quickly. Tell him? She wanted to, but it was so hard to show herself other than in command.

"I know Mitchell told me everything will be fine," she said at last, "but it isn't his land at stake. Crazier things have happened. Monica Edwards, who lives just east of town, inherited her parents' entire estate, but somehow her aunts and uncles and the executor of the will held up everything for two years in the fight over it—and they spent a great deal of her inheritance doing it, too."

"Mitchell is the executor and a good lawyer. And he's on your side. Besides, you can't spend land. It'll still be there for you."

Willa sighed. "I know. I'll just be glad when all this ugliness is over."

Trust, she thought, her gaze going to the boiling clouds above. Trust in the Lord to look out for her, trust in Hoppy to have seen to an adequate will, trust in Mitchell to do his job, trust in the law to be just. She didn't like it at all that her future was so completely out of her hands. That there was absolutely nothing she could do right now but trust in others.

"Jack, pull over. I think I'm going to be sick."

Immediately Jack pulled the pickup to the side of the road, and Willa hopped out, hoping to keep the truck between herself and Jack. She couldn't bear for him to see her. But as her stomach revolted against what little there was in it, she heard him step up behind her.

"Go away!"

"Willa…" His voice came gently. "Here." He handed her a handkerchief. His hand rested on her back.

She began to shake violently and felt terribly weak. She tried to wipe her face, but Jack took the cloth and did it for her. Then he was cuddling her to him.

"It's okay, Willa. You're not going to lose the farm. I won't let you lose the farm, honey."

"It's my home, Jack," she muttered into his shirt. "It's…" It was the one place on earth she felt secure, and with this thought came the memory of Jack's angry words of weeks before. She couldn't say this to him.

She looked up at him. "Thank you for coming," she said. She was suddenly very glad he was with her. His presence somehow made her stronger.

He smiled and nodded. "You okay?"

"Yes, I'll be fine now." Tentatively, deep within herself, Willa leaned on Jack's strength.

They met Darlene in the lobby of the courthouse, with her husband Ray and two men in dark suits, apparently their lawyers. If looks could kill, Darlene's even would have buried. Willa told herself she really should work on forgiveness as she sent Darlene an ultrasweet smile she knew would make the woman wild with fury. It was rewarding when Darlene's face flushed crimson.

With a hand at her elbow, Jack guided Willa across the lobby and down the hall. He felt her trembling. He hoped by holding her arm he could give her a bit of support. It frustrated him that there was so little he could do to ease her worry, and it was damn irritating to have to rely on Mitchell. But thank heaven for Mitch, he thought, if reluctantly.

He stopped to get a gummy bear from the bag in his coat pocket. "Guess I'll have to ration," he said, pulling out the bag and finding it contained only two of the candies.

"Oh, no, you won't," Willa said with a smile. Digging into her purse, she pulled out a small bag of gummy bears. "I bought them yesterday."

"Thanks, sweetheart." Right there in front of a good number of people, he bent to kiss her lips.

Willa's cheeks turned a bright pink, but she looked far from unhappy. "We'd better find Mitchell."

They bypassed the busy records office and several smaller offices, continuing on to one of the two courtrooms. Mitchell stood talking to a young woman just inside the double doors. After turning to greet them, he led them down the aisle to a table where his briefcase sat open. A vibrant excitement emanated from him, and it was clear he was in his element.

"When we were kids," Jack said to Mitchell when Willa had left to find the ladies' room, "all you ever thought of was becoming a lawyer. Why have you taken up banking?"

"Dad was getting on," Mitchell answered, looking up from the papers in his hand. "It seemed like a good thing." He glanced around the courtroom. "Until now I didn't realize how much I missed the practice of law."

Jack gave an understanding smile. "It's never too late to turn around when you find yourself on the wrong road, Mitch."

Mitchell looked at him with surprise. "No, I guess not." He gazed for a second into Jack's eyes. "It's food for thought, anyway."

"You still don't anticipate any problems with Hoppy's will?" Jack asked.

Mitchell shook his head. "By law it's Darlene's right to petition the court to hear her objections—not that I feel she even had grounds—and she did get a hearing, but that's all. In the end it could prove beneficial to Willa by securing her the farm once and for all.''

''This thing could go on, though, depending on what happens today, couldn't it? And even if the judge denies Darlene's petition, she could bring it up again, couldn't she?''

Mitchell gave a thoughtful look. ''Yes to both questions. But it will cost Darlene to challenge this will. We've got a good stand.''

Looking into Mitchell's eyes, Jack felt their rivalry evaporate as a strange bond took its place. In this moment he and Mitchell shared a unity of purpose, and that was to help and protect Willa.

When Willa returned, she sat between Jack and Mitchell behind the table. Cold chills raced down her spine, and her stomach felt as if it swarmed with butterflies. She refused to think about being sick again.

The courtroom process seemed very much like what she'd seen in movies and on television, except there was no jury, just a judge—younger than Willa ever imagined a judge— who sat and listened to one of Darlene's attorneys state his client's objections to Hoppy's will. It seemed more informal than what was portrayed on screen, and Mitchell simply sat back in his chair, relaxed, listening. It was up to Darlene's attorney to prove their objections valid, he'd told Willa and Jack before the hearing started. Mitchell stood ready should the judge have any questions afterward.

The judge stated he'd studied the wills cited in the case, both Hoppy's and that of Carter Lowe, father to Hoppy and Darlene, and the objections being raised. Then he listened as Darlene's attorney made his statement.

Willa was astonished to discover that Darlene wasn't, as she'd said, going for the entire farm and house. She was asking for only half the land, and she was citing her father's will as well as Hoppy's.

Listening, Willa could understand why the verbal skills of an attorney were so important. The man's voice was smooth, his tone even, his command of the language awe-inspiring. And she thought his southern accent added a great sense of drama.

While telling the factual truth, Darlene's attorney manipulated words to give his own interpretations of those facts. He cast a shadow on the circumstances of Willa's birth, making it sound as if she might not even have been Jimmy Lowe's child at all. He made Hoppy sound like a greedy ogre, a man who'd deliberately defied his father's wishes of splitting the farm with Darlene when she came of legal age. He also made him sound like a man who'd become, in his last years, of unsound mind.

The attorney made Hoppy's love affair with his drilling equipment sound like a crazy obsession, bringing up the way he'd been overheard talking to the rig. Hoppy had talked to his rig the way some people talk to their plants. And he'd talked to his plants, too, and had gone for walks in the rain, saying it was good for a person's body and mind. He'd also done what he called conjuring, a silly rain dance, when the land had gone too long without rain. Willa had never been entirely certain he wasn't teasing her and everyone else about it. And, yes, he'd been mean with a dollar and had, as Darlene said, kept a bit of money at home, having an abnormal distrust of banks.

The attorney cited all these idiosyncrasies, as Willa thought of them, and even produced a couple of witnesses to corroborate his allegations. He also put forward the supposition that Willa had used her knowledge of Hoppy's weakened mind and had preyed upon his grief at the loss of his only son to maneuver him into leaving her everything.

For the briefest instant she imagined Hoppy having one fine fit of anger at the attorney's portrayal of him. But now she thought sadly, he probably would have found all the commotion over him terribly funny. And he would have told her to look for the funny side, even if it killed her.

She looked at Darlene's flaming hair, fleshy face and long fingers adorned with rings. Ray sat nearby, seeming suddenly much older than Willa remembered. She turned her gaze to Mitchell, seeing his eyes sharp with interest, while his body appeared perfectly relaxed, even lazy. Then she looked at Jack and found him looking at her. His eyes held an unaccustomed warmth. Was it always there, and she'd been too caught up with maintaining her independence to see it?

He smiled and took her hand. She was glad, and her spirits rose with confidence.

When Darlene's attorney came to the end of his lengthy discourse, the judge was quietly thoughtful for some minutes and gazed down, presumably at the papers in front of him. At last, raising his eyes to Mitchell, he asked for comment.

Mitchell rose. "Your honor, Hopkins Lowe took Willa Lowe Cashion at the age of twelve into his home, and in every way, verbally, and by legal record, recognized her as his grandchild. We could bring a string of witnesses to swear to their loving relationship. It is true that Hopkins Lowe adored his granddaughter. He very naturally and legally gave her what was his to give.

"If there was an injustice done to Mrs. Woolard, it was by her own father, Carter Lowe, and is strictly a private moral issue, not one for the courts. Both wills are legal and binding, and there is absolutely nothing written in the will of Carter Lowe that would indicate he bound his son, Hopkins, to give to his sister any part of the Lowe farm. As for Hopkins Lowe's state of mind, everything stated thus far is true . . . and is the portrait of an independent man marching to his own drummer, not a man of unsound mind. And he very generously left his sister money from an estate that has very little cash. My client and I stand on the facts we have already submitted for your consideration, which are: Hopkins Lowe left his sister one thousand dollars; the remainder of his estate he left to his granddaughter."

Mitchell sat down, casting Willa a small, encouraging smile as he did so. She returned the smile, then looked to Jack and reached for his hand. She gave thanks for having both men on her side.

The judge rubbed his brow and looked down again at the papers in front of him. Finally he looked across his wide desk. "I must agree with your conclusion, Mr. Warner."

He turned his gaze to the three people at the opposite table. "Undue influence and unsound mind are very hard things to prove. From what I've heard today, Hopkins Lowe was indeed an unusual individual, but nothing counsel has presented shows him to have been incompetent. Now, while not quite fair in terms of equal shares to his children, Carter Lowe had left the family farm to his son, Hopkins. That will, naming both children, was legal and valid, and it made no mention of any of the farm being later endowed to Darlene Lowe Woolard. Under its provisions the farm was Hopkins Lowe's alone, and his to do with as he wished.

"The only person entitled by law to a certain portion of said Lowe's estate was his wife, and since she was deceased, it was his right to leave his estate to whomever he wished, which in this case is Willa Lowe Cashion. I find Mr. Lowe's will valid and binding and must deny the petition to overthrow it."

Willa heard his final word with rising euphoria and jumped when he slammed his gavel once as a sign of the hearing's end. Jack was grinning broadly at her, saying, "It's okay now, honey." He gathered her into his arms.

She wanted to feel relief, but she couldn't. She'd held the worry too long and too deeply to have it instantly disappear.

Then, without thinking, she put her arms around Mitchell and hugged him, too. When she did think, it came as a relief and a surprise to find Jack still smiling and reaching to shake Mitchell's hand.

Willa turned, seeking Darlene. As her gaze met that of the older woman, hate burned from Darlene's eyes, more strongly than Willa had ever seen it, as if in the months since Hoppy's death the resentment had multiplied in Darlene's heart. Willa turned away, knowing there was nothing she could do or say to change things.

She thought perhaps Darlene was morally entitled to part of the farm. Darlene's own father had been unfair, had made a choice based on the inequality of the sexes in his day, no doubt believing that Darlene, as a woman, would find a man to take care of her.

But Darlene's reasons for wanting the land were wrong. She certainly didn't need it. And Willa wasn't about to give it up. She would keep it for herself and Molly. And any other children she and Jack might have, she thought quite suddenly.

She gazed at his profile while he spoke to Mitchell, discussing matters of courts and trials and wills that Willa wasn't listening to. He'd come home, she thought, and he was still here beside her, despite all their disagreements. He'd remained

That night Willa stood within the circle of Jack's arm and stared out at the farm from the back porch step.

"You have your land, Willa," he said.

Her land. The words echoed in her mind. *Her* land, not *our* land.

She understood then, quite clearly, what Jack had been talking about all those weeks ago. It was *her* land. It was *her* company. And it was *her* life, a life she'd refused to change. She had insisted he make his life fit with hers, had refused to make any changes at all in her own way of living. Which, in effect, shut him out by taking nothing from him. Because, of course, the taking would lead to relying on him.

Quite suddenly Willa felt very sad. She didn't want to shut him out. She wanted to rely on him, to trust in him. She could never fully love him unless she did. He could never fully love her. Only she didn't know how to go about breaking down the tough wall of self-reliance she'd so carefully erected around herself.

She turned and pressed against him, wrapping her arms around his neck.

"Willa?" Surprise echoed in his voice. "Is something wrong?"

She shook her head. "No," she whispered. "I just want you to hold me, to make love to me."

His kiss came, hard and demanding.

The next day Willa rose early to go with Jack to the well site. She was anxious to begin drilling after losing time the previous afternoon. After all, she'd been the one to decide on taking the job, even though she'd been pretty certain they'd have to go very deep to find adequate water.

"We need the hydrofracturing equipment," Jack said at breakfast. "We could probably get enough water out of this well at this depth if we had it."

"We can't afford it," Willa said.

"There are such things as loans, Willa. And I have enough for the down payment."

"Loans require mortgages. We'd have to mortgage the company, because I'm not putting up the land."

"So take a little mortgage on the company," Jack said, and gulped down his coffee. "It's the way of business. We've got to spend money to expand."

"Maybe... I don't know."

Willa didn't like the idea, resisted the risk. She stabbed at her fried egg, but suddenly it looked unappealing. She looked up to find Jack's gaze hard and disapproving upon her. She recalled again what he'd said about her needing only the land and the company.

As if to escape the thought, she rose and began clearing the dishes from the table.

"For Doc." Molly tugged at Willa's pant leg. "For Doc..."

"Okay, darling, I didn't forget." Willa scraped her uneaten egg and toast onto a plate for the hound. "And how about a bit for Goose, too?"

Molly grinned happily. Allowing Molly to carry the plate for Doc, Willa took a plate outside for the goose. She looked up at the sky. It was dark toward the southwest, where a line of thunderclouds was building. The prediction was for scattered heavy thunderstorms all day. The humidity ha been high for days—no doubt the cause of her headache, she thought, wishing for the usual hot, dry Oklahoma wind.

Jack left first, and Willa followed, dropping Molly at Carrie's before proceeding to the well site. When she got there, Jack and Thomas already had the rig going.

"I think we need a new bit," Jack told her. "It's hard crystalline rock down there."

Willa nodded and bent to scoop a handful of cutting from the muddy pan around the drilling pipe. She examined the substance carefully.

"We've got to get the chips off the bottom faster," she said. "Let's try forcing down more water before we change to another bit."

Jack nodded. "I've already started that."

So, they would keep going. The bit worked at a depth of three hundred and sixty feet. They might have to go down several hundred more in this area, Willa knew.

The clouds rolled in, and Willa removed her wide-brimmed hat. Her headache was worsened, and her stomach didn't feel so good, either. She watched lightning flash far to the south, dreading the thought of the storm coming nearer. She wanted to finish this well.

Thirty minutes later, the wind began to gust harder. Jack spoke into Thomas's ear, and Willa saw Thomas raise the lever, bringing the drilling pipe to a halt.

"We got to take down the tower!" Jack hollered to her.

She shook her head. "No! That storm's going to pass south of us. We need to drill while we can, Jack."

With long strides Jack came toward her. She met him halfway. Thunder rumbled across the land.

"Let's not take chances, Willa. That storm is coming right over us."

"It's going to go around. We need to get this job done. We're getting paid by the foot, not the day."

Jack glared at her. "I said we're taking the tower down!"

About that time lightning split the air, seemingly right above them.

"I'll get the pipe!" Willa yelled, instantly stepping up onto the rig.

Jack moved to help Thomas uncouple the pipe from the piece in the hole. Large raindrops began to splat against Willa's head and shoulders and ping against the metal of the rig. The steel pipe swung in the air as Jack guided it toward her. She reached for it, guiding it toward the rack.

It seemed to take forever but actually was only minutes. The wind tugged at Willa's hair, and lightning forked across the sky. As the cable lowered the pipe, Willa guided it into position over the few others in the rack, but it landed crooked. She stretched and shoved. As it fell into position, it jarred another pipe, and in the blink of an eye the two pieces rolled, catching both of Willa's hands beneath them.

It was incredible, but it took her an instant to cry out in pain. And dear God, she couldn't move. Her hands were trapped, crushed beneath the heavy pipe. She screamed again. "Jack! *Jack!*"

Chapter Fourteen

The urgency of Willa's cries sent adrenaline pumping through Jack's body. He reached her in seconds. His stomach lurched when he saw her hands, fingers caught beneath the pipes that had rolled down upon them. He lifted the pipe ends enough for her to drag her hands free. Her movements were slow and jerky; her face was as white as a cottonball.

The wind whipped around the rig, and Willa seemed to sway with it. Jack immediately swooped her up in his arms and jumped down from the rig. He set her on the step and signaled Thomas to lower the tower. The still sparse rain splattered on his hair and shoulders.

Bending down in front of Willa, he took hold of her wrists. "Let me see." Her hands were encased in tan leather gloves, and dark stains were spreading on the leather.

She closed her eyes, then opened them. "Take off my gloves," she said in a hoarse whisper.

Jack shook his head. "No. Leave them on."

Her eyes widened. "I'm going to be sick." Her voice rose with panic. "I don't want to be sick, Jack. Oh, Lord, I don't want to be sick."

He grabbed her shoulder. "You won't be. Take some deep breaths. There. Deep and slow."

Thomas had come to stand near Jack's shoulder. "You handle things here," Jack told him. "Close up, then take Willa's truck. I'm taking her to the hospital."

"I will, don't worry," Thomas said, raising his voice above the wind and crackle of lightning. "Call the house as soon as you can."

Jack nodded he'd heard, then again bent to sweep Willa up into his arms.

Willa couldn't hold on to his neck, couldn't do anything but hold her hands out and feel her strength draining right out the bottoms of her feet. Her head whirled, and she had to work at not fainting. Her hands throbbed almost unbearably.

Jack helped her into the truck, and she leaned against the seat, resting the backs of her hands against her thighs. Nausea again swept over her, and she fought it down. The wind whipped into the cab before Jack could close the door. Lightning repeatedly shot across the purple sky.

"Thomas..." Willa began when Jack slipped behind the steering wheel.

"Thomas is fine. He'll finish shutting down. He'll go home. Now, sit still and be quiet."

"My truck, Jack. And Molly."

"We'll take care of it, Willa," Jack said sharply.

The truck bounced as it pulled out onto the road, jarring Willa's hand against her thigh. She bit her lip against crying out. Tears welled in her eyes. She blinked, and several tears streamed down her cheeks. Her head again began to whirl, and she closed her eyes.

When she felt the pickup stop, she realized she'd been unconscious. She opened her eyes to see that Jack had stopped at a cross street. Then the truck surged forward

Minutes later Jack was carrying her through the doors of the hospital emergency room.

He refused to relinquish her to a wheelchair and carried her straight into a small, curtained cubicle, where he placed her on a bed. He stayed and helped her provide information to the nurse. He rubbed the tears from the corners of her eyes because she couldn't. She could do no more than lie there and pray to the Lord to make the pain stop. Almost immediately a person appeared to inject her in the arm with pain medication. A doctor came and cut her gloves away.

Her fingers were a mess, bloody and swollen. After one look, Willa turned away, and this time she was sick. Jack held her head and then bathed her face with a wet cloth.

He went with her to the X-ray department and later listened as the doctor told them two fingers on each hand were broken, another two had the skin crushed and torn but the bones were intact, and the others were simply badly bruised. He got her some ice water and held the cup to her lips. His hand remained resting upon her right calf, giving an occasional squeeze, as her broken fingers were set and her hands encased in huge bandages. He signed insurance forms and took the instructions for follow-up care.

Willa left the hospital walking but leaning heavily on Jack. Her legs seemed to have little strength, and she felt exceedingly groggy. Her hands resembled a prizefighter's, encased in white boxing gloves. Jack helped her into the truck, and they drove home through pouring rain. Once home, Jack again lifted her from the pickup seat and carried her into the house and to the bedroom, where he set her upon the bed.

Looking down, she watched him untie her heavy work shoes and tug them from her feet. Her legs and arms felt weighted with lead, and she seemed to see everything through a haze. Jack removed her socks and helped her stand so he could strip off her overalls. Unbuttoning her shirtfront and cuffs, he carefully worked the sleeves over her bandaged hands. Lastly, he removed her bra and panties, then slipped a cotton nightgown over her head and eased her hands through the armholes. He pulled down the covers and fluffed the pillows. It all seemed so strange; she felt like a doll.

"Molly..." Willa murmured as she settled her head on the pillow.

"I'll have Carrie bring her home," Jack said softly. "Get some sleep."

Exhausted and drugged from the pain medication, Willa fell immediately into a deep sleep.

She awoke to the jangling of the telephone. Automatically, she reached for the extension phone on the nightstand beside the bed. She banged her bandaged hand, sending pain streaking up her arm.

"Owww!!" She couldn't see anything because the room was dark.

Suddenly the hall light came on. Jack poked his head in the doorway. "I'll get it, Willa." He reached down and lifted the receiver. "Yes, she just woke up. Okay, that'll be fine." As Willa struggled into a sitting position, he replaced the receiver and switched on the bedside lamp. "That was Carrie. She'll be around later." Moving quickly, he adjusted the pillows behind her back.

She struggled to clear her head. Worries tumbled into her mind. "Where's Molly?" She'd always been there to take care of Molly. Relief followed the question when she saw her daughter peeking around Jack's legs. "Hello, sweetheart." At the greeting, Molly smiled and hurried to throw herself on the bed.

"Careful of Mama's hands, Squirt," Jack cautioned. He regarded Willa closely. "You need a pain pill?"

She shook her head. She'd rather endure the small throbbing she experienced now than the swirling head she got from the medicine. "How long did I sleep?"

"A good six hours." Jack sat on the edge of the bed. "Thirsty?"

Willa nodded. "I'd love a glass of iced tea—lots of sugar." Her words came out in a strange whisper.

Jack smiled. "Coming right up."

As he left, Willa opened her arms and motioned for Molly to come close. Then she enveloped her daughter against her chest and wished very much to be able to stroke Molly's hair. At least she could take comfort from holding her.

"Mama..." Molly pulled away to look at Willa's bandaged hands. Then very slowly she lowered her tiny mouth and placed a gentle kiss on each bandage. "Better?" she asked, her deep blue eyes filled with concern.

Willa smiled, tears threatening. "Oh, much better, Squirrel. Thank you."

Jack returned and sat on the side of the bed. He peered closely at her face. "You in pain, Willa?"

She shook her head. "I... Would you wipe my eyes?" She couldn't pick up a tissue to do it for herself.

He smiled gently and reached for a tissue, then dabbed at her eyes, his big hands plainly unaccustomed to such acts.

Willa fought back further tears. "Just reaction," she said.

He nodded, started to hand her the glass of iced tea, then stopped. She couldn't take it, couldn't hold anything. He lifted the glass to her lips. She took several sips, then leaned back on the pillows.

"Thank you." Her eyes were suddenly very heavy, and she simply had to close them.

Willa fell asleep while Jack and Molly stared at her. "Come on, Squirt," Jack said, lifting Molly in his arms. "Let's let Mama rest."

Jack did his best to bathe Molly. He'd never done it before, felt anything but certain, and he thought they got more water on the floor than remained in the bathtub. He searched her drawers for nightclothes, but it was Molly herself who finally pulled a gown from the drawer. She shook it in the air. "This 'un. Mine."

He helped her into the nightie, then fumbled with getting a diaper on her. She plainly revolted against the diaper, but he used gentle persuasion—a gummy bear—because he was pretty certain Willa still put diapers on Molly at night.

He sat with her and read stories—five of them—before she fell asleep. He checked on Willa, and she was sleeping deeply. Then he cleaned up the dishes from the simple dinner of soup and sandwiches he'd made. Having made many a dinner for himself and cleaned up afterwards, he felt slightly more at home in the kitchen.

Carrie came by as she'd said she would, took a look at Willa and left after getting Jack's promise to call if he needed anything.

For fear Willa would need him, he showered quickly, but when he stepped nude from the bathroom, she was still sleeping deeply. Digging into a bottom drawer, he found a pack of cigarettes, took one out and lit it. It tasted stale.

The blue bedroom chair was more suited to a woman's slight form, but he sat in it anyway, on top of several of his shirts he didn't bother to move, and looked at Willa through the gray haze of smoke. After a few minutes he rose and stubbed out the half-finished cigarette in the decorative ashtray.

Very carefully, so as not to disturb Willa, he crawled onto the opposite side of the bed. Willa tossed slightly and gave a small moan. Leaning on his elbow, Jack studied her face. It was pale, her brows knitted. Her lips were very red, her hair curling over her brow and temples. He brushed a stray strand from her eye, longing very much to hold her, to take away the pain. After many minutes, he laid his head down and slept.

Willa awoke to the sound of soft moans and realized they were her own. Her hands throbbed unmercifully. The lamp was on, and she blinked as she looked around the room. A half a glass of watery tea sat on the bedside table. The window displayed the black of night. A cricket chirped from outside the house. Jack's nude body was stretched out on top of the coverlet. His arms hugged a pillow beneath his head, and he snored gently.

Willa lifted her useless hands and looked at them. She could feel only pain. Again she looked at the bedside table, hoping Jack had put the pain pills there. He hadn't. She licked her lips; her mouth felt as dry as cotton. All she could think of was getting something for the pain that now seemed to be pulsing up her arms.

Unable to lift the sheet, she pushed at it with her bandaged hands. Even this small action hurt, so she shifted her body into a sitting position, then stood, dragging part of the sheet with her and leaving it trailing on the floor. She swayed.

Oh, dear Lord, don't let me fall.

Nausea swept her, but with an iron will she swallowed it back. She tried a step, then another, and regained an adequate sense of balance. The pills would surely be in the kitchen, and if not, she could get aspirin from the cabinet—a half bottle of aspirin, she told herself with a low, ragged chuckle.

With the back of her wrist, she flipped on the kitchen light. The brightness was blinding. She stood quite still, allowing her eyes to adjust. Then she approached the cabinet, searching for the small vial she imagined would contain pain pills. Seeing nothing, she tried to open the cabinet where she kept a spare aspirin bottle. She couldn't, and the effort sent pain shooting to her elbows. She leaned against the counter, fighting the whirling in her head.

Where were the damn pain pills? And how would she get the bottle open? How would she even get a glass of water?

Tears of pain and frustration coursed down her cheeks. She wiped them from her face with the backs of her bandages but couldn't clear her eyes.

"Willa!" Jack's voice startled her. "What are you doing up?" With long strides he crossed the room toward her, as stark naked as, though much larger than, the day he was born. His expression angry, he swept her up into his arms as

easily as he would a Raggedy Ann doll. He turned and
headed back to the bedroom.

"I needed a pain pill," she said, gulping back her tears.

"Well, why didn't you wake me?"

"I didn't want to bother you."

"Bother me? Aw, hell, Willa!"

He put her back into the bed, glared at her a minute, then
stalked from the room. Seconds later he stalked back in,
carrying a glass of water. Willa stared at the pill he held out
to her.

"Open your mouth," he commanded.

Because there was nothing else she could do, she opened
her mouth and allowed him to place the pill on her tongue.
Then he held the water to her lips, and she swallowed. She
hated her helplessness, and frustration mounted even more
when she tried to wipe her eyes and couldn't do it ade-
quately. When Jack held a tissue up to her face, she turned
away.

"Come on, Willa. It's not going to kill you for me to do
this."

She remained still, eyes closed, while he dabbed at the
corners of her eyelids. Then he got another tissue and placed
it over her nose.

"Blow."

Furious now, Willa sucked in a deep breath and blew out
as hard as possible. Jack wiped her nose, threw the tissue
into the wastebasket, then looked at her. She stared at him
for a long time. Compassion and concern glowed in his pale
eyes.

She skimmed her gaze downward, to his wide shoulders,
bare chest, waist and lower. Slowly she began to chuckle.
"You're really not dressed for nursing."

He followed her gaze. "No, I guess I'm not. Or maybe I
am. It depends on how you look at it."

Willa's chuckling jarred her hands, and she lifted them
from her lap. "Oh, Jack, I really don't want to laugh. It
hurts."

"Shush. It'll feel better in a few minutes when the pill takes effect." He reached to fix the pillows behind her head. She caught his scent and breathed deeply, finding it oddly comforting. When he began to stroke her brow, she closed her eyes and let the pill carry her off to sleep.

When Willa awoke the following morning, the shades were pulled against a bright morning sun, and the aroma of coffee filled the room. The sounds of Jack's whistling and an early-morning children's television show floated through the open doorway.

She stretched her tense and achy arms. Her hands throbbed with pain, and her stomach gave a queasy lurch. Shifting carefully into a sitting position, she threw her feet to the floor, then stood, allowing the coverlet to fall behind her. After taking a moment to get her balance, she walked gingerly into the kitchen.

Jack sat at the table, Molly in his lap. They were both watching the small portable television on the counter. On the screen a pudgy, white-whiskered man with a blue cap argued with a rabbit puppet. Molly giggled, and Jack chuckled. He glanced up and saw her.

"You shouldn't be out of bed," he said, rising and setting Molly on the chair. He reached her in two long strides. Her face was pale in stark contrast to her curly dark hair. Violet circles were etched around her eyes.

"I hurt my hands," she said. "I'm not an invalid."

Still he held her arm and guided her to a chair. Her arm quivered in his grasp. She sat down, and Molly came to climb up on her lap. Without asking, Jack brought her a pain pill and water. She glanced up at him from beneath her long lashes, then opened her mouth and allowed him to place the pill on her tongue. He held the water to her lips.

Out of the corner of his eye, as he turned to get her a cup of coffee, he saw Willa hug Molly to her and speak softly. He brought the coffee, pulled his chair close and lifted the cup. Willa shook her head and turned away. He didn't know what else to do, so he left the cup on the table and rose to get her breakfast. He didn't ask if she wanted it; he knew she'd say no. And he also knew the reason. She didn't like the fact that he had to do everything for her.

Bringing a plate of bacon, fried eggs and toast, he set it on the table and chopped the food into small pieces. Molly watched television, and Willa watched Jack. Lifting a piece of bacon with the fork, he held it up.

"Open the hangar," he said, thinking it would make her laugh.

It didn't. She simply stared at him, her hazel eyes dark and round.

"Come on, Willa. You've got to eat. If you wait until you can use your hands, you'll be dead—or at least so skinny that we'll have to shake the sheets to find you."

She blinked. "Who's doing the drilling?"

He glanced at his watch. "Thomas will get the rig out there in about an hour." He sighed, knowing she wouldn't like the rest of it, though he had to tell her. "And I've arranged with Doyle Bartlett to be the licensed driller on site."

"Doyle Bartlett!" Dismayed, Willa stared at Jack. How could he do such a thing? "Doyle Bartlett is a competitor."

"I know that," Jack said, his voice taking on the irritating tone of an adult talking to a child. And he still held that stupid fork in the air. "But he's a good guy, and he's available. His brother can handle their work, and he'll help us—for a good fee."

"A good fee? We haven't made enough profit to pay him a good fee." Willa clamped her mouth shut.

"Willa, shut up and eat."

She glared at him.

"You have to have someone here. You can't get around that. Carrie can come some of the time, but she can't be here all day every day for the next several weeks. Now, it's either me or we hire someone." Jack regarded her sternly, and she hated his being right. He raised an eyebrow, and his voice dripped with infuriating sarcasm. "Do you want me to call your mother? Maybe she'll come."

"The moon would have to turn blue before my mother would do such a thing, and you know it."

"Let me do this, Willa. I want to do this."

His words, his tone, touched her heart. She was being pigheaded with pride, and she knew it perfectly well. It was just so hard not to be in control of herself. Jack gave a gentle smile.

Willa nodded. "I'm sorry." She lowered her voice. "Thank you, Jack."

"You'd do it for me—have done it. Remember the time I broke my arm?"

She could smile then. She looked at the bacon wobbling on the fork, and her stomach turned. "I can't eat the bacon, Jack. Please, just the toast."

He grinned broadly. "Okay. With lots of peach jam?"

"Yes, please," she said with a smile. "And I'll have coffee, too."

She eventually ate two pieces of toast and drank half a cup of coffee. Then, terribly tired, she allowed Jack to help her back to bed.

She slept for two hours, and when she awoke, Carrie was there. Jack had gone out to the well site, and that fact relieved Willa. It also wasn't nearly as hard to allow Carrie to help her drink half a glass of iced tea and eat half a bowl of chicken soup.

"Your stomach bothering you?" Carrie asked when Willa begged off eating more. "Jack said all you had for breakfast was toast."

"I'm not doing anything but sleeping, Carrie. How could I be hungry?"

Carrie regarded her curiously but said only, "I'll clear this away, and then we'll get your face washed and clean sheets on the bed. Everyone always feels better lying on clean sheets."

Willa slept most of the afternoon, Molly beside her. Jack fixed a dinner of toasted cheese sandwiches and cold fruit because that was what Willa had gotten a sudden craving for. He ended up feeding not only Willa but Molly, too, who'd decided it was a great game.

Between mouthfuls, Willa plied Jack with questions about the well. Were they getting any more water? Was it sucking out the water they pumped down? If so, it could be an indication of more water in the ground. What were the chips like? Were they making certain to get them out of the bottom of the hole?

Jack patiently answered all her questions. Yes, they had found more water but still needed to go deeper for an adequate supply. They planned to go to five hundred and fifty feet tomorrow and hoped that would be it. He'd put on a new bit, and yes, they were making certain to monitor the chips, trying to flush the drilled rock from the hole as fast as possible.

After dinner, Jack brought the portable television into the bedroom, and they all lay in the bed and watched television until Molly fell asleep. Willa insisted on joining Jack as he put Molly to bed, even though all she could do was watch. At least she could lean down and give her daughter a kiss.

"How about a bath?" Jack said as they left Molly's room.

Willa looked down at the gown she'd worn the previous night and all during the day. She really wanted a bath, but that would mean Jack would have to provide the hands. It was all so embarrassing.

But he gave her no time to answer. He simply steered her into the bathroom, saying, "You'll feel better."

Jack ran the water. Jack removed her nightgown and helped her into the tub. He sloshed water over her body, then lathered the washcloth with soap and rubbed it over her skin. His eyes danced with merriment. "You like this?" he teased.

She couldn't help but chuckle. "*You* certainly do." Her blood grew warm, and her breasts hardened slightly.

Jack leaned over and kissed her gently, then returned to washing her. He helped her from the tub and dried every inch of her skin with tender touches of the towel. Willa's legs began to tremble, half from desire, half from a strange, weak feeling. Without her saying a word, Jack lifted her and carried her to the bed.

"Which nightgown you want?" he asked as he walked to the closet.

"The white one with the pink flowers." Somehow wearing her favorite gown was a comfort.

After he'd pulled it over her head, he brushed her hair. Again and again the brush pulled through her curls in long, sensuous, relaxing strokes. Willa's eyelids grew heavy. Jack kissed the back of her neck and gently lowered her to the pillow. When he moved away, she called to him.

"Please, rest your hand on my shoulder."

And he did.

For the following days, except for a few hours when he saw to finishing the well and Carrie took over, it was Jack who fed Willa and held drinks to her lips. He cared for Molly, washed clothes, cooked and cleaned house—not perfectly, maybe, but the important things got done. In the perverseness of nature, since Willa couldn't scratch, she seemed to suffer an inordinate number of itches. It was Jack who scratched Willa's back, scratched her arms, scratched her nose. He dressed and undressed her, washed her body, washed and brushed her hair and even brushed her teeth.

It was the most frustrating time of Willa's entire life. She was totally helpless, totally dependent.

The second day after the accident, Jack walked into the living room, bringing Willa a cold drink, though she hadn't asked. She never asked for anything. He saw her staring down at the hearth rug, a tear slipping quietly down her cheek.

He knew immediately that the tears didn't come from pain. There was something she wanted or needed and that she couldn't do for herself. He knew this whole experience was about the hardest thing that had ever happened to her.

Very quietly, he retreated to the kitchen. She wouldn't want him to see her. It was a private moment, one he didn't think he should interrupt. So what he did do was after a few minutes get Molly to run to Willa. After another five minutes, he felt it safe to carry in her cold drink. She greeted him with a smile.

The days passed. A week after the accident the doctor examined her hands and put on new bandages that were smaller and left her thumbs free. She couldn't cut up any of the food Jack prepared, but she could manage a fork and could lift a glass or cup between her hands. She could turn the pages of a book and shift the sheet around herself as she wanted. Still, Jack had to do almost everything. And one of the worst things was that she couldn't stroke his skin when they made love.

He sure enjoyed stroking her, though, driving her crazy with desire before he satisfied her.

The days turned into two weeks. Weeks of frustration, times of embarrassment, moments of hilarity. And yet, Willa began to feel more and more moments of unique and wonderful magic. It was as if a curtain were being drawn away, allowing her an exceptionally clear view of herself she'd never seen before. For one thing, she was stuck with herself so very closely, and she *had* to look. And with Jack's constant presence, she began to see him more clearly, too.

With her extreme dependence on him, his extreme responsibility for her, a very special bond began to weave itself between them.

When Jack saw Mitchell's sedan pull into the drive, he went to meet him at the back door.

"I heard about the accident," Mitchell said. "I thought by now Willa might be up to seeing me."

Jack looked at him for a long second before he nodded. "She's in the living room." He watched Mitchell's back as the man strode into the hall. For a brief instant, jealousy tugged at him, and he wasn't proud of the fact that it was hard to put aside.

The soft beat of country music sounded from the stereo in the living room. Willa sat in her customary chair. She wore a pale pink jumper and appeared to have lost weight. Her hands rested, palms up, on her thighs. At the sight of the bandages, Mitchell's heart lurched, and he realized how helpless she must feel.

She smiled with surprise and pleasure. Her pale face seemed to have a certain glow. She was beautiful, and he wondered again if he could ever love anyone else. He couldn't say this to her, though. He'd come to say good bye. His only hope was to put some distance between himself and Willa.

Jack knew it wasn't to his credit that he lingered near the living room door, listening. But after hearing their greetings, he took firm control of himself and walked away to Molly's bedroom to check on her. She was sleeping. To give himself something to do, he opened a can of dog food, dumped it into a plate and took it out to Doc. When Mitchell came out ten minutes later, Jack was a bit surprised at the shortness of the visit.

Mitchell stopped and stuck out his hand. Jack accepted it without hesitation this time.

"Take care of her," Mitchell said, his deep blue eyes glittering.

Somewhat baffled, Jack answered, "I intend to. You going somewhere?"

Mitchell nodded and stepped away to his car. "Willa can tell you about it. Goodbye." He gave a small wave.

Jack found Willa in the kitchen, staring out the window. At Mitchell's car driving away, he thought. "Where's Mitchell going?"

"He's moving to Tulsa, accepting a partnership there," she said, turning to face him. "Did you encourage him to take up the law again?"

Jack shrugged. "Not really." A twinge of pleasure touched him at the news of Mitchell's leaving, and he wasn't sorry for it.

"He said you told him it was never too late to look for the right road."

Willa watched the surprise leap into his pale eyes. She wondered what he would say if she told him what she'd asked Mitchell to do. He probably wouldn't like having Mitchell handle it. But she hoped to please him by the course she'd decided to take. She'd asked Mitchell to handle the legalities of having the ownership of both the farm and the drilling company put in Jack's name along with her own.

"I may have said something to that effect," Jack allowed, breaking into Willa's thoughts. He smiled warmly in response to her own grin. He stepped over and swept her into his arms. "How about a bit of necking while Molly's napping?" He chuckled wickedly and murmured, "Careful of your hands."

Passion leaped through her veins like flames upon cedar branches, hot and furious. Love swelled her heart. She wouldn't tell him of her plans. She would show him. She would prove her love and acceptance of him into her life.

They were driving home from the doctor's office. Molly rested her head in Willa's lap, sleeping. Jack glanced over quickly, then returned his gaze to the road.

"How does it feel to have thumbs and little fingers?" he teased.

Willa held them up and wiggled them. "Wonderful! Maybe I can even cut my own food."

"Oh, the lady's playing fast and loose now!"

Grinning, she stared down at her hands and gave thanks for them. Again the new bandages the doctor had put on were much smaller than the previous ones and would allow her a bit more freedom. Still, she wouldn't be able to fasten her buttons, she thought ruefully. And how glad she would be to have the bandages completely gone and be able to feel Jack's skin again.

She glanced at his profile, thinking idly that his thick mustache needed trimming, though she liked it somewhat bushy. Then she stared out at the passing countryside.

Their anniversary was five days away—they would be married twelve years. It seemed quite a feat at that moment. And Willa had quite a present for Jack. At least she hoped he considered it a gift and not a burden.

The doctor had done something else for her besides rebandaging her fingers and freeing her thumbs. He'd taken a test and settled a question that had been plaguing Willa since the day of the hearing.

The nausea she'd experienced the day of the hearing and the days after the accident, much of which she'd hidden from Jack and Carrie, had not been from nerves or reaction to being injured. She was going to have a baby.

She hadn't planned it, though she'd been perfectly aware that she hadn't used birth control on a totally regular basis. Perhaps deep down inside she'd hoped to get pregnant, she thought now.

She was glad, terribly glad. But for some odd reason she hadn't been able to tell Jack. It seemed something so important that she couldn't find the words. Would he still want a child? Or would it be that, once confronted with something so settling as a child, he would change his mind? About her . . . about everything?

Thinking of her condition, Willa rested a bandaged hand against her stomach above Molly's head.

"Stop for the mail, Jack," she said as he pulled into the drive.

He complied, setting the batch of mail on the seat between them. Willa didn't look at it until they'd gotten into the house and Jack had carried Molly off to bed. Surely Mitchell would have been able to handle the legal requirements by now, she thought as she pushed the bills and advertisements away.

"Looking for something special?" Jack asked.

At that moment, her eye spied a white envelope with the bank's return address.

"Yes."

Willa tried to pick up the envelope, fumbled with it and at last Jack picked it up for her. He looked at the return address, then handed it to her with a suspicious scowl.

"Will you open it for me?" Willa asked. Her heart beat rapidly.

What if she were wrong? What if her actions didn't please him? What if they only made him feel tied down?

She watched him slip his finger beneath the flap and open the envelope. She had to do this, she thought. She had to take the chance. It was a way to bring her heart around with her will. It was a way to share her life with him.

Quite suddenly the fear evaporated. She loved him fully and without reserve. She could trust Jack with her love, her future, her life.

He pulled out the papers and handed them to her in an angry motion. She managed to straighten them out and look at them long enough to ascertain that they were indeed the papers she'd been waiting for.

"Jack, it hurts to hold them. Will you read them for me please?"

With a hesitant motion, he took the papers. He popped a gummy bear into his mouth before scanning the first page.

Like a slow-rolling wave on the shore, shock swept his face. He looked up at her and back again. Then he quickly looked at the second page. Willa felt tears welling in her eyes.

"What is this?" he demanded. His gruff manner shook her confidence.

"It's our future," she managed. "Happy anniversary." She didn't want to cry, and she fought the brimming tears.

Jack shook his head, threw the papers onto the table and turned his back. Willa's heart sank. What was wrong?

"Jack?"

Clutching all her courage, she moved around him to look at his face. He blinked and looked at her. There were tears in his eyes.

He shook his head. "The farm... the business... It's yours, Willa. You—"

She touched her little finger to his lips. "I didn't do it to hold you here, Jack. You must know that." She searched his eyes, and relief swept over her. He did know that. "You've put yourself into the farm and the business. And you are my husband. We are one. I love you... and I need you, Jack. I always have."

He crushed her to him and held her a long time. She didn't care if he never let her go.

But at last she pushed away from his chest. "I have to catch my breath," she said. Her heart pounded in her ears. "It's not good in my condition to be squeezed so hard, Jack."

He stared at her, and she knew he hadn't really heard.

"Jack, there's something else."

His face clouded with caution, as if he feared she was about to say something he wouldn't like. "What?"

"We're going to have to work harder to build the business. We're going to need more money."

"What have you gone and done now, woman?"

"Well, I didn't do it by myself, cowboy."

Perhaps they'd become close enough in spirit to read each other's mind, because the light of understanding seemed to creep across Jack's face. "Are you...?"

Willa nodded and smiled broadly. "Yes, we're going to have another baby."

Jack had the strange sensation of his legs going weak. Pulling Willa with him, he sat in the nearest chair and held her on his knee. He studied her face. At last, he thought. It was all happening. Another baby, another child—their child. But did she want it?

"You didn't tell me you'd quit using birth control," he said.

"I didn't really.... Well, I never was using it regularly, anyway." She touched the buttons on his shirt with her thumb.

"Are you happy about this, Willa?"

"Oh, yes, Jack." She nodded. "I hadn't really planned on it, but I know it's right. If it's right with you." For an instant she looked anxious.

"Oh, you bet, woman!"

He kissed her then, strong and hard and claiming. He was right where he wanted to be.

Chapter Fifteen

Willa replaced the telephone receiver and stood with her hand resting on it for a moment. Jack probably wasn't going to like what she'd just done.

Then, realizing the time, she moved quickly to slip on her shoes. They were brand new, cream-colored satin to match the dress she wore—a Victorian-style wedding dress in satin and lace. The shoes pinched her feet as she walked to the full-length mirror to study her reflection. Well, a little pain wouldn't matter, she decided, because she looked, well, exactly as she wanted to. Romantic, feminine, pretty—if a bit pleasingly plump. It was another wedding day for her.

She moved to the dresser and picked up the brush. Her gaze fell to the card there, the anniversary card from Jack. Laying the brush aside, she picked up the card and stared at it.

"Thank you for thirteen good years. I love you," Jack had written in his own hand down below the printed verse.

Willa wasn't certain exactly whose suggestion it was that they get remarried—hers or Jack's or Thomas's. But certainly she'd been thrilled with Jack's excitement over the prospect. He'd been the one to take care of the church arrangements, and Thomas had seemed to be the town crier, inviting everyone.

She was pleased, she thought now. Renewing their marriage vows was something very special. She only wished Hoppy were there with them. Perhaps he was in spirit.

There was a commotion in the hallway, and the bedroom door burst open.

"Willa, little Hoppy just untied my tie for the fourth time. Will you take him so I can finish getting ready?" Jack strode toward her, holding out their small son, who was giggling as usual.

"Come here, little one," Willa said, taking her son and holding him close. He was a big baby with dark hair and pale blue eyes like Jack's. Everyone said his eyes would darken and change with age, but somehow Willa doubted it. Just as Molly was very much like Willa herself, little Hopkins seemed very much his father's son.

"You'd better take care of feeding him before we go," Jack reminded her as he peered into the mirror and tied his string tie.

"I will," Willa said patiently as she held little Hoppy with one hand and moved two of Jack's work shirts from the chair with the other. Jack would never learn to put away his own clothes.

"Jack, there was just a telephone call for you."

"Who was it?"

"John Barton from Southwest Petroleum. He has an offer of a job down off the west coast of Mexico."

Jack grunted. "Did you tell him I wasn't available, or do I have to call him?"

"You have to call him—and I told him you were available." She rocked little Hoppy against her shoulder.

"You what?" Jack turned from the mirror, his expression exactly as she'd expected—grumpily disapproving.

"I told him you were available. I didn't take the job for you."

"Well, you sure stopped just short of that." He frowned. "Why, Willa? We've got drilling jobs backed up, and the kids—"

"Jack, lower your voice, please," Willa said as Molly bounced into the room. Smiling, Molly twirled in her new dress. "Isn't she pretty, Daddy?"

"She sure is." Jack sat on the bed and lifted Molly onto his lap. He gazed at Willa, and she felt a tingle deep within. She guessed he would always be able to do that to her. "Her mother is beautiful, too," he said in a husky voice. "I forgot to tell you."

"Thank you," Willa said softly. For a brief moment she enjoyed simply looking at him.

"You want me to take this drilling job?" he asked, obviously quite surprised.

"I think you should think about it. A vacation down in Mexico sounds awfully good for all of us, except, of course, only the children and I would get the vacation. You'd have to work."

He raised an eyebrow. "You'd go, too?"

"The farm and business would be here when we got back, Jack. Thomas is fully qualified to be boss for a while." She smiled. "Our home would be here when we returned. Besides, our home is anywhere we all are together."

He stared at her for a long minute, searching her face. Then he stood and put Molly down. "Let's get ready. We've got a wedding to get to. And since we're the main participants, we'd better not be late."

Just as they all walked out the back door, Jack reached for Willa and held her close.

"Thank you, Willa, for all you've given me."

"Thank you, Jack, for going through this life with me."

As Jack escorted her and the children across the lawn toward his waiting pickup, Willa knew they were two of the very few people who search for and find the wellspring of continual love. Love that enabled them to forgive and forget, and to accept each other just the way they were.

"Jack," she said as he helped her and little Hoppy onto the seat, "when are you going to sell those stupid cows—all of them?"

"Fifteen more are arriving tomorrow," he said as he slammed the door.

Anger immediately spurted through Willa. But as she watched him through the glass, she couldn't help but chuckle.

He mouthed to her, "I love you."

* * * * *